NINA HAYES

The Wisteria Wedding

The Old Bat Chronicles Book 3

Contents

Preface

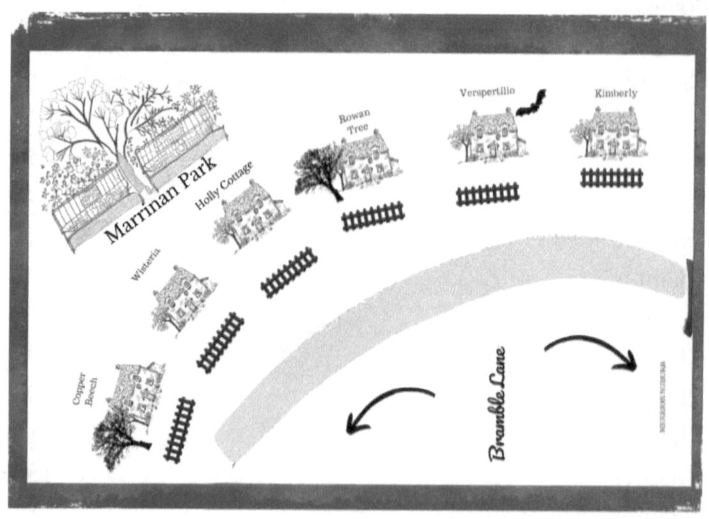

Bramble Lane, showing the new Marrinan Park

This is the third book in the Old Bat Chronicles, and in many ways the one I've enjoyed writing the most. As ever, the folk magic and folk traditions are all based in authentic, Irish traditions. If you are interested in them, there's a section in the back explaining both the magic used by The Old Bat and her friends, and the Irish wedding traditions mentioned. And there is a glossary below that will help with some of the Irish slang and Hiberno-English turns of phrase. We Irish have a rich, and sometimes bonkers, turn of phrase!

The Wisteria Wedding owes a lot to a trip to the USA in 2023. As I drove with my husband and kids from Connecticut to Niagara Falls, we passed by some towns that had fabulous names. We began a game of weaving together these names into a story, and the fictional "Jerusalem Hill, tough guy detective," was born. Humphrey Sterling, his author was named by the Cozy Mystery Village Facebook group (one of the best places to talk all things cozy!)

I hope you enjoy reading this book, as much as I did writing it. And while every effort has been made by dedicated people to remove any spelling, grammar and formatting errors please take any that slipped through the net as proof that this was written by a gloriously fallible human, not a perfect AI bot.

GLOSSARY

A Chairde! - **(Pro. Ah Car-djeh)** Formal greeting in Irish (Gaeilge) meaning "Friends!" Often used to open a meeting or event.

Bean Feasa - Wise Woman, (woman of knowledge) *pronounced Bann Fahsah.* The Irish equivalent of a witch but with very specific role in the community. See back section for more information.

Draíocht Ceoil - literally "Music Magic" this is the ancient

Irish tradition of using sound to create magic or commune with the Otherworlds. It is rooted in the role of the Poets (Filí) in Old Irish Society, and has evolved over the centuries into an intrinsic part of Irish Folk Magic.

Part of it is **Isteach** - *"ISS-tyock"* meaning Inside and **Amach** - *"Ah-mock"* meaning Outside. This refers to: to take in, Isteach, also listening and to emit sound, Amach, sending out sound.

Dreck -Yiddish word that comes from the German Dreck, which means both "dirt" and "manure." Became part of Dublin patois in the 19th century.

Eejit - a silly, foolish person, a complete twit
also **Gobdaw** - An eejit.

Fáilte Romhaibh - Fáilte (fawl-tcheh) means welcome in Gaeilge and Romhaibh (Row-iv) means "to ye" (plural)
Fáilte romhat, (row-ut) means to you (singular). Céad Míle Fáilte (kayd meela fawl-tcheh) means a hundred thousand welcomes.

Gallute - (gahl-lewte) A big awkward lump of a person, usually a male.

Garda - The Irish police is "An Garda Síochána" (*gar-dah shee-uh-chaw-nah*) or Guardians of the Peace. Individual members of the force are called Gardaí (plural) or Garda (singular) Detectives are addressed formally as Detective Garda.

Gobnait - This is a real name. Pronounced "Gub-nit" it is the name of a medieval saint, who is associated with Bees. She was born in Co Clare, descended from a great king, Conaire Mór, and was generally described as a decent auld stick. Her feastday is Feb 11th. Unfortunately the name Gobnait is generally regarded as a bit ugly and not a flattering name for a young woman. As the word "gob" means beak in Irish and is Hiberno-English slang for a mouth, generations of Gobnaits have been teased in school, and nicknamed "big Gob" and the like.

HB/Hazelbrook Farms - Iconic Irish Ice cream company, an integral part of every Irish childhood.

Hurl and Sliotar - The great national sport of Hurling is a uniquely Irish invention and one of the oldest ball sports in the world. It's also one of the fastest, and most exciting! The stick is called a Hurl and the ball is a sliotar, sometimes spelled sliothar.

Poitín - (Pro. Putch-een) Illegal drink made from potatoes, and legendary in Ireland. Still made in hidden stills around the country, but rarer now than in older days. Lethal if you over indulge, but fishermen in particular, and others who laboured outdoors, swore by its restorative powers if taken in moderation.

Seanchaí (sometimes spelled in English as Seanachaí) A traditional Irish storyteller

Sláinte -(Pro. *Slawn-tcheh*) Irish for "Good Health!" derived from Slán meaning safe or well.

Sleeveen - A weasel, a slimy or untrustworthy person

Whisht - "hush" - attributed to Ireland and Scotland and often thought to be rooted in Gaeilge, but also found in Middle English.

<u>CAST</u>
Eve Caulton, 50-ish, Artist and owner of Kimberly Cottage
The Old Bat(s)
Dymphna Moriarty, Next Door Neighbour and the unofficial leader of the Wise Women
Niamh Caulton née Boyd, Eve's mother. Scatty but shrewd.
Claudia Warren, Brigadier General of the Irish Women's Brigade, steady and reliable.
Greta Goode, incorrigible and famous for her true crime podcast Greta's Gory Truths
Neighbours
Tom MacDonagh (Retired)
Detective Ronan Desmond (Garda)
Margaret Furey (Teacher)
The Marrinans, Ellen and Finn, with their kids Boyd (16) and Melly (14)
Gardaí
Detective Cullen, Ronan's partner
Sergeant Jo Maguire, Greta Goode's granddaughter
Literary Festival
Emer O'Neill, well known author
Humphrey Sterling, famous crime novelist
Helen Dunphy, poet
Liam Quigley, Festival Organizer
Phyllis Dennehy, PA to Humphrey Sterling

Damian Burke, Literary Agent
Aidan Lowe, Journalist.

Chapter 1

Eve Caulton shifted slightly in her chair, her back aching. The Merrion community hall was draughty and rather grim, despite the large, slightly off centre, plastic banner emblazoned "Merrion Literary Festival." The seating was pure torture, hard and rickety and very unyielding even to a well-upholstered posterior. Eve moved again, hoping to discreetly massage some feeling into her extremities. Her mother Niamh glared at her, elbowed her sharply in the ribs and hissed, "Stop fidgeting, Eve!"

Sandwiched between Niamh and Dymphna Moriarty was an uncomfortable place to be at the best of times. Dymphna was Eve's next door neighbour, a close friend of her mother's, and a force of nature who believed in making herself as comfortable as possible. The elderly lady had one elbow firmly lodged on Eve's hip, her shopping bags under Eve's feet and had placed a large bag of boiled sweets in Eve's lap, "So Niamh can reach them too." Dymphna had of course secured the front row, centre seats. Originally a young couple had been foolish enough to claim them, but a glare from the old lady had sent them scurrying to the far side of the hall.

It wasn't quite how Eve had intended to spend the evening. There was plenty to do at home, for a start. She had started to renovate the spare bedroom in Kimberly Cottage earlier that month, and Spring had brought the usual jobs to be done in the garden. And she could have called in to visit her friend, Tom. Her *boyfriend*, she giggled to herself, although at fifty years of age that sounded a bit juvenile. Partner? Paramour? Well, at any rate, things were going very well there and she would have liked to meet up for dinner or a stroll around the newly created Marrinan Park, at the back of Bramble Lane.

Tom had designed the flower beds for the park and loved to keep a close eye on them, and it had rapidly become the meeting place for the whole neighbourhood. On a Saturday afternoon, the young people would be hanging out, the playground would be full of happy kids and they could grab a coffee and pastry from "Lola's Mobile Cafe" - a tiny van crammed full of treats and serving hot drinks that parked up there most days.

Or, Eve thought with a pang, she could have spent the evening with her other neighbour and friend, Margaret Furey, and poured over bridal plans for the wedding. Margaret was to marry Ronan Desmond - yet another neighbour - in just two weeks' time. As a result, Bramble Lane was at a fever pitch of excitement. Eve loved helping the young bride pick out colours, and flowers and even, to her great surprise, accompanying her to buy her wedding dress.

"I've no Mam to go shopping with, Eve - although, I know she'll be with me in spirit. I'd be so grateful if you'd come with me?" Margaret had asked, and Eve had jumped at the chance. It would be years before her own daughter Mairead would settle down, and when that day came, Eve doubted her advice on wedding dresses would be required. Mairead was more likely to get married on a bog, in her best overalls. Margaret was no fashionista but she shared Eve's love of textiles and they had a ball, choosing between various types of satin and lace. When Margaret completed the day out by asking her to be Matron of Honour, she almost burst with pride. Yes, she could have been in Wisteria Cottage, sipping coffee in the April sunshine and giving advice on the thorny issue of the seating plan. Or the relative merits of centerpieces for the reception, not to mention the vexed question of wedding favours for the guests.

Instead she was here, in a draughty community hall, chaperoning an overexcited gaggle of senior ladies.

Eve glanced once more at the leaflet that Niamh had thrust into her hand earlier that day. Her mother had a bad habit of calling in unannounced to Kimberly Cottage, and an even worse one of volunteering Eve for all kinds of things. Between making herself tea and ferreting out Eve's secret stash of good biscuits, Niamh had informed her that she was to attend a book reading by someone who rejoiced in the name "Humphrey Sterling." In typical Niamh fashion, her mother had plunged straight into the topic with no context provided.

"Claudia is bringing her Women's Brigade book club and some of those old dears are quite ancient, you know." Niamh was in her early eighties but refused to accept that the normal rules of aging applied to her or her closest friends. She viewed everyone else as fragile, decrepit, old biddies. "And Dymphna will be coming straight from town, so she'll need someone to help her carry the shopping home. She's buying presents for the wedding, from all of us. I'd do it myself but I can't get into town, not at the moment, with your brother needing me."

Eve's brother Conor lived in their childhood home with their mother, and up until recently had led a quiet and happy bachelor life. This had all changed when the lovely Ray appeared on the scene. He was gorgeous, outgoing, popular and for some reason seemed to think the sun rose and set with Conor. The pair were getting along just fine but Niamh had weddings on the brain now and she was convinced without her there to guide Conor, he would let this chance slip away.

"Just think, Eve, *we* could have a Big Day Out soon. Well, obviously, we're having one with Margaret and Ronan tying the knot but I mean in our *own* family. I do think Ray is ready to settle down, he was dropping hints to Conor about moving in together. Conor barely noticed, but I told him - *that lad has plenty of offers, don't let the grass grow under your feet!* I would love them to move into mine but sure, they probably want to live in one of those trendy apartments. I said to Ray, in my day we didn't move in together until the Banns were at least called, and guess what he said?"

"Eh, "mind your own business, you appalling nosebag?"" Eve suggested. "Honestly, Mam, you shouldn't interfere -"
"Nonsense. And you're wrong, Miss Smarty Pants. He said, "Don't you worry, Mrs. Caulton, we'll get him there yet." See? Ray is definitely on the same page."

"Oh my God." Eve groaned. "Poor Ray. Poor Conor, for that matter."

Her mother was too pleased with herself to bother rebuking her.

"I have high hopes, Eve, high hopes. Maybe a Winter wedding - or a destination one. Caroline Murphy's young one got wed over in Mauritius. She said it was brilliant - all the fun of a wedding and a holiday at the same time. Except the heat brought out her prickly rash and her Dan was raging because they missed the football final. But none of us are that into sports so it won't matter will it? Oh look at the time! I can't be standing here gossiping with you all day, you know. Mr. Sterling will be speaking at six o'clock sharp, so we'll see you there. Now don't be late, Eve, he's a very important literary figure. Here, these are my copies of his books. I don't want to be lugging them around all afternoon. You bring them to the hall for me. *Oh*, just imagine. I can get Humphrey Sterling to sign them..."

Her mother sighed like a lovelorn teenager and wandered off again, having first reminded Eve several times not to be late and not to forget the bag of books. Eve waited until she had left before opening it up and examining the contents - large books, with glossy covers, each adorned with a scene straight from an old film noir, from the golden days of Hollywood. One featured a detective holding a fainting girl, the next a femme fatale clutching a gun and in one case, a detective holding a femme fatale *and* a gun, with a fainting girl prone at their feet.

It wasn't her cup of tea and she had never heard of the books before. In fact, they looked like the last kind of book she would ever want to read. But here she was, wasting her Saturday evening waiting for the famous author himself. There was a frenzied air in the community hall, a low key ferociousness, as the mainly female audience chattered and milled about. Claudia Warren, another of her mother's cronies and the Brigadier-General of the Irish Women's Brigade, had filled most of their side of the hall with excited Brigade members, in rows behind Dymphna and Niamh. Each wore the dark green and gold uniform of the Brigade, with a Humphrey Sterling book clutched in one hand and a pen in the other. It seemed Niamh wasn't the only one determined to get her books signed. Eve hoped the author was prepared for the onslaught of besotted fans.

Eve glanced discreetly at her watch. The event was due to start at six pm with a short poetry reading from a local poet, one Helen Dunphy, before the main attraction took the stage. It was already twenty minutes past six and she pitied the unfortunate woman who would soon attempt to read her work to an impatient hoard of super-fans. She glanced at the stage - really just a raised platform at one end of the hall, with a set of red curtains creating a shallow wing either side. Peeping around the curtains was a nervous looking young woman, her fair hair tied up in a messy bun and her rather shapeless dress half-hidden under a baggy cardigan. She caught Eve's eye and blushed. Eve gave her an encouraging smile and nod.

Eve was used to displaying her paintings, which was nerve wracking enough but she had the deepest aversion to public speaking. Her sympathies lay entirely with the poet, prompting her to turn around and speak to Claudia.
"There's a young poet about to read. I'd say she's dreading it, with all this noise. It's not fair to her."

Claudia sighed. "There's no proper organization, as far as I can tell. The Festival committee seem to be twiddling their thumbs. Hang on a minute." The Brigadier stood, looked around her until she caught sight of one of the Community Hall board members and bellowed at him across the room.

"Liam Quigley! Over here, please!" She remained standing as the harassed looking man bustled across to her. "What's the story, lad? When do you intend to start?"

The "lad" - a man aged sixty-five if he was a day - rolled his eyes.

"We would be started by now, Mrs. Warren, if the audience would only quieten down a bit. I understand people are excited but really, we cannot ask Ms. Dunphy to shout over them."

"Is that all? For goodness sake, man, why didn't you say something." Claudia turned and addressed the crowd. Eve was expecting a repeat of the stentorian tones used to call Mr. Quigley but instead Claudia simply spoke in a quiet, authoritative voice.

"Ladies, Gentlemen. We are very lucky to have not only one but two literary treats tonight. One of our own, Helen Dunphy, is about to read her poems to us."

She paused and fixed the crowd with a cold stare. Her tone of voice did not brook any argument. "You will listen, and show your respect and appreciation."

The audience dutifully fell silent, those still standing scuttling back to their seats. An unseen hand pushed Helen Dunphy on to the stage, to polite applause. The poet stood blinking for a moment, looking deeply uncomfortable, but finally made her way to the mic and turned it on.

"Ah. Hi. Hello. My name is Helen Dunphy and I would like to read some poems for you today." Another smattering of applause seemed to give her courage. "My poems are inspired by local events - politics, community, history but I hope they have messages that have universal appeal. Um, let me see- Yes, I'll start with this one. Lost Days…"

The poem was brief, quite neatly crafted in Eve's opinion, with a message of compassion for those among them who had lost their way in life. It was well received, and the girl's voice grew a little stronger. Her next poem was much better, Eve felt, and even Dymphna nodded at one or two lines. It dealt sharply with issues of local politics, striking quite a chord with the locals in the hall.

Her cheeks pink, and her eyes shining, the girl read her

last offering of the evening. It was different again from the previous two offerings, a fantastical piece filled with rich imagery. Eve didn't follow all of it, but she enjoyed the sound of it immensely and some of the images it conjured up touched her deeply. The applause at the end of the reading was sincere and prolonged, and Helen Dunphy exited the stage in triumph.

"This isn't as bad as I feared," Eve thought. *"Maybe this chap will be as good."*

After all, all these people were devoted fans. He had to have some talent as a writer. She tried to ignore the throbbing ache in her back and the fact that Niamh had added a packet of bon-bons to the bag of sweets on her lap. She was half sorry she hadn't read any of the books in Niamh's bag before the reading.

It was a short lived regret.

Barely had the poet exited the stage than a tall, gaunt figure strode on, outlandishly clad in a cape teamed with a battered fedora. He swaggered as he walked, using an ornately carved walking stick in exaggerated gestures as he went. He reached the edge of the stage, basking in the cheers and clapping that had greeted his appearance. In one practiced movement he bowed, sweeping his hat from his head and bowing to the audience. This stoked the flames of their adoration to fever pitch and it was a full ten minutes before anyone could hear a word from the great author. Eve covered her ears with her hands in an attempt to drown out her mother's screams of "Humphrey! HUMPHREY Sterling" and Dymphna's whoops.

She also took a moment to contemplate a world in which Dymphna Moriarty would be heard whooping in public.

By the time everything had calmed down, there were several other people on stage. To her shock - and Dymphna's outrage

- Eve recognized one of them as Greta Goode, the fourth member of her mother's close knit group. Greta was a minor celebrity herself, as the presenter of Ireland's favourite true crime podcast, Greta's Gory Truths. Usually, the incorrigible old lady loved to let them know about her public appearances - even making it as far as the top rated evening chat show in the country, albeit for a brief appearance. However, judging by the sharp intakes of breath on either side of her, Eve deduced she hadn't breathed a word to the other ladies about this.

"What's that auld rip doing up there?" Niamh whispered loudly, bending across Eve to speak to Dymphna.

Dymphna pursed her lips and narrowed her eyes. " Making a holy show of herself as usual, no doubt."

Niamh sat back and muttered, "Well for some."

Eve felt like a mother trapped between squabbling kids.

"I think it's great she's involved in the Literary Festival."

Dymphna snorted in derision.

"She never said a word," Niamh snapped, "Which I for one find underhand."

"I'm sure she had her reasons," Eve soothed. Both women looked at her scornfully.

"Hush. We'll miss himself."

Humphrey Sterling raised his arms dramatically.

"Please, dear people, please. You humble me. But we must have a little quiet..."

His pleas weren't quite as effective as Claudia's but the crowd did quieten down enough for him to continue talking.

"I stand before you today, a mere wordsmith. A jobbing writer, peddling his wares..." He had to pause again as a tumultuous protest erupted from the crowd. One of the Brigade members roared, "You're a genius!" Eve was only a little surprised to realize it was Claudia.

"You're too kind," the famous author beamed down at them. "Too kind." His voice was rich and unctuous, a strange mix of upper class Irish and a transatlantic twang. A man who had spent much time on the other side of the pond, Eve thought, or who wanted to give that impression. Perhaps he was American by birth, and had picked up the Irish along the way.

"I still say though, I am but a mere scribe. If my scribbles have brought you joy, perchance uplifted your hearts, and dare I hope - elevated your minds? Then I am truly grateful!"

Eve grinned. For a modest man, he managed to cram quite a boast into one speech. She doubted very much anyone's minds were "elevated" by the kind of book he wrote. Somewhat smugly, she watched her mother and friends lap up every word.

"My latest offering - *Devil's Town* - marks the return of…yes, you've guessed it! Jerusalem Hill, the greatest detective in modern literature." A woman screamed and Eve was fairly sure someone fainted at the back of the hall. She felt sure this must have been what it was like to be at a Beatles concert back in the day, except instead of handsome young men gyrating to pop music, it was an elderly writer holding court.

"Who is Jerusalem Hill?" She asked Niamh, who took a break from shouting and clapping to stare at her.

"You don't know who - Eve Caulton, do you never read? Jerusalem Hill is the main character in all the "Death Cities" and "Trick of Treat" series. He's the tough, wisecracking, gorgeous hero - he makes James Bond look like a boy scout, so he does. Oh, you have no idea what you're missing."

Eve digested this. "I take it he's popular then?"

"Oh, for goodness sake. Eve, he had his own television series in the eighties! Sure, you used to watch it with me. Do you not remember?"

A faint bell rang at the back of her mind. Her mother was addicted to all kinds of murder mystery shows, from the great Agatha Christie to - well, this kind of thing. Jerusalem Hill…an image sprang to mind of a disheveled but sexy actor, with the stubble and ponytail so beloved of the period. It wasn't quite set in the classic nineteen-forties style of "hard-boiled" detectives - she could recall a lot of neon lights, jackets rolled up to the elbows, and eighties pop music - but yes, now she thought about it, the main character was called Jerusalem. Although the TV show had wisely shortened it to Jerry in most scenes.

By the time she had worked all this out, Humphrey Sterling had moved on to reading an extract from one of his classic novels. A rapt hush fell over the Hall as that distinctive voice rang out.

Chapter 2

Sterling cleared his throat, adopted a pose reminiscent of a hammy Shakespearean actor about to butcher Hamlet, and began.

"It was a dark, stormy night. Jerusalem Hill watched the world go by from his vantage point on the roof of Carrington Manor. A long night stretched ahead - surveillance on the new, young wife of Millionaire Brad Carrington, suspected of adultery with her personal trainer. It was filthy work, but needs must - rent was due on the office and Elmira was dropping hints about a vacation. A woman like Elmira Heights couldn't be taken for granted. Sure, she was loyal in her own way but with a body to die for and a face that haunted men's dreams...he wasn't going to take any chances. If Elmira wanted two weeks in the Bahamas, then that's what he'd give her. Jerusalem Hill wasn't the settling down type, but he knew he'd never get another chance with Elmira if he screwed it up. Again. The man who could have any woman, with the flick of an eyebrow and the ghost of a smile, had finally met his match in the Bombshell of Broadway...a walking doll, with soft bosoms and wide hips, a tiny waist and big Bambi eyes. Street smart but not one of those boring intellectual dames."

Eve tried not to giggle. If her mother had ever heard any

male in real life refer to a woman as a "walking doll," and "not one of those boring intellectuals" she would have removed his spleen with a rusty spoon. Add in "soft bosoms" and he'd be eating through a straw to boot. But as long as it was between the pages of a Jerusalem Hill novel, it seemed to be okay. In fact, Niamh was in heaven if her smile was anything to judge by.

"Jerusalem Hill was afraid of no man - a crack shot, a boxing champion who could have gone pro, he knew he could take down any opponent. But the luscious Elmira had found his weak spot - his only weak spot. He couldn't resist a hot dame!

"Far beneath him, light spilled across the driveway as the door to the opulent mansion creaked ominously open. Peering over the edge of the crenelations, Hill saw the unmistakable shape of Cornelia Carrington - née Watkins - slink out towards a waiting car. She paused for a moment, tilting her face upwards as if to absorb the silver rays of moonlight. He caught the sweeping curve of her cheek, the clean line of her jaw and raised an appreciative eyebrow. She had the face of an angel - no wonder the elderly billionaire had snapped her up. But if rumours were to be believed, she was a devil in disguise. On her way to an illicit tryst with famous tennis pro, Glen Jamestown. That young man had ripped his way through the LA nightclub scene in recent months, Jerusalem mused. Made quite a reputation for himself as a womanizer. Handsome, in an obvious way - easy to imagine a bored young woman, tied to an old man, falling for his charms..."

Sterling continued in this way for some time until he paused and closed the book. "Alas! That really is all I've time for this evening..."

The festival organizer that Claudia had spoken to earlier, Mr. Quigley, made a move but he was no match for Greta

Goode. She was in her mid-eighties but had a turn of speed Usain Bolt would envy. Before anyone else could react, she was in front of Humphrey Sterling, microphone in hand and her blue eyes twinkling with mischief.

"Greta Goode, of the podcast "Greta's Gory Truths." A wonderful reading, Mr. Sterling, wonderful. I speak for all of us when I say it was an absolute pleasure to hear you read. For my listeners, I just wanted to ask a few questions, if you wouldn't mind?"

Sterling preened. "Not at all, not at all. Delighted…"

"Great. First off, however do you think of the plots? So many Jerusalem Hill novels, each one unique."

"Ah. Well, it isn't easy. I do draw a lot on my own imagination, ha ha. But sometimes, an old case or a strange story comes my way and I get an idea."

"Have you ever based any of your books on real events?"

"Real? As I said, I've picked up ideas from old news stories. Hollywood mysteries, unsolved cold cases…but not directly from any one particular true story. I am fascinated by old, unsolved crimes, though…"

The author spoke at length about various obscure cases from the nineteen forties and fifties that he had researched and used as a basis for his books. Eve's attention wandered. It would be listening gold for Greta's fans but she couldn't pretend to care about long ago murders, in far away cities. In the past twelve months she had encountered two real life murderers, right here in Dublin, and that was quite enough.

Finally the interview drew to a close - after a few more questions by Greta, designed to draw out the writer and get some semi-scandalous anecdotes about his many celebrity friends. It was not, strictly speaking, her purview but Eve suspected she would weave it in cleverly to her usual mix of old and current crime.

"You've led a fascinating life, Mr. Sterling," Greta purred. "I'm surprised you haven't written a memoir by now."

Humphrey blinked, obviously surprised at the question.

"Ah. Well, perhaps some day."

"Well, I'm sure we'd all love to read your autobiography. Or a biography, if you don't fancy writing it yourself?"

"Ah. I think it's better to read a person's own words, rather than some hack's version of events." Sterling replied.

"Of course, totally agree," Greta murmured.

"Now!" Mr. Quigley seized his opportunity to regain control of the stage, "I know you have already given us a reading, but perhaps a brief reading from another of your classic works? I thought perhaps, and this is my personal favourite, Pistols at Syracuse."

He held out a copy of the book.

Sterling gave a regal nod, and accepted it. While he thumbed through the pages looking for a suitable extract, Niamh took the opportunity to explain to Eve, "After the original "Trick or Treat" trilogy - what we Silver Sterlings call "The Triple Ts" - there's the "Elmira Heights" books, *Pistols* is the best of those by far. Then there's the "Death City" books…all of those are good. Oh, he's ready to start. Hush now."

Eve didn't even bother to point out that she hadn't uttered a word.

"It was a hot, dry day, the kind you only get in the arid heat of the dessert…" Sterling had obviously used this chapter for readings many times, he barely needed to glance at the page. Whatever the quality of the prose, or the fact that the story bore a startling resemblance to the extract he had given them

from his new work - the fictional detective sitting on a rocky outcrop, watching a suspect from above and musing on the attractiveness of Elmira - he read it well. He should have been an actor, not a writer, in Eve's opinion.

"Jerusalem drew his trusty Glock 17, and faced the thug with a nonchalant shrug of his shoulders.

"Get back, Sweeney, or I'll plug you. Don't try me on this."

The hardened gangster met the ice cold eyes of the detective and hesitated. Even his tiny brain could see, Jerusalem meant business...
"

The crowd roared its appreciation, Humphrey bowed to them, and shut the book with a resounding slap.The organizers of the event moved around on stage, congratulating each other and the author in turn, and Eve achieved a measure of freedom by handing her mother and neighbour their bags of sweets and stretching out her legs.

"Isn't he marvelous?" Niamh asked her.

"He's something else," Eve replied. "I've never heard anything quite like that."

"You should read his earlier work," Dymphna advised. "I've every one of them, I'll lend them to you."

"Oh. Well, that's very kind of you but I doubt I'll have time to read much…"

"Nonsense. There's always time for a good book. I'm surprised your mother hasn't already got you started on them."

"Eve is a dreadful snob about books," Niamh said. "I did offer her the Trick or Treat series - Angel City is the best place to start the Jerusalem Hill series."

"I'm not a snob! I just am not into - well, that kind of crime fiction."

"Classic literature isn't for everyone," Dymphna remarked.

"But sure, you'll be surprised how quickly you get into it."

Claudia Warren appeared, having abandoned her brigade members to the queue.

"How did Greta swing that, do you think? Up there on stage with Mr. Sterling, the lucky wagon."

Dymphna sniffed. "She pushed in, like she does. Brass neck, that's what she has."

Unfortunately Greta Goode chose that exact moment to join them, with Dymphna's words still lingering on the air.

"What's this, ladies? Who has a brass neck?" Her wrinkled face was a picture of innocence but Eve was prepared to bet good money she couldn't possibly have missed what was said. Dymphna looked slightly discomfited but rallied.

"I was saying you have a brass neck, Greta Goode. Up there on the stage like you were the main attraction. How did you manage it?"

Greta winked.

"Ask me no questions and I'll tell you no lies!"

"For goodness' sake, Greta, would you ever grow up?" Dymphna snapped. "It's clear as day you just wanted to get him all to your self. Humphrey has no idea who you are, he probably thinks your silly wee podcast is about books. If he knew it was about murders, I bet he'd have run a mile."

Greta's eyes glittered. If her granddaughter, Garda Sergeant Jo Maguire, had been present, she would have warned the ladies to take a step back and then erected safety barriers. Long experience of the irrepressible old woman should have taught her close friends not to underestimate her, but Dymphna Moriarty was in no mood to pander to anyone. Her nose, Eve thought, had been put well and truly out of joint by Greta's coup.

"That's all you know, Dymphna. Humphrey is a big fan of *Greta's Gory Truths* and he was well aware that I was going to interview him. It's not my fault no one told that old fusspot Quigley. In fact, Humphrey and I have been corresponding for weeks now - and he's coming to mine for his tea after this event." She paused to let this sink in. "You're such a big fan of Humphrey's, I was going to invite you along as a surprise, but you know what? I don't think I'll ask you to sully yourself listening to talk about my "silly wee podcast!"

Dymphna went red, then white, then red again in quick succession. Eve groaned silently. It was rare that her neighbour lost her temper or "allowed spite to wag her tongue," as Niamh would say, but she had put her foot in it this time. Greta was usually a laid-back creature but any slight to her podcast – the very show that had helped them so many times in the past year, solving seemingly inexplicable crimes – was like insulting one of her kids.

"Ladies, please." Eve put her hand on Greta's shoulder. "Dymphna was out of order, and she shouldn't have said that. Your podcast is brilliant – sure, aren't you practically famous now? You're our very own celebrity, and we're terribly proud of you. Dymphna, tell her! You didn't mean it, did you?"

Dymphna pursed her lips. As clearly as if she had spoken, Eve could hear the war raging inside her friend. She knew she was in the wrong and should apologize but if she did so now, it would look as if she just wanted to be re-invited to tea with Humphrey. And if she didn't apologize, she would be doubly in the wrong, but her pride would be intact.

Niamh broke the deadlock by pinching Dymphna's arm, hard.

"Ow!"

"You would be the first to give out if I said something like that about Greta," Niamh snapped. "It was very rude and unfair."

Eve caught her mother's eye and Niamh had the grace to blush. "Oh, okay, full disclosure, I said that you probably tricked him into giving the interview. But not because we don't like your podcast, honestly. Just because we didn't see why a fiction writer would be on a true crime show, that's all. And it was a surprise, seeing you up there."

Eve narrowed her eyes.

"Oh, very well. And we were jealous. Mad jealous. Eaten up with it. Green with envy."

A twitch at the corner of Greta's mouth encouraged Niamh to continue.

"So jealous, in fact, Dymphna almost choked on her boiled sweets. And I distinctly heard Eve say, "The lucky cow!"" She shot a triumphant look at her daughter. "Eve is new to Jerusalem Hill and she's absolutely mad about the books now, aren't you pet? It would be awful hard on her to exclude her from tea."

"I wasn't aware I was excluded?" Eve pointed out. "In fact, I wasn't aware I was even invited in the first place. But – I'd love to go, Greta, if everyone else was going…"

Oh heavens, she thought, a whole evening watching them fawn over the aging author and his fictional detective. Still, in the interests of peace – she watched Dymphna, willing her to make an overture to Greta.

"Greta, I apologize." Dymphna said it with the air of a Monarch admitting a minor flaw. "I was very unfair to you, and I – well, I am a huge fan of your show. I totally understand if you don't want me to attend your tea party, but I do hope you'll accept my sincere apology."

She assumed a slightly martyred air, but after a few seconds added, "I'm a jealous auld cow, Greta, sorry."

A huge grin wrinkled Greta's round face.

"Ach, sure, I admit it – I didn't tell ye *precisely* because I wanted you all to be as jealous as cats!"

Eve laughed. "Well, you certainly achieved that. Honestly, Greta, I thought Mr. Quigley would choke when you started interviewing Mr. Sterling."

"He was like a scalded cat," Greta said complacently. "With a big red face on him. I've owed him one ever since he objected to my little garden – my special one - and then said keeping chickens in a suburb wasn't appropriate. Officious little toad. He tried to keep Humphrey to himself, you know, wouldn't let anyone else correspond with him. But one of my Goode Hunters works in publishing, and put me in touch." Greta's podcast fans were notoriously loyal, covered the globe, and were willing to do anything for their heroine.

"And – are you really having him round for his tea, Greta? Tonight? And can we all come?" Niamh asked.

"Yes, Yes and…oh g'won, then, yes. Seven thirty sharp."

The ladies burst into excited chatter over the prospect of meeting their favourite writer. After basking in their gratitude for an appropriate time, Greta bustled off to talk to the other dignitaries and the few local reporters covering the book festival. Eve tucked her arm through Dymphna's and the old lady smiled.

"I made a show of myself," she said.

"No, you had a moment. We all have them. Greta's fine about it now."

"I admit it, I was jealous. Greta deserves her success, though."

"She's some woman," Niamh said admiringly. "Good on her,

going around Quigley like that. He's a very annoying man."

"He's a pain," Dymphna agreed. "Still, I do wonder – it's not like Greta to stray from the True Crime path. It wouldn't surprise me if she had something else in mind, besides annoying people."

Eve said nothing. Dymphna did like to be right, and if it salved her pride to think Greta might yet have a hidden agenda, so be it. At least everyone was happy and on good terms again, even if it meant sacrificing her evening to Humphrey Sterling.

Chapter 3

Greta had invited quite a few people to tea, it turned out. She lived five minutes walk away from Bramble Lane, in a large Victorian redbrick villa, with bay windows, and basement kitchen, sweeping steps up to the front door and what estate agents liked to call "Period charm" which just meant it needed a good lick of paint.

Her garden was magnificent though, Eve admitted. Spring had come late to Dublin, after months of bitter cold followed by a three week run of sleet and rain. Just as the city had despaired of seeing any good weather that year, April had brought bright sunshine and warmer than average temperatures – and the gardens and parks had responded with a display of colour and foliage beyond everything Eve could remember in previous years. She was justifiably proud of her own garden, absolutely lush with late daffodils and Hyacinths, but it paled compared to Greta's. Bluebells grew everywhere, mixed with primroses and tulips, a bed of Aquilegia nodded in the evening sunshine and Clematis grew against the garden wall and over an archway that led to the back of the house.

"Wow," Eve wished her friend – partner, she smiled to herself – Tom was with her. He was an avid gardener and while he preferred growing vegetables, he had an appreciative eye for a well tended flower bed. She was sure he would love Greta's garden. Whether it would have been adequate compensation for an evening in the company of the over-excited octogenarians and their favourite author, she was less convinced.

"Isn't is lovely?" Niamh remarked. "I do think Greta has a touch when it comes to flowers. If I planted them all higgledy-piggledy like that, it would look a mess. Her version looks like a cottage garden from a fairy tale."

"It *is* lovely," Dymphna agreed, ringing the doorbell. "Her poison garden is excellent as well."

Eve blinked. Poison garden? was that the "special garden" Quigley had objected to? – but before she could ask, the door opened and Greta waved them inside.

"He's in the drawing room, ladies. Go in and be introduced. He has some kind of assistant with him, a right streak of misery – you'll have to go through her first. But he's lovely, once you get to him." Greta disappeared into the kitchen, where she could be heard loudly and happily ordering her army of offspring and in-laws around. Anyone who married into the Goode family had better be prepared to roll up their sleeves and muck in.

Eve pushed open the door of the drawing room but neither of her friends made any attempt to follow her. She looked at them in surprise.

"Come on, then. Isn't this what we came here for."

"I don't know, Eve. Oh dear. Maybe we should wait for Claudia."

"Claudia won't be here for ages yet, Mam. She has to sort all those Brigade women out first. I'm not standing in the hall for an hour. Dymphna, tell her."

"Your mother has a point." Dymphna looked quite flustered, a red spot on each cheek and her dark eyes shifting. "Um. I'm not ready yet." She pulled at her collar and flattened her grey hair with one bony hand.

"What? Oh my god! You're like love-struck teenagers the pair of ye – " Eve shook her head. "Enough. I'll do the talking, until you recover yourselves. Honestly, I can't believe you've lost the run of yourselves over some auld fella."

"He's not some auld fella, and I'll thank you to speak about Mr. Sterling with a bit of respect!" her mother snapped.

"That's the spirit," Eve said approvingly. "Now, in we go."

The drawing room was already well populated, mainly with people Eve recognized as committee members and volunteers from the Merrion Literary Festival. There were some faces she vaguely knew, including other authors and poets roped into the event. She was fairly sure the plump, blonde woman trying to balance a cup of coffee and a slice of chocolate sponge had been on the Late Evening Show the previous Saturday. Emer O'Neill, she was nearly sure of it. The presenter had called her "a voice of her generation," and then went on to patronize the writer for appealing to "women of a certain age."

Eve had enjoyed watching the writer take him down with a series of polite, but acerbic, comments. Making a mental note to try to be introduced to her later – if only she could be sure of her name! – Eve scoped out the room quickly. Apart from those associated with the Festival and a few well-known faces, there were a handful of women clutching copies of the latest Jerusalem Hill novel and gazing adoringly at the guest of honour.

Humphrey Sterling sat in the best armchair on one side of the fireplace, facing the assembly. The "good chair," Eve noted with some amusement, the traditional place of honour in any Irish home. Several empty seats were ranged on either side of him. Mr. Quigley was there, of course, fussing over him. The author looked thoroughly bored and visibly winced as the man murmured something to him. He looked around the room and his face brightened when he saw the newcomers.

"Come on," Eve instructed. "Now's our chance."

As she moved forward, a tall thin woman dressed in a scarlet jacket and a tight black pencil skirt, her brown hair scraped into a severe bun, grabbed at her arm.

"I'm sorry," the woman sounded anything but sorry, "Who exactly are you?" She waved a clipboard under Eve's nose. "We have a list, you know."

Eve's eyes met those of Mr Sterling. The author looked embarrassed and she thought there was a touch of pleading in his gaze. Usually, someone so rude would have provoked a sharp response from either of the older ladies but they were uncharacteristically meek in the presence of their hero. Eve sighed. There was no point in making a fuss, was there?

"My name is Eve Caulton. This is Niamh Boyd, and Dymphna Moriarty. I think you'll find Mrs. Goode put us all on your list."

Unless, and it was a horribly plausible thought, Greta had allowed them to come only to be turned away by this clipboard wielding weapon – it would have been a delicious revenge.

"Oh. Yes. You're here." A tight smile flitted across the assistant's face. "I'm Phyllis Dennehy. Mr. Sterling's Personal Assistant." She stressed her title, obviously expecting them to be impressed.

"Nice to meet you," Eve lied politely. "Well, now we've sorted that out, my mother and Mrs. Moriarty need to sit down.

Excuse me." She strode across to where Humphrey was sitting and indicated the empty chairs beside him. "Excuse me, do you mind if my friends sit here?"

"Oh, not at all," He sprang to his feet, and gave a tiny bow. "Dear ladies, please do make yourselves comfortable."

Quigley scowled at Eve, obviously annoyed at the interruption of his tete-a-tete but couldn't do much about it. He stood up stiffly and said "We'll talk later."

Humphrey smiled at him, but as he walked away, muttered, "Not if I can help it!" He grinned at Eve. "Thank you! I was running out of polite ways to answer him. Very impertinent man – kept asking me about my family, personal life, all kinds of things."

"He's a nosy git," Eve agreed, "though in fairness, it's probably just for his annual write up on the festival. He's pretty much the main organizer."

"Ah, perhaps that explains it. Anyway, never mind that – who are these lovely young women?" He turned the full force of his charm on Dymphna and Niamh. "Dare I hope – fans of my humble scribbling?"

Eve tried not to giggle. He was ridiculously theatrical, but there was something endearing in it. And the reaction from her older friends was delightful – she would have given up many an evening in front of the television to see her mother and the redoubtable Dymphna Moriarty blush like schoolgirls.

"We adore your work," Niamh managed. "And we've been reading you for…for *decades*!"

"I've read everything you've written, including short stories," Dymphna added proudly.

"Oh, my. True fans. How wonderful! Tell me, which of my books is your favourite?"

Eve sat back and relaxed. The question had opened the floodgates and the pair of senior literary critics were now in full flight, arguing passionately over the relative merits of *Sin City* versus *Angel's Dream* while the object of their obsession basked happily in the glow of their admiration.

"It was when Jerusalem finally admits his feelings for Elvira, when he says, *"You're all right, babe."* That was – well, it brought a tear to my eye. Pure romance, so it was."

"But that's nothing compared to when he finds Merriot has betrayed him. His best friend, his army buddy, his right hand man. Oh my god, when he says, *"the bullet came from your gun, Merry –"* I screamed!"

Realizing she was surplus to requirements for the time being, Eve excused herself and took the chance to mingle.

She was glad to recognize some familiar faces in the guests, especially her neighbour Ellen Marrinan. Ellen greeted her enthusiastically.

"I was beginning to think I was the only one under sixty who had come!"

"Are you mad? The auld women wouldn't miss this for the world. It's quite a gathering, isn't it? I assumed it would just be a handful of neighbours."

"Greta has invited everyone associated with the festival and then some. There are quite a few publishers here and agents."

Eve glanced at a few serious looking individuals dotted here and there, looking a little out of place.

"See!" Ellen inclined her head in the direction of one of them, a short stout man with a thinning head of hair, and a smooth unlined face that made him look curiously young, like a schoolboy dressed up in his dad's clothes. Round gold-rimmed glasses were perched on his nose, and in a fashion flex unseen in Dublin since the nineteen seventies, he sported a red bow tie with his gray, three-piece suit. "It's your man off the telly. Oh you know him – the one they always get on The Evening Show to talk about books."

"Ah." The penny dropped. "Damian something. Damian Burke? Something like that. I wonder what he's doing here?"

"Sure, he's Humphrey's agent – well, on this side of the pond at least. I assume he has an American agent too."

"How do you know that?" Eve asked.

"Oh, I just picked it up somewhere. Or maybe Greta told me? I can't remember. "

"Grand. For a moment I thought you were going to tell me you're one of his super-fans." Eve laughed. "Look at my mam and the rest of them. They're all completely batty about those books. Honestly, I just don't understand it."

Ellen looked away. "Ah, they're not that bad. Excuse me…I just want to grab a cup of tea."

She smiled and moved away, leaving Eve standing alone. Feeling rather as if she had put her foot in it – but unable to say how – Eve sighed. She decided to make herself useful, picking her way through the throng and into the kitchen. Greta smiled at her as she entered, but continued to berate a red-faced girl – one of her granddaughters, Eve thought – with the words, "Don't ever make tea without boiling the kettle properly!"

"It had only popped a minute ago," the unfortunate defended herself.

"60 seconds off the boil is sixty seconds too long. Now, make it again, fresh tea with boiling water and bring it in to the guests." She turned to Eve, her usually good-natured round face quite cross. "Honestly, Eve, she spends one summer in the States and forgets how to make a proper pot of tea. Stone cold, it was."

"How can I help?"

"Ach, we've everything under control. Well, you might just bring in these –" she thrust a platter of tiny sandwiches at Eve – "Hand them around. And try to stop that pain-in-the-neck Quigley from annoying poor Humphrey. Honestly, he can't get a moment's peace from the man."

"I saw that. Dymphna and Mam are chatting to him now. They'll owe you big time for this, Greta. I've never seen them so happy."

"Hah! Well, they'll have to admit my little podcast is good for something, eh? No, no – I'm not really annoyed. I knew I was going to make them sick with envy, so I can hardly blame them."

Eve went to leave, clutching the tray of sandwiches.

"Oh -Eve! Here's one thing, Humphrey asked me especially to invite Ronan and Margaret."

"Really? That is interesting. He asked for them by name?"

"Well, yes. Said he would be most grateful, he knew the family. But he didn't say which family – Ronan's or Margaret's. They'll be here shortly."

Eve was curious but then, it wasn't that surprising that the man might know people in Dublin. "I suppose, it might explain why he agreed to do the Merrion Festival. He's a big name for such a local event."

"Yes, I thought the same…" Greta hesitated. "Look, Eve, I wasn't quite up front about –" the ringing of the doorbell interrupted her. "Oh bother, that's probably Claudia. I'll tell you later, okay?"

Eve smiled as her friend went to answer the doorbell. It was typical of Greta to have some intrigue and drama swirling around the most innocuous of events. She would get around to confessing whatever she had been up to in her own good time, and in the meantime there was no point in speculating.

A familiar voice rang out from the hall – Claudia Warren had indeed arrived, accompanied by her daughter Jennie. Eve was very fond of the younger Warren, having had occasion to rely on her legal advice in a very tight spot. There were other voices too – Margaret Furey's and Ronan Dempsey's.

"We all met on the doorstep," Claudia was saying cheerfully, "like a little neighbourhood delegation. I must say, Ronan, I didn't have you pegged for a Jerusalem Hill fan – or is it you, Margaret?"

Eve passed by with the tray of food, deposited it on a table in the living room and returned to the hall, just as Margaret confessed, "I actually don't really know much about him, Claudia. I have heard the name – but I haven't read anything of his. But we were delighted to be invited, weren't we Ronan?"

Ronan nodded, catching Eve's eye with a wry glance. "Yeah. Sure, it's a change from seating plans and sorting out meal choices from the RSVP cards."

Eve gave him a sympathetic wink. "Well, Mr. Sterling has no shortage of adoring fans. I've never read any of his books either, but Mam is absolutely cracked about them."

Jennie Warren rolled her eyes. "This one too," she said, pointing at her mother. "If I've heard once that Jerusalem Hill reminds her of my Dad when he was young –"

Claudia snorted. "You only knew your father when he was old and conservative, God rest him. He was a wild man in his youth. He was the only lad in four parishes to own a motorbike, and he wore black leathers…"

Jennie shook her head and hissed at Eve, "It was a glorified pushbike, with a motor that wouldn't power a hairdryer."

Claudia ignored her daughter. "Greta, the younger generations always think they invented a good time. But we could tell them a thing or two."

Greta laughed – cackled, if Eve was being honest. "Heh. They haven't a notion, Claudia. The things we got up to in our day – well! They'd never cope." She opened the door to her living room turned literary salon. "Come meet Humphrey, Claudia. Now, there's a man who appreciates age and wisdom."

Stifling a fit of the giggles, Eve ushered Jennie and the young couple into the room in Greta and Claudia's wake. As the Brigadier was introduced to the author, Eve fancied she could see the years, indeed the decades, melt away leaving a star-struck girl instead of the self-confident, slightly bossy older woman.

"Ah, they're having a great time," She whispered to Jennie, who nodded.

"I know. I complain, but sure, isn't it great to see them enjoying themselves like this? He's not my cup of tea but I suppose, each to their own."

"It's awful dreck," Eve agreed.

Jennie shrugged. "I watch reality TV to relax. I can hardly criticize someone for reading a bit of purple prose."

"Hmm." Eve couldn't help reflect a little smugly that she didn't watch reality TV – or at least, not the worst type of the same, just the good stuff, the ones with the chefs and the bakers, and maybe the romance ones or that one on the island with the ex-boyfriends. Nor did she read silly books about impossibly charismatic detectives. "Oh, that reminds me – I think I saw Emer O'Neill here. And there's a lovely poet who read earlier – Helen something."

"Oh. I would love to meet Emer O'Neill. Did you read her last book?"

"*Butterflies?* Yes. Loved it." Eve took a discreet look around. "She's over there, on her own. Shall we go say hello?"

"Be rude not to," Jennie grinned.

Emer looked rather pleased to be approached, especially as both women were at pains to show that they had actually read and enjoyed her work. Before long they were a happy trio, exchanging book recommendations and talking about the Literary Festival. As soon as she could catch the poet's eye, Eve called over Helen Dunphy and complimented her on her poetry reading. Helen was as shy in person as she had seemed on stage, but Eve was pleased to note that she relaxed a little as she contributed to the discussion. A pleasant half hour passed, until Margaret tapped Eve on the shoulder.

"Eve, there's something really weird…"

"That's my department all right," Eve smiled. "What's up?"

"I know – I mean, I can swear to it – I've never met anyone called Humphrey Sterling in my life. And I've never read his books, or anything. But I can't shake the strangest feeling that I know him. I keep staring at him, and I know the poor man has clocked it once or twice, he must think I'm a lunatic. But – well, I'm full sure I know him." Margaret peered at her anxiously. "I can't explain it, it's the oddest feeling."

"It happens," Eve smiled reassuringly. "I once said hello to a woman in Dunnes, I was convinced I knew her. Turned out to be that newsreader off the telly – the one with the big helmet of blonde hair. The look she gave me! She must have thought I was a crazed fan."

Margaret laughed, but was obviously distracted. "Maybe that's it – maybe he just reminds me of someone."

"Well, let's narrow it down. An actor? No? Someone you worked with?" Eve paused. She was trying to think of rational explanations, always her first response. She found reaching for less mundane solutions always made her a bit self-conscious. It was hard to trust her intuition, look beyond the surface. Something, in fact, she had promised her mother and Dymphna that she would work on. Now was as good a time as any.

"Give me your hand," she instructed Margaret. "Now let's think. It isn't someone you met recently, or you'd remember. So what are you feeling? How far back is it?"

The hand in hers felt smaller, lighter, and Eve immediately guessed, "Childhood? Someone you met once as a kid – or he reminds you of someone from then?"

Margaret snatched her hand away, and stared at Eve, eyes wide.

"Oh. OH! Eve, he reminds me of – Dad. Of my Dad. His face, a bit, but his build and his mannerisms – and it's not just that. Oh my God! I *have* met him before."

The young woman turned on her heel and crossed the room to where the author sat, pushing her way unceremoniously past her neighbours, past a sour-looking Phyllis Dennehy (still clutching her clipboard) and even squeezing past her hostess, Greta. Humphrey Sterling raised his eyes to hers and Eve thought she saw a flicker of apprehension in them, mingled with something else – hope, excitement? She wasn't sure. At any rate, he didn't protest as Margaret grabbed both his hands and squealed, "Uncle Paddy! It is you! It is! Oh my god, Ronan, it's my uncle Paddy!"

Chapter 4

A mild outbreak of chaos had greeted Margaret's announcement. The media present – two local journalists, one arts editor from a national newspaper and a few book related social media influencers – had pounced on the story. For at least half an hour, Margaret and a gracious Humphrey – or as he used to be known before fame and fortune claimed him, Paddy Furey – answered questions, while the rest of the guests enjoyed a hearty gossip.

"His real name is Paddy Furey?" One woman, a self proclaimed "super fan," considered this. "I knew he wasn't born Humphrey Sterling, of course, but his real name has been a closely guarded secret. For decades."

"Closely guarded?" asked Greta pointedly, "Or merely, no one thought to ask?"

Her guest ignored her. "I suspected of course, that he was linked to this area…."

"How?" Greta interjected. "Margaret Furey isn't from this area, she only moved here a few years ago."

The woman pursed her lips and snorted. "I suppose you know all about it."

Greta grinned. "I know more than you."

Her rival flounced off in search of a more appreciative

audience and Greta turned to her friends. "Can't stand people like that, always trying to muscle in on someone else's story. Well, now we know why Sterling wanted me to invite Margaret and Ronan. He must have been hoping for a chance to meet her."

"It's rather sad, isn't it?" Niamh said. "I mean, he obviously didn't want to approach her directly, so he must have been afraid that she wouldn't want to know him."

"I think you're right. I wonder why he fell out of contact with the family? I suppose, from Margaret's point of view, it must hurt a bit. I mean, that he wasn't around when she lost her parents. She's been awful lonely, so she has." Greta looked over at the Uncle and niece, standing arm in arm for photographs. "She doesn't look like she's bearing a grudge, though."

"She looks ecstatic. Oh, Ronan, there you are. Isn't it amazing?"

The detective gave a nod, but looked less than enthusiastic. Eve touched his arm, and he turned to her, his face troubled.

"Is everything all right, Ronan?"

"Yes, of course. Well, at least – it is, I suppose. I'm just a bit…well, Margaret has had a pretty rough time of it over the years. She is very trusting for someone who hasn't had much reason to trust people. Look what happened with the O'Reilly's!"

Their former neighbours, a couple called O'Reilly, had befriended Margaret but only to use her. It had very nearly had disastrous consequences for the young teacher.

"But this is different, Ronan. Humphrey – Paddy – is her family, and he's a successful author with no reason to want anything from her. It's a shock, but really, there's no reason to be suspicious."

"Suspicious?" Ronan laughed suddenly. "Am I being suspicious? Ah, it's probably just the Garda in me, Eve. A cop is never off duty, eh?"

"Go over there and introduce yourself to your new in-law," Niamh advised. "And stop fretting. It'll be lovely for Margaret to have family around."

"Oh!" Claudia's face lit up. "I expect he will be at the wedding."

A hush fell over the senior ladies of the group, and Eve did not need to employ any special powers to know that each and every one of them was rapidly revising what they planned on wearing to the event.

"And –" Dymphna said, "And if he's sticking around, it really behooves us – as Margaret's mentors and advisors, and the closest thing she's had to family until now – it's really our duty to take him under our wing."

Eve winced. Poor Mr Sterling thought he had found a long lost niece, but in reality had inherited a neighbourhood of incorrigible old bats.

"Steady on, ladies. He may be flying off in the morning to another festival for all we know."

"He's staying for a week at least," Greta informed them. "I got his itinerary out of Lemon Face, his personal assistant. And - he's accepted an invitation to stay with me for the duration."

The other ladies greeted this announcement in silence, but Dymphna managed a gracious smile. "That's lovely, Greta. I'm sure we'll all help you entertain him."

Greta rewarded her friend with an equally gracious "Ye can all call in whenever you want." Her eyes sparkled, her triumph complete.

The niceties observed, Dymphna gestured to the tall brunette with the clipboard, and winked.

"Speaking of Phyllis. She doesn't look too happy about all this, does she?"

The woman in question was standing to one side, hovering around her employer and looking as if she would like to push Margaret aside.

"This is probably interfering with her precious timetable," Greta said. "She was like a tartar earlier, insisting that everything had to be done just so, ready half an hour before kick off, complaining if anyone took a minute to themselves."

One of her daughters in law passed by with a tray of sandwiches and Greta called her over. "Give us a few of them, before the savages descend. Sheila, tell them what that Phyllis one was like earlier."

Sheila, married to one or other of Greta's many strapping sons, a slight woman with a gentle expression, stuffed sandwiches onto the ladies' already full plates.

"She was a pain in the bum, Greta. My wee Charlie called in to help and she roared at him for putting the wrong napkins on the table. *Only plain white ones! Are you colour blind?*""

"Wee Charlie" was a six foot teenager, if Eve recalled correctly.

"What did Charlie say?"

"He told her to stuff her napkins, threw the white ones into the recycling bin, and went off to Hurling practice."

Greta nodded approvingly. "Good lad. I see she went with the red in the end."

Sheila moved on and the ladies considered the abrasive personal assistant.

"It's odd that someone as charming as Humphrey would

have her around," Niamh remarked.

"I don't know. Sometimes you need a weapon like that, especially if you're easy-going." Everyone turned to see who had spoken and Emer O'Neill blushed deeply.

"Oh, I'm so sorry. It's such a bad habit – eavesdropping. It's the peril of being a writer. I was so interested in what you ladies were saying, and it just popped out…"

"Not a bother," Greta said. "I eavesdrop all the time. The things you hear!"

"Me too," Niamh agreed. "I once stayed on a bus three stops past my own, because the woman beside me was telling the most *riveting* story to her friend over the phone. I couldn't bear not to hear the end. Here, squeeze in there beside Eve."

Emer grinned and joined the group. "Thanks. Anyway – I know what it's like at book signings and events. You can be treated really well – or you can be walked over by staff and the public. I have an agent, she's brilliant, lovely woman. But if you met her at an event where they were being rude to me, or hadn't set things up properly, you'd swear she was a right cow."

Eve eyed Phyllis from afar, rather doubtfully. "You think Phyllis has a nice, pleasant side to her?"

"It's possible. Or maybe she's always like that. But I bet Humphrey there is often glad to have someone around who will be demanding and picky, while he gets to be the nice, gracious famous author."

"That's a point," Dymphna conceded. "It isn't easy to be the one who has to get everything done on time."

"Still doesn't explain why she's giving the evil eye to Margaret," Niamh sniffed. "Look at her. You'd swear she was jealous."

"Maybe she is." Eve sighed. "She's his right hand, at the moment. She probably has a say in a lot of things, and now, in her mind, someone else will have influence over him."

Niamh went to answer but Greta hushed her. "I'm trying to hear what he's saying,"

The representative of the larger, national newspaper was now taking his turn to interview the reunited family members. Ronan had joined them, Margaret clutching his arm on one side and her uncle's on the other, looking the picture of happiness. Humphrey too looked delighted, Eve was glad to note.

"Mr. Sterling, Aidan Lowe of The Evening Times – this is an extraordinary moment, worthy of any of your mystery novels. Can you tell us – how is it you and your niece – Margaret? – lost contact?"

Margaret looked a little embarrassed. "I was too young ... I can't remember."

Humphrey shook his head and patted her arm. Avuncular good-nature personified, Eve thought, then immediately felt guilty for being snide. The man was obviously delighted that his niece was happy to acknowledge him.

"It was my fault, entirely mine. I was – well, young and arrogant. Our family were good, solid, middle-class people. Teachers, Bank clerks and the like. I didn't fit in, to put it bluntly. My parents didn't understand the burning desire – nay, the need – to write. My brother, God rest him, was also bewildered by it but he encouraged me as far as he could. He was a lovely man." He stared into space for a moment, seemingly lost in memories. Then with a little laugh, he continued, "But when I decided not to do some kind of course after leaving school – or get a "good job," in a bank or whatever it was they suggested – even poor Lorcan lost patience with me. He gave me a lecture, as I saw it, on the foolishness of thinking one could just run away and become a successful writer. In my defense, I was hurt – very hurt. But I know now he meant well. He was only looking out for me."

A murmur of sympathy went through the guests, and Eve could have sworn she saw Dymphna dabbing a tear from her beady eyes.

"I lashed out, Margaret. I was cruel and said things – hurtful things. All due respect to your father, Lorcan never once retaliated. He just said over and over, he wanted me to be happy but that maybe I should get a job and work on my writing in my spare time." Humphrey sighed. "Perhaps – perhaps he was right. But I thought the only way to be successful was to leap in, both feet. So – I did. I went to London first, and then to America. I was one of the hundreds of thousands of young Irish immigrants, fighting their way to a better life – and in many ways, it made me the man I am today!"

A round of applause greeted this statement, with Margaret now hanging on his every word, and only Ronan still looking slightly skeptical. The Detective Garda was not easily swayed.

"Ah, long story short, once my first novel was published and I was full of my success, I came home on and off. But if I am honest – I was insufferable. I boasted. I preened. Your father and mother made me welcome, put up with my antics and they were the ones who minded my parents into their old age. They lived quiet, peaceful, kind lives. As time went by, I thought about them less and less, and was swept up in all the glamour of my life as a bestselling author, with books that made it to the Big Screen."

"I thought it was a TV series?" Eve whispered to her mother.

Niamh glared at her and ignored the question.

Humphrey drew a shaky breath. "By the time I realized what a fool I was, how I had ignored the best friend I would ever have, my own brother – it was too late. He was gone, and his dear wife Alison. I tried to get in touch with Margaret but I couldn't find out much about her. It was before the age of instant information, before we all became so easily connected online. But when I was invited to come here, I started to research her again and – a miracle!"

"You found out that I lived right nearby!" Margaret interjected. "Oh, isn't that just amazing? It's meant to be, Uncle Pad- I mean, Uncle Humphrey."

"Ah, yes. I was born humble Patrick Furey, I admit it. I don't mind you calling me Paddy, my dear. It reminds me of your father." He added pointedly, "Although I shall of course remain Humphrey Sterling to everyone else."

The journalists moved around the room, getting a few quotes from the other literary figures. The man from the Evening Times approached Emer O'Neill with a familiar smile.

"Lovely to see you again, Emer," He winked conspiratorially. "A bit much, eh?"

"It's a lovely story, though," she replied politely. "A family reunited."

"Hmm. Very convenient though, isn't it? Here, in front of an audience? The girl seems genuine enough, I would say she had no idea. But I wouldn't put it past the old fox to have arranged it all. Of course, his niece could just be a good liar."

Oblivious to the sudden frostiness in the air, the man ploughed on. "And it must gall you a bit, eh? Playing second fiddle at a "literary" festival to an old hack like Sterling?"

The writer, despite being rather short and a little plump,

managed to look imposing and stern as she drew herself up and faced down the journalist.

"Mr. Lowe, I have respect for every genre of writing, and every writer. If I can look back on a career as long and as successful as Humphrey Sterling's, I'll be very grateful."

"Hah." Lowe just grinned, not a whit abashed. "Yeah, right. Of course, you're wise to be careful what you say. I've heard some of his fans are positively rabid, absolutely mad old bats."

Eve instinctively took a step backwards. Dymphna and Niamh didn't, as she had half feared, launch themselves at the literary correspondent, but their expressions would have "frozen the blood of a martyr," as her Dad used to say. She didn't need to exercise any form of psychic ability to know Mr. Lowe was about to regret his life choices, and very soon.

"Well, bye for now," he gave them a little wave of his hand. "Off to file copy. We'll puff it up, of course, it's too sweet a story not to run it, but mark my words, Sterling is a slippery one."

"Mind how you go," Dymphna said. She managed to make it sound like a warning.

"Yeah, be careful out there," Niamh added. "Wouldn't want you to trip and hurt yourself."

"Mam…" Eve said pleadingly.

"Be well," Claudia said pointedly, patting the journalist on his shoulder with a friendly pat that made him wince. "Lots of awful doses going around. I heard there's a terrible outbreak of strep throat."

"And a stomach bug," Greta piped up. "I really hope you don't pick up any stomach bugs."

"Oh. Um, well – yes, thank you. Good evening." Lowe bustled off and Eve shook her head at her mother and friends.

In front of Emer and Helen, she couldn't say anything, but she hoped they hadn't gone for overkill on the (admittedly, unlikable) hack.

"He's an awful pain," Emer remarked. "But he's terribly influential. He can make or break a new author with his reviews."

"You stood up to him, though." Dymphna gave the younger woman an approving smile.

"Ah, I'm lucky enough. My books sell well, and now even if he hates one, his reviews don't have as much impact. But I dread to think what he'll write about poor Humphrey's latest - I got the impression he didn't like him much."

"He's a cynic, all right." Claudia said. "And how dare he even suggest our Margaret would lie? Or be part of a – a publicity stunt?"

"In fairness, he doesn't know her," Eve pointed out. "And maybe, we should give him the benefit of the doubt a little?"

The older ladies just sniffed and looked disgusted.

"Ah well," Eve told herself, "I tried. Maybe Lowe won't wake up to a world of pain tomorrow."

But she wasn't hopeful.

Chapter 5

Monday morning and time for more wedding planning. The excitement of the Saturday night had kept everyone up late but a leisurely lie in the next morning had soon revived her. She and Tom had spent Sunday having a lovely time, first gardening and then a trip to the cinema. Mondays were usually quite busy, with her art classes in the afternoon, but the morning was earmarked for wedding prep. She was determined to get as much done on Margaret's behalf as possible. It would be nice if the young couple could have a relaxed few days running up to the big event.

She was pressed into action as soon as she arrived at Wisteria Cottage, Margaret having a last minute crisis about her veil.

"It's definitely ivory," Eve insisted, holding it up to the light and casting a critical, artistic eye over it.

"It looks white to me." Niamh snatched the veil from her and examined it in the sunlight herself. "Are you sure it'll match?"

Unfortunately, her mother had turned up on the doorstep just as she was leaving, and had invited herself along. This was not proving helpful. Eve fought the urge to strangle her mother. Margaret was already wound up – the last thing she needed to worry about was if the veil matched the dress.

"Mam. I am an artist. Colours – down to the tiniest nuance

– are my business. I am telling you, that veil is the exact shade of ivory to match the dress."

"Well, if you say so…" Niamh looked unconvinced but laid the offending headdress down carefully and settled back into her chair. Wisteria cottage shared the same layout as all the houses on Bramble Lane – a tiny hall with a staircase leading up to the bedrooms (two, the same size, one facing the front garden and the other overlooking the back garden) with a door leading off the hall into the sitting room at the front, the kitchen at the back and a small scullery to the side. In Eve's house the old scullery was a storage room for her artist equipment. In Tom's it was an extension of his gardening shed. In Ronan's it was – well, no one was sure but Eve guessed it was probably a junk room.

In the Marrinan's place, Holly Cottage, Finn and Ellen had extended the house out into the garden, which enabled the family of four to stay on Bramble Lane where they had made friends since returning from the United States – the scullery made a little storage area for sports gear including Boyd's hurl and sliotar. In the USA, Boyd had played hockey, but in Dublin, he had found his true vocation as a Hurler – his combination of speed, agility and absolute fearlessness earned him a place on the local team and perhaps the county board, all going well. He lived and breathed the sport now.

In Wisteria Cottage, Margaret had turned the space into wedding headquarters. With Eve's help, she had made her own invitations, party favours, centerpieces and place-names. On one wall hung a large whiteboard, covered in a "work in progress" seating plan. By far the worst part of planning any Irish wedding is the intricacies of who should sit where, and with whom. Put your single friend at a table full of couples, and risk a falling out. How can they be expected to meet anyone at a table full of people already taken? Put them at a table with other singles, and risk the same. How could you isolate all the single people like that?

Put Aunt Mary beside Auntie Joan, when they haven't spoken in forty years over the issue of who broke Granny's turkey dish, and all hell might break loose. If Uncle Joe was at the same table as young Pat, he might be so shocked by the young fella's off colour remarks, the wedding could end with an ambulance being called.

Family feuds lasting generations had been kicked off over seating plans at weddings.

Margaret had a very small pool of immediate family – a few elderly cousins, and her newly discovered Uncle made up the bulk of her guest list on that score – but she had a great many friends. Ronan had a lot of family, all excited to descend on Dublin from the far-flung reaches of the West of Ireland, Cork, Belfast and in one case, the Aran Islands. Added to this was a large list of colleagues, all Gardaí. Ronan had, in strictest confidence, provided a list of cousins that it might be unwise to seat beside, or even near, an officer of the law.

"Mam, we really need to get on with this. Margaret is too polite to tell you to go away, but really, you need to go away."

"Sure, I can help with the seating. I'm very good with things like that. Show me the plan again."

"Mam!"

"Oh, all right. Tell you what, I'll pop the kettle on and make us all a nice cup of tea…" She wandered off, humming to herself while Eve buried her head in her hands.

Margaret gave Eve a sympathetic look. "It's all right, honestly. She's not in the way."

"She's in my way. Ah, never mind. Let's see where we are. I think we've nearly cracked it, you know. If we put Ronan's Aunt Claire and her plus one with the Marrinan's, that leaves a space at table nine for Superintendent Kelly and his wife. Then Jo Maguire can enjoy herself away from her boss, with DS Cullen and his guests. Isn't it lovely though – Cullen has been seeing Ashleigh and Sean's mother since Christmas and it looks like it's going to go the distance..."

"Oh, they're made for each other. Poor woman – very difficult to date again after losing your husband, but Cullen is very sensitive underneath that tough exterior. Now I've got to know him properly, I think he's a dote. And Ronan wouldn't have any other partner, you know, he and Cullen are like brothers."

"Well, that just leaves the issue of Ronan's cousin, Dessie. Now, as I see it, the main issue is he can't stop making jokes about policemen, and he loves to wind up Ronan. It's not like he's actually a criminal." Unlike the Poitín-smuggling cousin from Clones, she thought, or his brother with the very dodgy line in used cars. "I was thinking about it – instead of trying to fit Dessie in somewhere else, which throws out all our other seating arrangements, let's put him at table five, with the rest of Ronan's workmates. Let's see him make his snide comments with nine Gardaí staring at him."

"Oh. Genius."

"And...we're done!" Eve stared at the plan. "As long as no one falls out with anyone before the wedding, we're good to go. One thing, though – I assume your Uncle will be at the high table with you and Ronan and your parents-in-law?"

Margaret's face lit up. "Yes! It'll be so nice, Eve. Having a family member there, when honestly I thought – sure, it's just perfect now."

"You're getting on well then?" Niamh had come into the room so silently, despite the laden tray of cups and plates in her hands, she made both women jump. "You and Mr. Sterling are doing well?"

Eve rolled her eyes. The mystery of Niamh's sudden desire to help was solved. No doubt she had promised to ferret out the news and report back to the others. They had already tried to pump Eve for information, but she had deemed it none of their business. After their reunion, Margaret and her uncle had spent the Sunday together enjoying a catch-up, with Ronan hovering on the sides. Eve still wasn't sure how he felt about his new uncle-in-law but he seemed determined to put a friendly face on it all. Eve and Margaret had texted back and forth a few times, but Eve had tried not to be inquisitive. Now, when she might reasonably have expected a nice chat with Margaret about the situation, Niamh had stuck her oar in.

As she had feared, Margaret withdrew a little.

"Yes, of course. He's so nice, and he's agreed to stay until after the wedding. Which is really lovely, considering how busy he is."

Niamh nodded. "So we'll definitely get to see a bit more of him, then?"

"Yes, absolutely. And I was going to ask Greta could she have us all over for our tea some evening this week, have a proper visit with ye."

Eve had to admit, this seemed to satisfy Niamh, who could hardly wait to gulp her tea and wolf down a few biscuits before hurrying away.

"She's off to tell the ladies that their idol is not only attending the wedding, but they'll get to have a private tea party with him soon. Without having to wait on Greta's invitation." Eve's lips twitched as she added, "Very neatly done, Margaret."

"Hah. I've picked up a few tricks for dealing with those ladies," her young friend admitted. "I love them to death, I do, but –"

"But they also make you want to emigrate to the furthest reaches of Antarctica?"

"Sometimes. Nah, that's churlish of me. They're great craic, really and I'm truly fond of them all. But – I wanted to talk to you about Uncle Paddy – he likes me to call him that, as long as I say Humphrey in public – and about Ronan."

"Ah. Yes. I did notice that Ronan seemed a little…undecided, about your uncle?"

"I can't understand it. Normally, he's the most supportive person on earth and he knows how much this means to me. But he hasn't warmed to Uncle at all. He's very polite and if you didn't know him, you'd say he was being friendly but – it's all on the surface. Whenever I talk about Paddy, about how successful he is or how kind he's being, Ronan says "yes," and "Of course" but I can tell it's not what he's really thinking."

Eve was taken aback. It didn't surprise her that Ronan was a little wary of the newcomer but that it was so deeply rooted, so quickly, came as a surprise.

"He's a detective. Gardaí are all a bit like that, you know. They are naturally suspicious." Eve considered Ronan, and laughed. "And in fairness, he's the most Garda-like Garda there ever was. Sure, Dymphna will tell you – he lived on Bramble Lane for nearly five years before anyone knew he was a cop!"

Margaret brightened up. "You have a point. And he's very protective. He can't help it."

"There you are. I'm sure once he gets to know your uncle properly, he'll be different."

Privately, Eve was torn between thinking that Ronan's nose was a little out of joint, with Margaret so enthralled by her famous relative – and thinking perhaps he was right to be cautious.

"I'd say you're enjoying getting to know Humphrey better?" she asked, as casually as she could manage.

"Oh yes! He's led the most fascinating life. Wait til you hear some of his stories. He's been everywhere and done everything. He must think I'm an awful hick in comparison, don't you think? But he's so nice about everything – says Wisteria is a beautiful home, and that it reminds him of a cottage on the grounds of some huge estate in Connecticut! He admires your paintings, Eve, says he saw some of them in an exhibition in London. He loves Dublin, too. I think he might even plan on buying a place here, at some point. He says he has been awful lonely, despite all his fame. He would love to spend time near family. Isn't that such a compliment?"

The bride-to-be rattled on happily, extolling the virtues of her uncle, while Eve listened carefully. Try as she might, there was no hint of anything underhand in any of his dealings so far, she decided. Just an elderly man, past the flush of his success, delighted to be back on good terms with his only close family.

And maybe just a tad too fond of embellishing a good story, if Margaret's second hand versions were anything to go by. Perhaps that's what was throwing Ronan off, Eve thought. The detective was honest, and straightforward, with little patience for what he would see as falsehoods. The harmless tall tales of the author, trying to impress his niece, might make Ronan feel uncomfortable.

Feeling she had solved the mystery, and promising herself to have a wee chat with Ronan when the opportunity arose – convey to him that the creative temperament was prone to a little exaggeration – she took her leave of Margaret, conscious that she had a lot of work to get through. Without meaning to, Eve had created quite a busy schedule for herself between giving paid art lessons in the Community centre, unpaid tuition to some of the local schoolchildren with talent that outstretched their parents' means, and volunteering on various local committees. It was unbelievable that less than a year earlier she had arrived on Bramble Lane, divorced, uprooted and rather lonely. It gave her a sort of fellow feeling with Humphrey Sterling – if she had found safe harbour here, then surely he could too.

Chapter 6

Greta Goode was waiting for Eve on her doorstep. Her usual air of irrepressible mischief was absent, instead she looked worried. She cut short Eve's surprised greeting, and pointed to the front door.

"Talk inside," she said rather shortly. Eve took her cue from the older lady, but not without a discreet eye roll. Her mother, neighbours and friends seemed to treat Kimberly Cottage as the headquarters for every crisis, major or minor. She didn't begrudge them her time but really, they could try to ring or text in advance, just once.

"Okay, Greta. Shoot." Eve had closed the front door firmly, led the old woman into the sitting room and settled her into one of the two large, comfortable armchairs. "What's up?"

"You know the way Humphrey Sterling is staying with me?" Greta said. "He has decided to stick around for the wedding, so he'll be at mine for a while."

"Oh. Well, that's nice I suppose. Though I'm surprised he didn't opt to stay with Margaret, now."

"With the house turned upside down, for the wedding? Sure, what would a man of his age be doing, surrounded by fabric samples and flower arrangements?"

"Fair enough. So, he's staying with you and…?"

"And – ah, here. I'd better start at the beginning. But I'm trusting you not to go gossiping around with this. No telling your Mam, or Dymphna or Claudia, you hear? Not yet, at least."

"Okay." Eve was interested now, despite herself .

"You remember I interviewed Humphrey for the podcast, at the reading?"

"I do."

"And you remember how annoyed the others were? They were convinced I was up to something. They weren't entirely wrong."

Eve resisted the urge to drop her head into her hands and groan aloud.

"Greta, what have you done?"

"Me? Nothing. Really, Eve, don't jump to conclusions. All I'm doing is my job, but it's all getting a bit complicated. So I wanted to talk to someone about it, and you're the only one I can tell who won't go blabbing it around."

"Ah Greta – if it's important to you, Mam and the others wouldn't gossip about it!"

"Maybe not. But they wouldn't like what I'm doing, and I'd sooner not have them wading in with their opinions just yet." She gave Eve a sly grin. "Time enough for that when I have all my ducks in a row."

Eve gave up. "Okay. Fill me in. Start at the beginning and don't stop until you reach the end."

"You sound like your mother when you say that." Greta sniffed. "I don't suppose you'd stir yourself to make a cuppa tea, while I tell you?"

One pot of tea brewed, a plate of biscuits (the second best ones) in front of her, and Greta was finally ready to start.

"You know how occasionally I cover old unsolved cases? Usually Irish based ones, or the UK, because that's what my listeners are interested in. But every now and then I cover the famous ones, especially the American ones. The Black Dahlia, The Zodiac, Room 1046, that kind of thing. Then a few years ago I heard of a little known case, The Microwave Murder."

Something of Eve's thoughts must have shown in her face, because Greta broke off to add sharply, "I didn't name the case, Eve, that's what the media called it. Anyway – in nineteen ninety five, almost thirty years ago, the vice-president of Brighton House Publishing, at the time a very well-regarded, literary publisher, was murdered. His name was Cornelius Watkins. The method was almost unbelievable – it looked at first as if there had been some kind of electrical fault that caused a fire to spread throughout his house. But even back then, there were rumours. It was labeled an accident, then a murder, and then finally, an accident again. But the rumours have never subsided, and there are still a few people around from that time who are convinced it was a murder."

"Interesting stuff, but what does it have to do with our famous author?"

"Ah. Well, firstly – he was originally signed by a top literary agent, touted around as the next Hemingway or something. When he failed to produce a great literary novel, he was dropped like a hot potato. The story goes, it was Cornelius Watkins who absolutely trashed his manuscript and that prompted the agent to kick him. In desperation, Sterling wrote the first Jerusalem Hill novel and the rest is history."

"Wow. So when you interviewed him, you were going to use it as background for a podcast on the cold case?"

"Yes. No. Not exactly. There's a bit more to it than that. You see, that manuscript of Humphrey's that Cornelius Watkins read, I've been told that it was a very early version of the Jerusalem Hill books, but dressed up to be lofty and highbrow. It was about a writer who despairs of ever achieving critical success, so he decides to exact revenge on those who stand in his way. It was supposed to be a searing commentary on the publishing industry, and the fickleness of fame, but Watkins hated it. Called it shallow, pulp fiction, ridiculous..."

Eve stared at Greta. "Oh my. Let me guess, you think Humphrey had a motive to kill Watkins?"

Greta sighed. "No. I don't think so. Probably not. Look, it was all just fascinating connection and rumours, something to pad out for the podcast, until he turned out to be Margaret's long lost relative. Now, he's staying in my house and I feel a bit..."

Eve spluttered. "Greta! Are you trying to tell me you feel a bit guilty?"

"Whisht. You're a cheeky young wagon. Oh, okay, I do feel a bit...underhand. And also a bit worried, I mean, should I tell Margaret? or Ronan?"

Eve shook her head in horror. "For the love of - No! Absolutely not. Greta, no offense but you've spun a tenuous connection between Humphrey and this unfortunate man into something it's not."

"You really think so?"

"I do. And whatever your original motive in inviting him to stay, now he's Margaret's family..."

"You know what? You're right. I've been fretting over nothing." Conscience salved, the old woman perked up. "Make us a cuppa there, like a good girl. And a decent biscuit, I know you have them somewhere."

Greta left half an hour later, in high good humour. It was Eve who was left with an oddly unsettled feeling.

* * *

Later the same day, Eve knocked on the door of Rowan Tree Cottage, Tom's cottage on Bramble Lane. While the cottages were all built to the same specifications over a hundred years earlier, each had their own distinct character from the different designs in the gardens to the colours chosen to paint the exteriors.

Tom's cheerful colour choices, in both plants and paint, made his home a warm and welcoming place. Whereas many now overlooked the humble spring flowers of daffodils, hyacinth and crocus, Tom had planted a riot of yellow, white and green from tall to tiny, with patches of purple and yellow adding to the scene. His back garden was dedicated to vegetables and herbs, a hobby which had recently extended to the new allotments beside the park, and Eve frequently wondered what on earth he planned to do with the mountain of food he was growing. Judging by the tomato plants alone they would be drowning in homemade ketchup in September. But it made him happy, which made her happy, so if she had to sell them by the punnet to every neighbour to get rid of them, she would.

This made her think of Wexford strawberries, sold in punnets on the side of the road for miles around the county of Wexford, and further afield, still warm from the Summer sun. When she was young, they would always buy two punnets, she remembered. One they would share in the car, her mother popping a plump red and green treat into her Dad's mouth as he drove and Conor bickering with her over the biggest ones. The second punnet they would bring home and eat with ice cream – a block of vanilla by HB farms, back in the day when there really was a Hazelbrook farm, wrapped in its brightly coloured cardboard covering.

Tom opened his front door to find Eve lost in thought, a rather wistful smile on her face.

"What's up, love?"

"Oh, don't mind me! Sorry, I was miles away. Something reminded me of Sunday drives out with my parents and Conor…strawberries and ice cream…you know how it is!"

"I do. You start off thinking about what size nail you need to fix a fence and end up in the attic looking through old photo albums and you're not entirely sure how one thing led to another. It's a sign of getting old, you know."

"Cheek. I'm in my prime." Eve kissed him and added, "But let's have strawberries and ice cream soon, okay?"

"Absolutely." Tom eyed her quizzically. "You sure you're okay?"

"I'm grand. Stick the kettle on though – I've had a day of it."

She sat in the peace of Tom's sitting room – more elegant than her own rather eclectic one, with it's comfortable but mismatched armchairs and tables– and waited until he placed a steaming mug of coffee and a plate of biscuits in front of her.

"I shouldn't," She said, taking a chocolate covered offering. "But I will."

"Sure, you've a great figure. You walk everywhere, you're very active. Have a biscuit and enjoy it."

"I'm a hypocrite," Eve grinned. "I make all the right noises about giving up sweet things but then I insist we get strawberries and ice cream!"

"Life's too short," Tom choose a shortbread with a jam filled centre and bit into it with gusto. "As long as you're healthy overall, it won't hurt. Now, pleased as I am to see you, what's on your mind? You didn't call around just for the love of my biscuits."

"Not entirely," Eve admitted. "I just wanted to talk to you. Ever have a feeling something bad is going to happen? Or that something isn't quite right, but you can't decide what or even if you're imagining it?"

Tom nodded. "Occasionally. I always think it means that subconsciously I've picked up on some detail that I'm not fully aware of. Like once, when I was still running the antique shop, a man tried to sell me an antique dresser. It was a lovely piece, just perfect, and came with impeccable papers. Full provenance, it all checked out. But still, I couldn't shake the feeling that there was a problem – I examined it twice, I hummed and hawed…I was so tempted but in the end, I passed. The man was furious, but I felt sure I was right. It turned out, it was a stolen piece and I had read about it months before and promptly forgotten the details. But when it was in front of me, my brain kept trying to tell me it was dodgy. Best forged paperwork I've ever seen, though. The man was an artist in his own way."

"So, you reckon it's not so much instinct as buried knowledge?"

"Ah. I think it depends on the person. Now, an auld plodder like me – I don't get inspiration, as a rule. But someone like you – or Dymphna – then yes, I think sometimes it's more than just your subconscious."

Eve blushed. It was a tacitly avoided subject, that of the rather special abilities she shared with her mother and the older ladies. And now with their young friend Ashleigh showing every sign of being a very talented young lady, there was a new generation to think about. But she had never spoken to Tom about any of it. It was a relief to hear him be so matter of fact, and unfazed.

"I do have moments where I just know – like, *know* – something," Eve said quietly.

"Ah." Tom sipped his tea and then added, "When I was a lad, my dad sent me off to live with my Aunt Philomena for a Summer. It's a long story, but my mother was sick and he thought it was for the best. And she did recover, probably the faster for not having a rambunctious twelve year old under her feet, so he was right. But at the time, I was furious. Hated him for it. I felt rejected, I suppose. At that time, he and I weren't close but I was very fond of my mother. So, when I arrived in Kerry to Philomena's small farm, I was hell bent on being as rude and unpleasant as possible."

"So she would send you home?" Eve guessed. Tom laughed.

"Exactly. But oh, my – I met my match in Aunty Mena. She was a little bird of a woman, looked like she was carved out of bog oak, tough and sinewy and as strong as any man. She also had a will of iron, and a heart of gold. And I wasn't there a week before I realized, she had the ear of every neighbour, and they relied on her. She had the cure for animals and humans, she knew what to do about disputes and fights, she helped the young ones pair up, she helped them deal with the in-laws too – she was what that generation and the ones before her knew as a Bean Feasa."

"A wise woman, a woman of knowledge…" Eve murmured.

"So you see, I'm not unaware of the power of a good woman with a will of iron and a heart of gold. " His eyes twinkled at her. "Let's start from the premise that I won't dismiss what you feel, and tell me what's bothering you."

"Tom MacDonagh, I do love you." Eve blew him a kiss, and settled down to tell her woes.

"I have very little to base any of this on, but – Humphrey Sterling. I know the auld ladies are mad about him, but his turning up has stirred a lot of things up. Greta just told me that she interviewed him, because she's investigating a cold case for her podcast and he's connected to it. And it's a mad, silly connection, at that – apparently some publisher may or may not have been murdered and he had recently rejected Humphrey's work." She paused to allow Tom digest this. "I told her it's not worth worrying about, and I mean it. But ever since Humphrey turned up, I've felt…worried. And then there's Ronan. You must have noticed, he's not a bit pleased that Sterling is hanging around. I can't help but wonder if it's insecurity or just his natural caution or – does he know something we don't about Margaret's uncle?"

She waited for Tom to speak. He liked to turn things over in his mind before jumping in, and while she was impatient to hear his thoughts, she knew there was no point in rushing him. Eventually he set his coffee cup down and leaned forward.

"Okay. It's only been a few days, Eve. Ronan doesn't like change, and probably is a bit suspicious of Mr. Sterling. I don't think he would let Margaret befriend the man if he actually knew anything to his detriment – so, I would say, give it time. They've the wedding to get through, then the honeymoon and so on, plenty of time for the gloss to wear off and for Margaret to find out for herself if he's all he pretends to be. Now, where Greta is concerned, you know what she's like. Wonderful woman but she does get a bee in her bonnet about things. Remember when she hounded that Councillor about the death of his Aunt ? Or was that before you moved here? She got a bee in her bonnet about him, and how he might have poisoned the poor old lady…she went after him like a terrier with a rat. He got an injunction against her, two of them in fact, and she ignored them. It was terrifying to watch. No one could reason with her."

Eve felt the knot of worry she had been carrying loosen. "You're right. I'm worrying about stuff I can't do anything about. Margaret won't hear a word against her Uncle, and why should she? He's done nothing but be nice to her. Ronan knows his own mind, and nothing I say will change that. And Greta – the last person she ever listened to was her mother, and that was about seventy years ago. By the way, what happened with the Councillor?"

Tom grinned. "Oh, she presented a mountain of evidence to the Gardaí and they exhumed the body. Turned out he had poisoned her."

Chapter 7

Margaret Furey patted her waist, and gave herself a metaphorical pat on the back. With only a week to the wedding, she had definitely managed to tone up her stomach. She was generally happy with her appearance but the beautifully fitted wedding dress was a little unforgiving and add to that a two week honeymoon in the Seychelles, in a swimsuit. The most confident person would be a little worried, she thought.

She had set herself a target – many sit ups and push ups and abdominal crunches later, that target was well within reach. She had intended to go to the gym after work but a long hard day had defeated her good intentions. Still, she wasn't too worried now, looking at her figure. She'd make it up tomorrow.

A noise downstairs alerted her to the presence of her Uncle.

She had given Paddy- Humphrey, she corrected herself – his own set of keys to Wisteria cottage now, so he could pop in and out with ease. It was awfully good of Greta to put him up until the wedding, she thought, but the poor man needed to get away every now and then. Ronan had been a little shocked at her handing over keys to someone she had only known a day, but she had insisted. Somewhere along the line, she had picked up the idea that family called in and out of each other's houses without warning, and now here she was, with her own family member popping in whenever it suited him. She smiled at her reflection.

"Better let him know I'm here," she told her mirror image. "He'll have heart failure if I suddenly appear."

Leaning over the banisters and peering into the hall beneath, she was just about to shout out *"hello!"* when she heard her uncle speaking. Only his side of the conversation was audible, and that was pretty hard to miss. Gone were the measured, rich tones – his voice was pleading, urgent.

"...I can't right now. Things are a little tight. I just need a bit of time..."

There was a pause, as someone on the other end of the line spoke.

"Just give me some time - I have it all in hand. My new book - yes, I swear, it's sold...yes. Just need some time..."

Margaret withdrew hastily, her heart beating fast. She hated hearing any kind of row, and added to that was the embarrassment of being an unwilling eavesdropper. Should she go down and explain that she overheard? Perhaps Uncle Paddy – Humphrey! – would like a shoulder to cry on. Or would he just be annoyed that she hadn't made her presence known?

As she dithered, footsteps echoed on the tiled floor of the hallway followed by the sound of the front door quietly closing. Her uncle had left the building.

* * *

The Literary Festival was still in full swing, with a poetry reading in the Marrinan Park on the Wednesday afternoon, some other minor events on the Thursday and Friday with the grand finale on Saturday night - a panel discussion with local authors. Emer O'Neill was the main attraction for the latter, with Humphrey Sterling taking second billing, but Eve was pleased to see that Helen was included in the list of poets for the park event. Up until then, she had supported the festival dutifully, as she would any local event but having met all three writers she felt a personal interest in attending. Tom was happy to accompany her to the evening discussion on the weekend but his face clouded over slightly when she mentioned poetry.

"I've never quite grasped it," he confided. "I mean, we did all the famous ones at school…Your man wandering around looking at daffodils, Yeats and his terrible beauty…but I prefer prose."

Eve rolled her eyes. "Fine, I'll let you off that one. I'm going though, and if I'm going alone, you'd better have a nice dinner waiting for me!"

Tom grinned. "Thanks, love. I'll cook you a steak as big as your head, how's that? You go enjoy the angst-ridden poets. Oh, and if you see Quigley about the place will you ask him to ring me? It's all very well holding these events in the park, but he let them put up a podium right on top of my new bulbs – if young Boyd hadn't spotted it, it would have been a disaster." He grumbled about the cheek of people prioritizing their activities over the needs of the precious plants and wildlife until Eve distracted him with talk of the wedding.

"Margaret is going to ask Humphrey to give her away," This latest nugget had been divulged during a text exchange about the place settings. "Ronan still hasn't warmed to him, but sure it's been less than a week."

"I think it's a lovely idea. And Ronan will come round, wait and see."

Fortified by a kiss from her Tom and clutching a thermos mug of coffee, Eve made her way to the park. It felt rather nice to be at something so cultured as a poetry reading, she thought. She wasn't sure what to expect, the festival's organization having been a bit hit and miss so far, but someone had certainly put effort into this event. Bunting hung from the lampposts and trees, marking off the far right corner of the space, and drawing the eye to a large banner advertising, "Poetry in the Park / Merrion LIT festival." A podium had been placed in front of a semicircle of chairs three rows deep. A one sheet programme for the event had been laid out on the seat of each chair, and some of the local teenagers were acting as ushers.

To one side, there was a row of tables, covered in white cloths with brightly coloured embroidered flowers, each bearing a selection of slim books. Each pile was tended by a person she guessed to be the author. Picking up one slim volume entitled "Dancing to Pipes, A Collection of Poetry," she smiled at the nervous looking young man behind the table.

"Is this yours?"

"Ahem. Yes. Yeah." He smiled at her. "Um, it's my first collection."

"It looks great." She read the blurb quickly and looking at his hopeful face, made up her mind. "How much?"

"Oh! Eh, nine euros. I mean, if you don't mind –"

"Nine is fine!" She wagged her finger at him. "Don't sell yourself short. Here, I've got it in cash if that helps." She waited while the delighted poet took the money and handed her a book in a plain paper bag.

"Thanks so much." He looked like she had given him a

thousand euro, rather than less than a tenner. "I'm Eoin Fogarty – well, sure, you know that. It's on the book cover. Anyway, let me know what you think of them. The poems. I'd love to hear."

Promising to email him when she'd read them – and promising herself to actually read them and not forget – Eve made her way along the line of sellers. Some few were traditionally published, albeit with small, literary presses, but many were what one girl explained to her as "Indie published."

"All the hard work, but then again, I get most of the royalties…" the girl said, grinning. "Do you write, yourself?"

"No, no. But – I'm an artist. So I get it – I have sold through galleries and exhibitions but I make my real living selling directly to clients."

"Well now, Indie publishing is a bit like that."

By the time she took her seat, Eve was filled with admiration for the writers she'd met, even if their work wasn't to her taste. And she was fascinated by the insights they had given her into publishing. There was an idea bubbling at the back of her head – it had been for a long time – but she had assumed it was too difficult to even contemplate. Her students were producing work that really deserved to be seen and admired – amateurs, yes, but artists in their own right. She had toyed with the idea of an exhibition, but also of a book, a coffee table type production, filled with prints of their work.

If these brave souls could learn how to self publish, and put their work out into the world, why couldn't she help her artists do the same…

A sharp squeal of feedback from the podium's microphone brought her back to the present. Mr Quigley, his face radiating disapproval, was engaged in a discreet but quietly vicious tug of war for the mic, with Greta Goode his opponent. Eve choked back a laugh, watching as the irate festival organizer finally conceded defeat to the short elderly woman. Greta beamed out at the audience and in a voice that barely needed the amplification, announced, "Welcome! Fáilte Romhaibh!"

The audience murmured back at her, while Eve wondered what Greta was up to now. She had never expressed any interest in poetry, but Greta was always interested in winding people up. Looking at Quigley's red angry face, Eve felt sure Greta had muscled in solely to annoy the officious man.

Greta waved her hands and continued, "Hush now. Well, I'm so pleased so many of ye have turned up today to help us celebrate our local poetic talent. I personally can take or leave most verse – although I do like a nice birthday card with a rhyme, don't you? – and frankly a lot of modern poetry just sounds like a shopping list to me. But I appreciate the skill it takes, even when it's not obvious that much skill went into it. Poetry used to rhyme, didn't it? I remember in school we learned a wee ditty –

"Who has seen the wind, neither I nor you,

but when the leaves hang trembling, the wind is passing through."

"Now that's poetry. Christina Rossi, it was. She was some woman, wasn't she? Hah. But sure, here they are, our own local poets, and they have all made a huge effort. So my advice is to suspend your criticism and let them have a chance to wow us, eh? Great stuff. Now, first up…Helen Dunphy. Oh, wait, I've heard her before…she's not half bad. You'll enjoy this."

Greta pressed the mic into the unfortunate woman's hand, and sat herself down firmly on a chair in the front row. Helen looked to Eve as if she was torn between laughing and crying at Greta's introduction. Laughing won.

"Thanks, Mrs. Goode. Appreciate your willingness to suffer through our humble offerings." She glanced at her notes, then looked out over the crowd and sighed. "I had a speech all prepared but…well, it wasn't very good. I'm not good at public speaking, you see. But what Mrs. Goode said made me think – what is poetry? In Ireland especially…why do we still value it so highly? Because we do – look at you all here today, on a Wednesday afternoon. Look at the poets we still produce, in both English and Irish. The ancient Filí – the old Irish word for a poet – they were more than writers. They were…magicians, courtiers, keepers of our history and culture. The power of the word – the power of sound itself – is an integral part of our folklore and possibly our one unique and abiding contribution to the world. And, just so we're clear, their poetry didn't always rhyme either."

An appreciative chuckle greeted this.

"We have inherited poetry that was used in law, in medicine, and in battle. It was our magic. Poetry kept the flame of revolution alive. Poets fought and died for our freedom. So when you hear us here today, even if you don't like our words, respect them. Respect all the poets about to lay themselves bare for you. We speak for ourselves, and for the past, and for the future."

A huge cheer went up, not least from Greta Goode, who turned in her seat, caught Eve's eye and gave her a wink. She looked thoroughly pleased with herself.

Helen seemed to come back into herself, blinking at the audience as if she'd forgotten they were there. When the noise subsided a little, she started to read one of her poems – not one she had used at the Humphrey Sterling event, Eve noticed, but with similar themes of poignancy and loss. She was very well received and Eve felt a stab of pity for the next poet – she would be a hard act to follow. She saw young Eoin Fogarty take the mic from Helen and crossed her fingers.

"Thanks, everyone. Wasn't Helen amazing? Well, I hope you're not expecting more of the same. My poetry tends to be a little more…well, sure let's get on with it and you can decide for yourself."

With a mischievous grin he launched into a short, slightly dirty, but hilariously funny poem about a young man lost in a big city at night. The audience was impressed, especially when he followed it up with a sharp, and probably libelous, attack on the foibles of certain politicians, with a longer poem, almost a sonnet in form, bewailing the vagaries of the newest motorway tolls.

Eve felt rather smug that she had bought his book. It wouldn't be much of a hardship to make her way through his work.

The next poet produced some pleasant but in all honesty, forgettable work, and Eve found her attention wandering. She glanced around her, picking out familiar faces. Ellen Marrinan was seated a few rows away, and she was pleased to see her young friends Jenny and Ashleigh among the volunteers. Boyd Marrinan, Ellen's teenage son, was hovering by the flowerbeds and sternly reminding people not to trample on them. He was Tom's devoted helper, and took his role very seriously.

To her surprise, near the front and looking interested, was Damian Burke. It was curious that a small poetry gathering had attracted such a famous literary agent – and critic, she supposed, considering his regular appearances on Irish television. He was a fixture on the kind of shows where three or four well known faces earnestly discussed something highbrow. Her own work had made an appearance on a late night arts show, much to her mother's delight. Eve had received nothing but praise although some of their interpretations of her work left her scratching her head. Writers seemed to have it harder, she reflected. Burke was a fair commentator but if he disliked a book, he was very vocal about it.

Which made it even more odd that he represented the author of the Jerusalem Hill novels. Burke was not known for a love of genre writing. Eve filed this away under "things to think about later," and applied herself once more to the poetry.

A short interval was announced, Quigley clutching the mic as if his life depended on it. He glowered at Greta who just grinned back. "There are refreshments available at the Irish Women's Brigade table, to your left…" his words prompted a small stampede, no Irish crowd unable to resist the lure of tea and homemade cakes. Eve stood, more to stretch her legs than from any desire to join the throng around the tea urns. She eyed Quigley, who was fussing around the stage, but the volunteers were taking their orders from a tall, dark-haired figure. Phyllis Dennehy, Humphrey Sterling's PA, still clutching her clipboard and looking severe, was marshaling the young ones and overseeing crowd control.

Eve was not by nature an intrusive woman, but she had a stab of pure nosiness, she admitted to herself. What on earth was Sterling's PA doing, helping out at the poetry event? She made her way through the chattering groups, but before she could reach her, Mr. Quigley called out Phyllis' name. The girl rolled her eyes but obeyed the summons, leaving Eve rather stranded.

She turned to find Claudia Warren at her elbow, smiling

widely. For a large lady, she could move quietly and quickly when she chose.

"Enjoying it?"

"Yes, quite a lot. Helen was very good, wasn't she?"

"Yes, she's got *quite* a talent." Something in Claudia's tone made Eve's eyebrow raise.

"Oh."

"Greta bet me a pint she could get it out of her," Claudia shook her head. "When will I learn not to bet against that woman? You saw it, of course?"

"Her…moment?"

"Imbas, my dear. Inspiration. She opened herself up and let the words flow through her. Extemporaneous."

Eve made a mental note to look up what extemporaneous meant but she understood the gist. "I thought Greta was up to something."

"Isn't she always?" Claudia elbowed her in the ribs. Eve tried not to yelp in pain. "Look at that one, Phyllis is it? Did you know she helped organize this?"

"Ah. I thought it was a bit above the usual level."

"Quigley was like a bear over it, but she was here when there was all the fuss over the podium – stupid man placed it on the flowerbed, and young Boyd almost threw it into the pond. Phyllis stepped in, saw the general chaos and took over. Next thing we knew, there was bunting and lovely tables. She had the good sense to ask me to invite the Brigade to sell refreshments – no charge for the table, and all proceeds to the Brigade charitable fund."

Eve was impressed. "She's efficient. And that was kind of her, to help out."

"I think she's at a bit of a loose end. Humphrey is spending all his time with Margaret at the moment and Phyllis can't get a look in."

"Well, maybe get her even more involved, Quigley is a nightmare to deal with and she seems to have the measure of him." Eve pointed towards the podium, where the festival organizer was being quietly but firmly managed. Phyllis handed him a sheaf of leaflets and pointed at the passersby who had stopped to hear the poetry. Quigley started to hand out festival programmes while Phyllis shepherded the next three poets up to the podium and gave them instructions.

"Neatly done," Claudia agreed. "She's a dark horse, that one. She was borderline surly at the meet and greet in Greta's house. But here she's as cool as cucumber and quite pleasant."

"What do you make of him?" Eve nodded at Damian Burke, still seated and earnestly reading the programme.

"That's an awfully short leaflet to need so much attention," Claudia remarked. "I bet he's just trying to discourage anyone from talking to him."

"I suppose, he is a well known face. It must be tiresome to have people at you all the time, especially at events like this. Do you think he's here to…well, talent spot?"

Claudia shrugged. "I would have said he only dealt with novels, but it's possible. He certainly seems to be interested."

There was no more time to discuss it, as a call went up from the stage to return to seats and the readings resumed. Putting aside thoughts of Burke or Phyllis, Eve took note of another poet whose work she felt like perusing. As the event wound down, she made a point of buying Helen's book and this other one to add to Eoin Fogarty's.

"Look at me, a literary connoisseur," she giggled to herself. "Still, never too old to take up something new."

Before she left the park, a cheerful Greta informed her that she would be hosting another reception, this time to mark the close of the Festival.

"Everyone's invited! So come to mine the moment the thing finishes, okay? My lot want to see the last event, but they'll be over after to lend a hand. If you and Tom could pitch in first, we can manage."

Promising to help, Eve took her leave. All the earlier unease had disappeared and she felt a bit silly for having given into it. Feeling pleased with her afternoon, she headed to Tom's for her promised slap-up dinner.

"It was really good," she assured him, over a delicious steak. "I'm actually looking forward to Saturday night. It'll be great fun."

And that, she thought later, was her mistake. She had tempted fate.

Chapter 8

On Saturday, the community hall had once again been pressed into service but this time Eve thought she could detect the hand of Phyllis Dennehy in the decorations. The Merrion Literary Festival Banner was still hanging over the stage, but now attractive garlands of balloons and ribbons framed either side. Fresh flowers stood in large containers – Eve recognized the ornate vases as props from a rather ambitious staging of The Mikado by the Merrion Musical Society – and the place looked like it had been subjected to a good sweeping and dusting. The audience still had to make do with plastic chairs but someone had placed six sturdy wooden chairs with matching red cushions in a semicircle on the raised dais.

Even Tom was mildly impressed. "It looks quite nice, really," he nodded approvingly.

"I bet it was Phyllis – you know, Humphrey's young assistant. I told you she helped out with the poetry reading on Wednesday."

"Well, it's a step up from Quigley's attempts…oh, thank you, yes –" Tom accepted a small brochure from one of the teenagers milling around the seating area. "Oh, a programme – that's a nice touch. Your friend Emer O'Neill is on, I see, and that man who writes about animals…that'll be worth hearing…"

"Programmes cost money," Mr. Quigley's sour tones cut across the room. He was waving a sheaf of the offending items, his face almost purple and covered with a faint sheen of sweat. He was vibrating with rage, to all appearances.

"It cost precisely twenty euros," Phyllis drawled, her south Dublin accent more pronounced than ever. "Which I paid out of my own pocket, so I fail to see what your issue is?"

"I – You have no authority to print these!" Quigley threw his bundle on the floor and several of the young ushers scrambled to pick them up. "Who gave you permission to –"

"I don't need your permission," Phyllis cut across him. "I have every right to promote any event that my employer attends – check his contract if you don't believe me. It's under "Marketing and Public Relations," subsection "promotional material." Would you like me to find it for you?"

The man drew back, trembling with rage, and for a terrible moment Eve thought he was actually going to strike the young PA. Tom stepped forward, placing himself firmly between the warring parties, his face stern as he towered over the shorter man. Eve watched Quigley's face, as he tried to compose himself. The man was far angrier than was reasonable.

"You're nothing but a jumped up little pup!" he snarled, peering around Tom at the girl. "You're nothing but a jumped up, interfering, officious wagon. I turned my back for a few minutes, to look after our authors and guest speakers, and you pushed in. Throwing your weight about and making a nuisance of yourself. Wait until I speak to Humphrey about this."

Phyllis shrugged. "Knock yourself out. He'll tell you the same thing - it's my job to make sure any event he's part of is properly run. It's his reputation on the line, if it turns out to be a complete shambles."

Liam Quigley's face turned an even darker shade. "I know him far better than you do, ya wagon! If you think he'll take your side over this – well, you're in for some land, Missy."

He shot a nasty glance at Tom, and muttered something uncomplimentary under his breath. Tom chose to ignore it, continuing to stand firmly planted between the agitated committee man and the young PA.

"I've more important things to do than stand here arguing with the likes of you," Quigley snipped. With that he strode off, leaving a rather shell shocked group in his wake.

Eve noted with interest that the journalist they had met at Greta's reception - Aidan Lowe - was present. Was it her imagination or did he look pale? He had watched the altercation between Phyllis and Quigley closely, but hadn't moved to intervene. She watched as he squirmed in his chair, in some obvious discomfort. She felt a pang of guilt until he caught her looking at him and scowled nastily in return. It reminded her of his rude comments about Margaret and she shrugged off any sympathy for him.

Eve took a few minutes to chat to the young volunteers, glad to see they were more amused than upset by the organizer's temper tantrum, up to the point where he had seemed to threaten his opponent. That, she was equally glad to see, they did not find funny in the slightest. As more people entered the hall, their attention was soon turned to their duties as ushers – it took four of them to wrangle the Irish Women's Brigade members into three rows, as the ladies popped in and out of seats, swapped places and darted up to have a closer look at the stage.

Eve and Tom took their own seats, Tom rather silent as they settled themselves.

"You did well, there." Eve patted his arm. "I'm glad you stepped in."

"I can't abide any man who will even speak to a woman like that," Tom said. "Let alone step up to her in that way I'd have – I'd have burst him, if he'd actually raised a hand to her."

She squeezed his hand, "Phyllis didn't seem at all fazed by it, did she?"

"No. And Quigley made a total donkey of himself, talking like that. And saying he would report her to her employer. But sure, why would that matter? The great Sterling isn't going to sack someone as efficient as Phyllis to please Quigley!"

"I didn't know they even knew each other that well," Eve mused. "Quigley and Humphrey, I mean."

"Do they?"

"Well, Quigley said – what was it? That he knew Humphrey better than she did…I thought they only met this week."

"Ach. Liam Quigley is a narcissistic gobdaw, Eve. He thinks he's the king of Merrion. In his head, he's so important, even world famous authors will obey him."

Eve laughed. "You're right. Let's forget about them. Look, the first author is Michael Flynn, the politician. He's written an autobiographical account of his time in office – it says here, *"Laying bare the truth behind Ireland's greatest political scandals!"*

"Oh, good." Tom cheered up. "I was afraid it was all going to be either romance or murder. Politics and wildlife, that's far more my speed."

The first author did not disappoint. The ex-cabinet minister, who had retired in a flurry of allegations and rumours, had written a book that Eve could only assume was truthful because if not the man would have been sued several times over. It was well written, possibly by a ghostwriter, and above all, it was scurrilous. Very few of his erstwhile colleagues came out of it with their reputation intact, and Tom was particularly delighted to hear apparent confirmation that his least favourite TD was indeed the indecisive, venal twit he had always suspected. Eve was less interested, but enjoyed the reading, and to her delight, Greta Goode was chosen to ask some searching questions in the follow-up session. Dymphna, Niamh and Claudia were scattered throughout the room, but Eve could pinpoint their exact location by the cackling every time Greta landed a hit.

The wildlife expert spoke briefly, using his time less to promote his book and more to emphasize the importance of protecting the environment. He had to be reminded by Quigley to hold up his book and tell the crowd where it was available for purchase. This did him no disservice in the eyes of the audience, who could recognize genuine passion. He received a round of applause that made him blush.

Helen then read a short poem, followed by a reading from Emer's new book, a witty and irreverent take on family life. Both were very well received, to Eve's delight. At this point, she felt personally invested in the writers and their success. She was pleased to see her mother and Claudia applauding loudly and made a mental note to look for both authors' books when it was time to buy birthday presents.

Next up was Humphrey Sterling. Eve was happy to see that Margaret and Ronan were front and centre, applauding with most of the crowd as he stood to approach the mic. If Ronan was still lukewarm about his new Uncle in Law, he was hiding it well for Margaret's sake. Sterling paused until the applause died away, the picture of a modest, reluctant celebrity.

"Again? Oh my dear people, have you not tired of me yet?"

The roar of denial from the Brigade alone made the old windows rattle.

"Well, I am honoured. Humbled. Truly. This has been – I say this from the bottom of my heart – this has been a homecoming for me." He waved at his niece in the audience. "My darling Margaret – many of you will have read of our happy reunion. And soon I will have a nephew to add to my little family. I never dreamed when I accepted the kind invitation to headline the Merrion Literary festival, that it would lead to such a joyous event."

Eve smiled at his claim of "headlining" the event, but in fairness, he was one of the best known writers there. He seemed sincerely happy to have found Margaret, which was all that mattered.

"I chose this event to launch my latest book," the author continued, "because Ireland holds such a special place in my heart. And I have wonderful news to impart, news that I know my dear fans will appreciate." He smiled archly.

"Dear lovely people of Dublin! I have thought long and hard about this. Success has brought me far from home, to the sunny climes of California, and to the busy streets of New York. Now, I feel the time has come – to return home. I cannot bear to think of parting from my darling niece, having found her again. So – if you will have me – I intend to make my home in Dublin, close to my family. Yes, I am coming home…"

It would be difficult to describe the bedlam that erupted at this. Cheers, foot stamping, applause, Margaret rushing to the edge of the stage to hold Humphrey's outstretched hand. Eve couldn't help it, she turned instinctively to look at Ronan

Dempsey. The look of dismay on his face was almost – but not quite – comical.

Humphrey waited until the noise faded away. "Now, I've taken up quite enough of your time. I shall now read from my new novel. This is a sneak preview of Jerusalem Hill, "*In Mortal Peril, Sin City Book Two!*"

A shriek of joy came from several ladies in the audience, including some of the Brigade members. Claudia frowned at them, but her heart wasn't in it. Humphrey's fans were clearly overjoyed at the prospect of a new Hill novel, and from the whispered conversations all around her, a sequel to Sin City was particularly good news.

Tom raised an eyebrow in query and Eve shrugged.

"Haven't a clue, Love, but it's made the old dears happy."

Humphrey started to read, and despite herself, Eve couldn't help but be drawn in. It was the same style as his other work (overblown prose, in her opinion) but there was something about the story – something compelling.

The scene he chose saw Jerusalem Hill creeping though a darkened house, a feeling of dread building as he moved from one empty, shadowy room to the next. His nerves stretched to breaking point, he cracked open the door to the kitchen, peering through the opening. An outside lamp cast an eerie glow over the room, highlighting the gleaming white marble of the countertop and the shiny metal of the appliances. He stifled a gasp of shock as it lit on a figure, bent over, searching through a drawer. As he went to withdraw the person straightened up, and turned, the glow from outside illuminating a face he knew all too well, a face that had no more business being there than he had. He hesitated but decided to carry on his search for -the author broke off and smiled.

"I'm afraid if I read on, I'll give too much away. But for anyone interested, "In Mortal Peril" will be out soon – revealing all!"

The rest of the programme continued smoothly, Emer O'Neill being especially entertaining and the Q and A session provoking some lively banter but there was no doubt Humphrey had stolen the show. There were quite a few journalists present tonight, and they all gathered around the triumphant mystery writer as soon as he descended from the stage. Aidan Lowe was among them, a slight limp in his left leg noticeable as he made his way to the front of the hall.

Amid the clamour for his attention, Eve noticed Humphrey looking anxiously around the room until he caught Margaret's eye. It was rather touching, she thought, watching his face brighten once his niece waved to him. He must have been a little worried how she would take the news of him moving here permanently, she thought.

Dymphna Moriarty elbowed Eve in the ribs.

"Maybe he thought it was all very well having a long lost uncle for the wedding, but not so much when he's around all the time."

The old lady's habit of answering thoughts you had never spoken outside the privacy of your own head never failed to startle.

"What did you think of the new book?" Eve asked

"Hmm. It was very good, that goes without saying, but there was something …different about it."

"I've never thought of Jerusalem Hill as being scared, or creeping around." Niamh sidled up behind Eve, her blue eyes bright with curiosity. "It's definitely a *darker* kind of story, don't you think?"

"Mature." Dymphna said. "And modern. Hallmark of a great writer that is. He'll appeal to a younger audience too with this one."

Eve left them to their critique, having spotted Helen in the crowd, speaking to Emer O'Neill. They waved her over.

"Congratulations! You were excellent," Eve told them both.

"Thanks," Emer lowered her voice. "To be honest a few hours ago, I half thought the whole event would be canceled!"

Helen nodded. "It was bedlam back stage at the beginning. We weren't told anything, just left to wander around."

Eve raised an eyebrow. "That's poor form."

"If it wasn't for Humphrey's assistant, we'd still be running around like headless chickens!. Phyllis, is it? She got the kids to set everything up and then practically frogmarched us all on stage."

Eve laughed, congratulated them again on a great event and went to rescue the Wildlife Man from Tom's enthusiastic chatter.

"Sorry to interrupt, but we need to get going. I promised Greta we'd call in to her after this. She needs a hand to set up the reception. There'll be scores of people landing in on her soon. I saw her leave five minutes ago, she'll be tearing her hair out."

Tom rolled his eyes but let himself be led away.

"Very interesting chap," he told Eve. "Agrees completely with me about the need for more meadows and wild planting…"

Eve listened to Tom's familiar lecture on biodiversity with only half an ear, as they made their way to Greta's house. It was a lovely Spring night, and the walk was a pleasant change from the stuffy community hall. It was all very exciting, she thought, long lost uncles and famous writers. The Merrion Literary

Festival had got a lot of publicity out of it, surely beyond all expectations. It would have no problem attracting big names next year. You'd think Quigley would be pleased by that but the man had been as sour as ever, a face like thunder on him as they'd left. She was just wondering why, when a scream pierced the air.

"Help!" Greta's voice rang out from her house, and as one, Eve and Tom raced the last few feet and up the steps to her front door. It was ajar, and the hall beyond was dimly lit by a solitary lamp on the hall table. Eve rushed ahead, only to be pulled to a halt by a firm grip on her arm.

"Stay there," Tom said, "Let me past you!"

Part of her wanted to say no, and push ahead of him to find her friend, but the rational part of her brain acknowledged that if there was an intruder, Tom would be more able to handle them. So she compromised by letting him go first, but following close behind.

"Greta?" Tom bellowed.

"Tom? Tom, come quick!" Eve was shocked by the note of panic in Greta's voice. In her experience, nothing truly scared the older lady.

"I'm here!" Tom barged into the drawing room, fists clenched like a rather dapper, middle aged pugilist. He took in the scene and froze, arms still raised. "Oh."

Eve almost barreled into him, but managed to right herself. "What's going on -Oh."

She stared at Greta, who was on her knees on the carpeted floor, tending to…a body. It was definitely a body. The great big red stain visible on his white shirt, under his unbuttoned jacket, and the large knife protruding from his chest, made it doubtful that there was any point in Greta's frantic attempts at CPR. But it had to be done – Eve shook herself into action.

"Tom, ring an ambulance. And the Gardaí. And Ronan Desmond, get him over here. Greta, I'll take over now, you take a breather…"

Eve worked diligently, despite her near certainty that it was a pointless exercise. At some point, Ronan arrived, pushed her gently aside and took over. Then the room was filled with Paramedics, but their grim expressions confirmed Eve's suspicions.

Greta looked distraught as it dawned on her that they had failed.

"I tried everything I could," she said plaintively, "I thought there might be a chance…"

"I shouldn't say this," one of the paramedics said, "but ladies, he was gone before you found him. You couldn't have saved him, in my opinion."

Greta nodded, still looking miserable. Eve hugged the old woman's shoulders, shocked by how tiny and frail she felt under her arm. "You were amazing, Greta. Wasn't she Tom?"

Tom broke off a whispered conversation with Ronan and nodded. "Greta, you have nothing to reproach yourself for."

Ronan took a seat beside Greta.

"Listen, we don't have much time. Greta, my colleagues are outside, I've had a word with them but – we need to know. Who is he, and what happened here?"

Greta stared at him. "How the hell would I know what happened?"

The others exchanged glances.

"Greta," Eve said as gently as she could. "It's your house."

"Well, that's not my fault is it? You of all people should know that sometimes people turn up dead in your living room, without asking your permission first. I know *who* he is, It's Damian Burke – he's Humphrey's agent. He came to the reception last week, and then called around a few times during the week to speak to visit Humphrey. As for what happened here, I haven't a clue. I left the community hall a few minutes early, to get things ready here for the party. I came in here to make sure the fire was still going and – there he was. On my Axminster rug."

Eve looked at the men. "She's telling the truth – obviously she is. She only left about five minutes before we did."

Ronan nodded and took out a small black notebook. "Okay. It all depends how long he's been dead but I'm fairly sure she'll be out of the frame. The forensics team are on their way, I'll talk to Dr O'Toole when she gets here. So, what do any of you know about him? Where's Sterling by the way?"

Eve shrugged. "I don't know anything about Burke other than he's well known in literary circles. And of course, I've seen him on TV. Ellen Marrinan pointed him out to me, at the party here. She only knew him from the telly too, of course. Oh, Emer O'Neill might be able to help – she seems to know him. And Aidan Lowe – he was talking about him that night."

"Okay, that's a start. Now, Cullen will need to take statements from you, but we'll try to get it done quickly. Greta, this is a crime scene now. You can't stay here. Neither can Humphrey."

"Greta can stay with me!" Eve insisted. Tom nodded. "I'm happy to take Mr. Sterling. Or of course, he could stay with Margaret."

"He'll probably prefer Margaret, but I'll let him know you offered." Ronan snapped his notebook shut, a worried frown creasing his forehead. "I don't mind telling you, I don't like this. Greta, does anyone have keys to the house other than you and Humphrey?"

Greta gave a quick, sharp look towards Eve before answering. "Only my cleaning lady, Martha. I'll give you her number but she's on holidays at the moment, in Lanzarote. And a neighbour, Shirley, she lives at number 6. We keep each other's keys for emergencies."

"I see." Ronan bit his lip. "So – Humphrey was here earlier today? Before the reading?"

"He was." Greta's expression was unreadable. "As were a lot of people – Phyllis Dennehy, for one. And Quigley, fussing about tonight. Can't get that man out of here, in fact. He's been around almost every day, worrying after Humphrey for one thing or another. I'd people in helping to set up for tonight – oh, all that food will be just sitting there!"

"I'll take care of it," Eve soothed her. "I'll freeze what I can and hand out the rest."

"Good, good. Um, yes, that's about it – lots of people have been in and out recently."

"And Mr. Burke? Was he here earlier today?"

"No. Not that I know of, anyway."

"Okay. I'll ask Sterling too." Ronan paused, before asking in a casual tone, "About what time did Humphrey get to the community hall, did anyone notice?"

Eve stared at the detective. "Ronan, you can't possibly think –"

He cut her off. "I have to ask, Eve. You know that. Now, did any of you notice him arriving?"

Tom answered for all of them. "He was on the stage at eight-fifteen, along with the other writers. But you would have to ask Quigley or Phyllis – his PA – when he actually arrived at the Hall."

"Okay. Greta, what time did you leave here at tonight?"

"Seven-thirty." The old lady replied promptly. "I checked my watch. Humphrey was in the sitting room, reading over some notes, but he had his hat and coat on. He said he would be leaving right after me."

"Okay." The black notebook made another appearance. "Timing is going to be important, so please, if you think of anything – let me know."

A discreet cough at the door alerted them to the presence of Ronan's partner, Cullen. The older detective was a gruff, sturdy man with a deceptively sleepy appearance.

"Time's up, I'm afraid. We need to take statements and Dr. O'Toole is here."

"Thanks, Cullen, appreciate it." Ronan stood. "You take statements and I'll get O'Toole set up…"

Cullen shook his head. "Sorry, no."

He gestured to Ronan to step outside, and a whispered conversation took place in Greta's hallway. Eve could make out words here and there – especially Ronan's.

"That's a load of – I'll ring him now, Cullen. He can't take me off this!"

Eve looked at Tom, who shook his head slightly. "It's too close to home, I wondered if they would let him investigate."

"Well, it never stopped them before!" she whispered fiercely. "Didn't he solve the last two murders, they should be glad to have him on the spot, with local knowledge."

"There's local knowledge and then there's this." Greta said flatly. "Humphrey Sterling. His future uncle-in-law. There's only two suspects right now, me or him."

Tom was right, Eve realized. And soon Ronan was back in

the room, two bright red spots burning in either cheek and a steely look in his eye. Cullen looked resolute but miserable, taking charge of the crime scene without any further comment. Ronan waited, until all three had given statements and were released, then with a curt "Goodnight," to the unfortunate Cullen, ushered them out of the house and into the cool evening.

"Greta, they let Dymphna in to pack this bag for you, it's enough for overnight in Eve's. Although she was a bit put out that you're staying there and not with her. Also Niamh, who wanted you to go stay with her. And the Marrinans want you to come stay with them, although where they think they'd fit you in is beyond me. Finn Marrinan said to tell you if you need anything, including a lawyer, he's ready to foot the bill." Ronan said.

Greta sniffed and said "Nonsense" but her face belied the sentiment. Tom took the small overnight bag from Ronan, and held out his arm to her.

"Allow me to escort you to Bramble Lane, Madame."

Eve fell back to talk to Ronan as they made their way to Kimberly Cottage.

"They kicked you off the case."

Ronan growled. "According to my Super, three murders in the locality of my house in a twelve month period is bad enough, but he draws the line at allowing me to investigate when one suspect is a close friend and the other is my future wife's relative. Bloody Humphrey Sterling."

"Ah Ronan, that's not fair. The poor man isn't responsible for this – it's not his fault you can't take the case."

"Isn't it?" Ronan stopped walking and stared at her. "And if it turns out he did in fact murder Damian Burke?"

"But why? Why would he? Burke is his agent. Sterling has a new book coming out, and he has Margaret. You can't tell me he'd risk all that?"

Tom and Greta had also paused, listening to the heated exchange.

"Hmm. I'm not a bit convinced that the bold Humphrey has half these deals in the works."

"Ronan," Tom expostulated. "Don't you think you're letting your annoyance cloud your judgment?"

"You've never warmed to the man," Eve agreed.

Ronan executed an eye roll that would have been the admiration of every teen in the area. "Oh for goodness sake! Don't tell me you pair have joined the Sterling fan club too? The man is a smooth talking hack, that's all."

Greta drew herself up to her full height of five foot two, and with a horribly stiff dignity addressed Ronan. "A hack?" The ice in her voice could have reversed global warming. "You impudent young pup."

"Oh give over," Ronan said, ignoring Eve's frantic eye signals to back off and shut up. "You only asked him to stay because you're pumping him over an old murder. Yes, Mrs. Goode, I am well aware of his connection to that old case – and I am also fully up to date on the rest of his fascinating life. Like, for example, his bad habit of putting the advance of his books on broken down nags at the race course. He's up to his neck in debt. I'm also well aware of his reputation for being difficult, a walking ego in fact, and impossible to work with, according to those who know him well. Oh, and I happen to know the gossip in publishing circles is that Damian Burke was about to sack him as a client. And that he was only hanging around him was to let him down gently."

He paused, and seemed to become aware that the others were staring at him.

"What?"

"Ronan Desmond," Greta asked, her tone a mix of outrage and admiration. "Did you have your future Uncle in Law investigated?"

"Um –" the Detective Garda prevaricated.

"You did, didn't you? Oh, Ronan." Eve shook her head.

"Don't you "*Oh Ronan*," me. Margaret is my priority, and I wasn't going to let some randomer walk into her life and take advantage of her."

Greta grinned, laughter lines spreading from her twinkling eyes to her round cheeks. "Well, you've more gumption that I gave you credit for. Not that I agree with you about poor Humphrey, you're fierce hard on him. The man is an artist, and everyone knows writers are a funny lot. Sure, don't they all drink and gamble? That's nothing. And he's never been anything but charming to us, has he? So I wouldn't put so much store in him being difficult. That's artistic temperament. But I'm impressed. You'll make Margaret a good husband, so you will."

Ronan blinked, obviously bewildered by this mix of reproof and unexpected praise. Eve tapped him on the arm.

"Greta might be right, Ronan. I mean, about him just being a typical writer. He never claimed to be a saint. What worries me is – Damian Burke was about to sack him?"

"Like I said, It seems to have been common knowledge among publishing circles."

"But it's gossip, all the same. Not proof."

"We could ask Emer O'Neill, maybe she'd know?"

"Or we could just ask Humphrey...Um, I mean, the Gardaí

could ask him."

Three pairs of eyes avoided looking at the Detective Garda.

Ronan sighed. "Look, I don't have much patience tonight. Can we dispense with the formalities and just all admit we're going to investigate this anyway? Let's get some sleep and congregate at Eve's first thing tomorrow. Ye rally the troops and I'll fill you all in on everything I know."

Eve opened her mouth object, both to once more interfering in an investigation and to everyone using her home as their headquarters - again - but Greta beat her to the punch with an enthusiastic, "Yes!" Tom, the traitor, chimed in with, "Of course," and Eve found herself saying, "I'll ring Mam and Claudia before I go to bed. Greta, you and Tom tell Dymphna when you get to Kimberly. Ronan, are you going to bring Margaret into this?"

The young man hesitated. "I can't see any way to avoid it. She'll be out of her mind with worry."

"Call into her now, make sure Humphrey is with her. Warn them that Cullen will be hot on your heels. Ask her to stay with her uncle while he's being interviewed. Then get some sleep. Come over to mine first thing tomorrow morning."

And here we go again, Eve thought. The wedding would have to take a back seat until this was all cleared up. What worried her and what no one was saying out loud was, if her beloved uncle was arrested for murder, would Margaret call it all off? Would there even be a wedding at Wisteria cottage?

Chapter 9

Dawn had been streaking the sky by the time Eve got home, and she had collapsed gratefully into bed. Sleep had come quickly, but she jolted awake around eight o'clock, her heart thumping and remnants of a nightmare clinging to her brain. It was a struggle to get up and dressed, but if she knew her friends, they would be descending on the house as soon as was decent. Which on a Sunday, probably meant nine o'clock. If she was any judge, the older ladies would arrive expecting their breakfast and an endless supply of tea and coffee.

To her absolute horror, the doorbell rang at half past eight. She opened it cautiously, dreading the thought of entertaining anyone at that hour and on so little rest.

"It's me, pet," Tom grinned at her. He looked tired himself, but he was neatly dressed in his Sunday uniform of chinos, polo shirt and light jacket. He could have been on his way to a posh brunch, Eve thought sleepily. Except for the fact that he was carrying a large catering box, that smelt deliciously of bacon and sausages…

"I thought you wouldn't be up to dealing with that horde, not this morning. So I got up early and got to the Deli in the shopping centre. Lucky for us, they were only too delighted to whip up this lot - it's everything we need for breakfast, apart from eggs and I can do them. We'll stick it in the oven and feed them as they arrive…"

He disappeared into the kitchen, leaving a grateful Eve to sit and sip her coffee in peace.

"You're a genius," she called into him, from her armchair. "I am, no doubt about it. Ah, here they are -" the doorbell, an old fashioned shrill bell, rang out. Eve sighed and hauled herself to her feet. Her next door neighbour Dymphna stood on the doorstep, with a plate of scones.

"For after breakfast," she said, handing them to Eve. "The others are just behind me."

Within minutes the little cottage was full, and the noise level threatened to tip Eve's mild headache over into full blown migraine. But at least she could sit, and chat -Tom didn't even ask if anyone wanted tea, he just set about filling the kettle and fishing Eve's stash of good biscuits from its latest hiding place. The scones would only go so far. He buttered slices of bread, cracked eggs into the frying pan, and opened a pot of locally made Gooseberry Jam.

Dymphna elbowed Eve with a sharp, bony arm. "He seems to know his way around your kitchen. Very much at home here, isn't he?"

Eve ignored her neighbour. Ever since she and Tom had become an official item, the women of the parish seemed hell bent on getting them to move in together. Niamh and Claudia at least confined themselves to gentle hints while Dymphna made very pointed comments indeed.

Greta had just asked her outright, *Would they not shack up together and rent out one of the cottages?*

If Eve had been inclined to answer them, she would have said that they were happy with the way things were, and while yes, she would like to live with Tom, he didn't want to give up his vegetable garden and she had waited so long for a home like Kimberly Cottage, she couldn't bear to leave it. But she wasn't so inclined, because she had no intention of responding to their nosey questions.

The breakfast was demolished - Greta in particular had a hearty meal, Eve was pleased to note. Nothing could get the old lady down for long. Tom made a fresh round of tea and coffee, popping his head around the kitchen door to catch Eve's eye.

"Kitchen or Living room?" he mouthed silently.

"Good man, Tom, bring it on through -we can all fit better in the living room." She counted heads. Ronan was perched on the arm of Greta's chair, while the other ladies had ranged themselves around the room. Ellen Marrinan had arrived shortly at Kimberly shortly after breakfast, and her husband Finn was also on his way. Eve was touched, but surprised. A few months previously, they had turned to Eve and her friends for help when their son Boyd was accused of murder. She would have thought the last thing they would do was get involved in another case, but Ellen had insisted.

"We owe you and those auld biddies," she had whispered to Eve. "And we're so fond of Margaret and Ronan. Count us in on anything. I'm a good organizer and Finn has an entire army of strong young men on his building sites, in case we need some muscle."

All through breakfast, Eve's phone had lit up with a flurry of texts from concerned friends and neighbours, anxious to help. Gossip had spread through the area at the speed of light, and many of the frantic inquiries were from people who were under the impression that Greta herself had been murdered.

The rest were full sure that she was the murderer.

Eve was rather touched that in both scenarios, people were firmly on the old woman's side.

Sunday was usually a quiet day in Bramble Lane, with Sunday lunches and outings the order of the day. One of the reasons for the early meet-up was not to clash with Dymphna's long standing Sunday dinner with her daughter's family. Greta would normally be collected from Merrion Avenue by one of her many sons, daughters and in-laws. Her extended clan was already clamouring to come and whisk her away, but her granddaughter, Sergeant Jo Maguire, had told them to stand down until she called for them. Greta couldn't be persuaded to sit this one out but everyone agreed it would do her good to be surrounded by family for a while.

Niamh was also anxious to get home. Her first words to Eve hadn't been about the shocking events of the night before, but rather the prospect of some exciting events at home.

"Conor says Ray's parents are in town!" She could barely get the words out, her voice sounding squeaky and high-pitched. She clutched Eve's arm so tightly, her daughter winced. "Flew in from London this morning. He never said a word, the eejit. And now, they want us all to meet for lunch. Three o'clock in town, some posh place the lads like. I don't know what to wear, what do I wear to a posh lunch? Ah Eve, I could box his ears for him, springing this on me."

"Calm down, ya mad yoke. Ray is very laid back, I bet his parents are the same. Wear your green trousers, and the cream blouse I gave you for Christmas. And didn't Mairead give you a lovely cream cardigan, with pearls and embroidery …wear that over it."

"Right. Thanks, love. What about my hair?"

"Brush it and pull it back with a hairband. Honestly, Mam, it's not rocket science. Stop fussing and just enjoy meeting them."

"Hah." Niamh shook her head. "You think it's simple, but it's not. What if his parents think we're all mad, or don't want their son settling here in Dublin? What if Ray sees his parents and gets homesick for London? What if he leaves?"

"What if he takes Conor with him?" Eve asked mischievously.

"I'd hate it, frankly, but I would sooner he went there than him and Ray broke up."

"Ah, for goodness sake! Ray doesn't sound like he's going anywhere. And Conor is well able to manage his own affairs. Go to lunch and stop trying to meddle."

Niamh ignored her. "Do you think it'd be a good idea to give things a little…helping hand?"

Eve froze. "No. No, I do not. You're not to try any of that on Conor, Mam. Absolutely not. If he's meant to be with Ray, it'll work out."

"I suppose so." Her mother did not sound convinced. "I'll do nothing - for now."

I'll have to text Conor, Eve thought, and warn him. But there were more pressing concerns than her brother's love life. Doing a quick headcount, she noticed one person missing.

"Ronan, what about Margaret?" Eve asked.

"She's got her hands full with Humphrey. He had a full scale meltdown when he heard about Burke and then he had another when he was told he would be questioned about it. She says he was hyperventilating and wanted a lawyer present." His tone was dry and carefully neutral but it was clear his future Uncle's reaction had not improved his opinion of the man.

"Poor Humphrey," Greta sighed.

"Desperate hard for a sensitive man like him," Dymphna agreed.

To Eve's surprise, Ellen Marrinan chimed in, agreeing earnestly. "It's much worse for a writer like Humphrey. He must feel terrible."

Ronan looked at Eve, his face a picture. She was a bit taken aback herself at first, then remembered her friend's reaction at the tea party where they first met Humphrey. She had not appreciated Eve's joke about the writer. Perhaps Ellen was a fan of the Jerusalem Hill books, and Eve had inadvertently offended her - a thought that made her cheeks hot with embarrassment. Still, she had a right to her opinion surely? And it wasn't as if those books were what you'd call highbrow, either. She pushed down the guilt and applied herself to the task of getting this meeting under way. It had been a long night, an early start, and she was exhausted. Time to move things along.

"Folks, as I see it, there are several things we need to consider. The first is how and why poor Mr. Burke was in Greta's house. Did he call around to visit Humphrey? Who let him in? Greta, you need to talk to your neighbours, see if anyone saw him coming. Or if they noticed anyone at all - especially Humphrey. We need to find out his exact movements yesterday - we can ask him, of course, but we need to double check."

She paused to think. "Okay, we also want to know everything we can about Burke, and his relationship with Humphrey. Ronan, you can fill us in about that?"

Ronan cleared his throat. "Some of you know already but - I did a bit of digging into Humphrey. Don't glower at me, ladies. I won't apologize for protecting Margaret. Even he admits he was a bad brother, and he never once tried to help

Margaret when she was just a kid and had lost both parents. I don't like that. All very well to show up now and act the loving uncle, but I wanted to be sure he was on the level. So I had him checked out. Unofficially."

There was an uncomfortable tension in the room, as the older ladies were torn between outrage at the thought of him investigating their idol and a burning desire to hear every scrap of gossip he had uncovered.

"It's understandable," Greta said firmly. "And with him being a public figure, it's not like you were really snooping. Now, spill the beans."

"Well, as you know, his real name is Patrick Furey, Paddy to most people who knew him before he emigrated. As a young fella, there's nothing much on him. He ran up a few debts that went unpaid when he legged it abroad, but that's about it. When he was a struggling writer, he hung around with some seedy characters, no big gangsters or anything, just low level petty thieves and con men. Not that surprising considering the areas he lived in, in New York and then in Los Angeles. When he got famous though- that's where things get interesting. For a few years he lived the high life - and boy, did he live it! I spoke to a retired detective, an Irish chap who emigrated to the States and ended up working as a detective in San Francisco. He once arrested Paddy for drunk and disorderly, on some three day bender with his flunkies. He used to surround himself with hangers-on and flew them all over the place to party. My contact said it was a nightmare, Paddy - Humphrey, I should say - was screaming abuse and roaring, *"Don't you know who I am?"* before taking a swing at one of the uniforms."

He looked around triumphantly but if he was expecting the women to be shocked, he was in for a disappointment.

"Just like Clarke Gable, in that movie. The one where he has his shirt off, and some woman has brought him low, and he gets arrested..." Niamh said dreamily.

"It reminds me of stories about Hemingway," Ellen volunteered.

"Sure, Ronan, your generation wouldn't understand but he's a Man's Man. Men used to be rough and tough."
"We're talking about the nineteen seventies and eighties here, Dymphna - not the wild west."

"I remember seeing photos back then," Claudia cut across Ronan. "He was a real bad boy, wasn't he?"

Eve shook her head at Ronan. "Don't even bother," she told him. "They're besotted. Just carry on. What else did you find out?"

"He made a lot of money from the books and that TV series, but he ran through it. Gambling, wild parties, really bad investments - you name it. Then his books fell out of fashion, sales slowed down and he had made so many enemies in publishing, no one wanted to touch his books. The same in Hollywood - plans to make movies fell through, the television series was canceled, and so on. From what I heard, the only person to stand by him was Burke."

"How did they meet, do we know?"

"Years and years before, apparently. Humphrey was in a writing group, Damian Burke was the hottest young agent in Dublin. He also wrote a literary column in the papers.The story they both have told in the media is that he came to talk to the group, got interested in Humphrey and encouraged him. He didn't take him on as a client for a few years after that, but it's apparent he was a great influence."

"How did Humphrey take the news, Ronan?"

"Well," Ronan admitted reluctantly, "He did seem genuinely upset. I'll give him that. But - well, he was also concerned about his own interests. Like, his book that Burke was touting."

"Okay. So, fond of Burke, but maybe also a bit selfish about it?"

"Yeah. That's fair."

"What about this cold case, the one Greta was interviewing him about?"

"Nothing in it. Sorry, Greta. Like, the man died in very odd circumstances but I can't see there being anything there. Just - a weird coincidence."

Greta sniffed. "Maybe, maybe not."

Eve shrugged. "If Greta thinks it's worth pursuing, we should follow it up." In her experience, the old woman could smell a scandal from fifty feet and as many years. Greta looked around smugly, already perking up at the thought of digging into her favourite topic. Ronan didn't argue, perhaps realizing that it would do no harm to keep Greta occupied.

Dymphna spoke for the first time. "I think we need to find out everything we can about the Festival. It's the reason everyone involved was here, isn't it? Humphrey, Phyllis, Burke…"

"Agreed. We need to gather as much intel as we can, see how everything fits together."

"Well, there's not much we can do right now," Eve yawned and stretched. "It's Sunday, for one thing. It'll be easier to get a hold of people tomorrow, won't it?"

Ronan nodded. "Obviously my team - Cullen's team, I should say - will be working regardless but you're right. It'll be a lot easier for us to get moving tomorrow. Who are you looking at first?"

"I think you're right and the best way we can help is by talking to everyone involved. I know the Gardaí will too, but we're locals. People will tell us lots of things your lot wouldn't even consider important. And we have the advantage that Humphrey is Margaret's uncle. We can get all kinds of background on poor Damian Burke, from him."

"Hmm. If he's cooperative."

"Ah Ronan, there's no reason to assume he won't be."

"He was genuinely upset," Greta said firmly, "There was no faking that."

"Doesn't mean he'll actually be honest with us," Ronan said stubbornly. Eve decided it would be best to tactfully ignore the issue for now.

"Let's make a plan," she suggested. "Who wants to tackle Humphrey?"

Claudia's hand shot up. "Leave him to me."

"Okay. Dymphna, want to ferret around the neighbourhood tomorrow? We could catch up with some of the authors who took part in the festival too - I know for a fact Emer O'Neill is still around. Good. Mam, you know all the local teens - a lot of them were volunteers, so let's see if they heard or saw anything. Ronan, you need to pull in any favours you're owed, and find out what the Gardaí know."

She looked around the room. "And one last thing - Tom and I aren't clearing up this mess. I want every dish in the dishwasher and those pans washed, before anyone goes anywhere!"

Chapter 10

A full stomach and a nap in front of the TV gave Eve a new lease of life. There wasn't much left of Sunday by the time Tom headed home, but she thought she would pop over to Wisteria Cottage and see how the bride to be was faring.

Eve found Margaret sitting on the floor of the tiny utility turned wedding planning room in her cottage.A stack of rectangular, lilac coloured cards lay scattered around her, a silver calligraphy marker abandoned to one side.

"Having another go at the place settings?" Eve asked, trying to sound cheerful. Margaret gave her a forlorn look in reply.

"Stupid idea."

"No, it isn't. It has to be done, regardless of what else is happening." Eve lowered herself gingerly to the floor beside the bride to be. It was easy enough to get down, she thought wryly, it's getting back up again might be a problem. "Look, I'm as upset as anyone about that poor man, and I'm worried about Greta too. And Humphrey, of course. But I'm sure neither had anything to do with it all. We'll soon sort it out, and then we'll have the wedding of the century to look forward to. Ronan is going to be tied up with this investigation – we both know he can't leave it alone, not even for Cullen."

Margaret gave a wan smile. "He's raging, Eve, absolutely

raging. I've never seen him so angry and frustrated. I couldn't tell him, but I agree with the Super. He can't possibly be lead detective on a case that involves his own in-laws!"

"Of course not, but I wouldn't say it him either. That young man only cares about two things – solving crimes and marrying you. Let him work away with us to clear this up, and you make sure he has a wedding at the end of it."

Margaret hugged her, catching Eve by surprise and almost toppling them both into a box of silk flowers. "You always make me feel better, Eve. I'm so glad you're my bridesmaid."

"Matron of Honour, if you please. It's been a long time since I was a maid! And I'm honoured you asked me. Now, you have me for an hour, before I have to collapse in front of the TV. What can I do to help?"

Margaret thrust the calligraphy marker at her. "You're the artist – my attempts look like a drunk chicken wandered through some silver ink. Write fast!"

By the time she returned to Kimberly Cottage, Eve felt the better for an hour of wedding preparation. It seemed a little heartless, considering the events of the previous day, but that was life – you had to seize happy moments when they came, even when things were bleak. Kimberly was peaceful and welcoming, and she spent a half hour catching up on "Ireland's Hottest Chef's," her current guilty pleasure in reality TV. Watching beautiful people cooking while a famous chef roared at them was a welcome distraction, especially as they finally revealed to the contestants which among them had hidden the nutmeg in the previous episode.

During the ad breaks, she fired off a text to her brother.

"What were you thinking, springing that lunch on Mam?"

"Hah. Amateur. As if I'd give her time to plot." Conor replied.

"Okay. Makes sense. How did it go?"

"Grand. How's the murder going?"

"Fine. What you mean, grand? What are Ray's parents like?"

"Lovely. It went fine."

Eve sighed. Typical Conor, saying it was grand and no proper details. Her phone pinged and a text from an unsaved number popped up.

"Hi Eve! Ray here. Ignore Conor. Lunch was great. My parents love your Mam. They are obsessed with Conor. Staying for a week, hope to meet you. They will be back over for Conor's birthday. September. Keep date free."

Ray signed off with a series of wink emojis followed by hearts, smiley faces and…a ring. Eve clapped her hands in delight. Ray sent one final text:

"Don't tell your mum!"

There was no need to worry about her brother, Ray seemed to have everything well in hand, including Niamh.

Eve celebrated with a cup of decaf tea and a biscuit which tipped her over into sleepiness and she sank into her bed gratefully. A decent night's sleep went a long way to completely restoring her spirits, and Monday morning found her up and ready for action. She stood at her kitchen counter and sipped coffee, ruminating on the situation. A pot of freshly brewed tea and a single bone china cup rested on a saucer beside her coffee mug.

Margaret had been grateful for her confidence in her uncle, as much as for her reassurance regarding the wedding – there was no hint in her demeanour that she suspected Humphrey on any level. Blind devotion, Eve wondered, or did she just know him better than anyone else, despite their short acquaintance? There must be genuine affection on both sides for him to chose to remain in Dublin…

"Stop wool-gathering," Dymphna snapped, breaking Eve's reverie. Not for the first time, the old woman had managed to enter the cottage without making a sound and then to creep up on Eve, who was proud that she no longer yelped and jumped when it happened. Instead, she picked up the teapot, handed her neighbour a hot cup of freshly poured tea without comment, and noted that Dymphna's eyebrows twitched in annoyance.

Hah, thought Eve, score one for me.

"Any word from anyone?" Dymphna made herself comfortable at Eve's kitchen table and helped herself to a biscuit.

"Not so far. I was over with Margaret last night, she's taking it all quite hard."

"Hmm. Not nice, is it, finding your long lost uncle and then having him accused of murder."

"No. Dymphna…I know you and the others are mad about the man, but honestly, what do you think? What do you feel? Is he capable of …murder?"

Dymphna sighed. "Most people are, in the right circumstances. If someone hurt one of my kids, or grandkids, for example – but for money? Or in anger? I can't see it. He's got his flaws, has our Paddy Furey – Humphrey Sterling, I should say – but I don't think so. I could possibly see him lashing out in temper, but if he did that, could he be cold-blooded enough attend a book reading, make a big speech about staying in Dublin and finding family? He's more the type to panic, and run. He'd look after number one, first, in my opinion."

Eve blinked hard. "Really? I thought – well, you give the impression that you're as besotted about him as the others. All that guff about his literary genius…but you aren't, are you?

You're very aware of him."

Dymphna reached out calmly, poured herself another cup of tea and then whacked Eve sharply on the back of her hand.

"OW! What the – what was that for?"

"For being a complete and utter snob about Humphrey and his books. Stop it. Yes, I can see the man's faults but I'm not lying about enjoying Jerusalem Hill. I *love* those books. Oh, I'm aware they're not going to win a Booker Prize, or end up on the school curriculum to be studied, but so what? Let me tell you something about books. They are there to entertain us, to give people a break from their daily lives. You think all good books should be educational, and deep, and have messages – well, Jerusalem Hill is loyal, rough but fair, tough but kind. The villains are always caught, the innocent are always cleared, and justice is always served – I wish to God I could say the same about real life."

Eve felt her cheeks burn. "I'm not being a snob…"

"Oh, *yes* you are. The way you sneer at your mother about reading them, the little eye rolls when she talks about them. Well, you can thank Humphrey Sterling the next time you see him because when your Dad died, and your ma was left with two young 'uns and next to no income, when she worked as a cleaner, and then came home and did alterations for her middle class neighbours on their designer gear – when she could barely get out of bed for grief and worry – those books kept her going. They were her one bright spot, and she couldn't even afford to buy them, got them all at the local library. Jerusalem Hill made her feel like things would eventually turn out okay, even if they got pretty dark first. Did you know that? No? Well, you do now."

Dymphna smiled, the kind of grim, knowing smile only an

old bat can give. "So, you start reading them, and tell her you loved them, and thank every passing God that your mother found them when she needed them. Books are like friends, my dear. None of them are perfect, but all of them are valuable. And all of them deserve respect."

Eve was conscious of several feelings, from shame to embarrassment, to a fierce stab of affection for her poor mother. Over the years the fact of her widowhood had just become "one of those things," just the way things were, and the reality of what it must have meant, how hard it had been for her, was lost. They had known money was tight, but Conor and Eve had never been exposed to Niamh's terrors. Looking back, she couldn't remember wondering where food was coming from, or if they'd have a roof over their heads. Her mother had done everything on her own.

Before she could gather her thoughts to reply to Dymphna's quiet but brutal lecture, the older woman had stood, brushed the crumbs off her smart black skirt and blouse and picked up her handbag.

"Come on, girl. Time to get snooping."

* * *

If Emer O'Neill was surprised to be accosted on the doorstep of her Bed and Breakfast by Eve and her elderly neighbour, she hid it well. The author had the air of a woman who liked to go with the flow, and who was game for any adventure.

"Ladies," She grinned at them. "To what do I owe the pleasure?"

"Nosiness." Dymphna twinkled at her, doing her best kindly old lady impression. "Pure nosiness. Well, and concern too.

You know poor Greta, it was her house that man died in? She's one of my closest friends and she's in bits over this. I promised her we'd ask around, see if anyone saw anything..."

"Don't the Gardaí do that?" Emer asked blandly, her mouth twitching. "They were here last night, asking that everyone present at the Merrion Literary festival stay around for a few days. They seemed to be investigating thoroughly."

Dymphna shrugged. "I'm a huge fan of the local Gardaí, sure isn't Greta's granddaughter one? Sergeant Jo Maguire, you'd have seen her last night – she's on her way to being a detective herself, so she is. But…well, you know how it is. They're fierce narrow in their inquiries at times. Don't get the full picture about people, if you catch my drift."

"I think I do. In all honesty, I'm nosey myself and I'd be ferreting around given half a chance. Tell you what, buy me a coffee and maybe a bun, and I'll spill the beans. All the gossip I know about Sterling, and Burke, and the rest of them."

Eve felt fairly confident that bribery was unnecessary and the writer had been hoping to have a good chat about the murder, but she was happy to stump up for a coffee. There was something endearing and interesting about Emer, with or without gossip to share.

As it turned out, Emer had a wealth of the same, and a storyteller's knack for weaving it all together. In olden days she would have been called a *Seanchaí*, in Irish, one of those who kept old stories alive and collected new ones. She entertained them with a steady flow of chat until they reached The Parlour Café.

"This is excellent," the author looked around it appreciatively. It was small, but every inch of space had been skillfully organized without being cluttered. The décor was unusual for a Dublin cafe, avoiding the industrial or hipster looks and opting instead for the feel of a country kitchen, with jars of wildflowers on each table, and pretty bone china tea cups and saucers.

"It's a lovely place, and best of all, they serve coffee in a proper coffee pot instead of a measly mug." Eve waved a hand, "and it makes me feel like I've stepped back in time. This building is from roughly the same era as the cottages on Bramble Lane, you know."

"I didn't know that, but it makes sense. I do love this area. Okay, you've kept your end of the bargain – those cream éclairs are divine, by the way – so now I'll pay my debt. Let's see, where to start? With Damian Burke, I suppose. Poor man, I didn't know him very well but he seemed a decent stick. He had a great reputation, honest and very good to new writers. I actually submitted my first book to him, you know, hoping he'd represent me but he passed. He did send a lovely email though, very encouraging and very kind. Publishing is brutal so you remember the few agents who are nice. When my agent took me on, and the book took off, I got another email from him saying he was delighted to hear about it and that I had found the perfect person for it in Maud. I met him a few times after that. I would say he was genuine, businesslike but with a soul – not that common in this industry! It's hard to imagine anyone hating him enough to hurt him. I feel like, whatever the reason, it wasn't about *him*, if you follow me."

Eve wasn't sure she did, but she nodded. Dymphna was remaining uncharacteristically quiet, which usually meant she was busy in some unseen way. It fell to Eve to encourage their guest to chat.

"Now, that journalist, Aidan Lowe…oh my god. He's *slime.*

I told you before, he takes a particular pleasure in ripping authors to shreds, and it's an open secret he especially hates female writers who turn down his sleazy advances. Which is pretty much every female writer who has met him. Nasty man. Now, if he'd been murdered, I would have said it was richly deserved. He loves digging up dirt on people, too. Wait and see, I bet he'll report on all this and it'll be ninety percent scurrilous innuendo, with ten percent facts. And he'll probably have those few facts wrong."

"Did he – have you had any trouble with him?"

"Oh yes. I think I mentioned to you before, he blasted one of my early books? The week before, he contacted me, saying he wanted to do an in depth interview with me. I met him in a restaurant in town, in the middle of the afternoon – like, you'd think you'd be safe then, wouldn't you? Public place, broad daylight? Not a bit of it. The man was like an octopus from the start! And the personal remarks!…even the waiter asked me if I was sure I was okay at one point. When I say I fled the place, I'm not exaggerating. He was furious, sent me absolutely vile text messages for a few days and then a week later, that review came out."

"Oh wow. I'm so sorry." Eve glanced at Dymphna, whose face wore a grim little smile. The journalist had already fallen foul of her by sniping at their friends, now she was fairly sure a world of hurt was about to land on him. And when Eve got a chance, she'd add her own mite to that pile.

"It's grand. Well, it isn't grand, but you know yourself. Now, I make sure that any new writer is forewarned about him and I've made sure my agent and anyone else who'll listen is aware."

"Good for you. Thanks for telling us, although I'm not sure it has anything to do with the murder, do you? As you say, it'd be easier if he'd been stabbed, not poor Mr. Burke. He seems to have been genuinely popular. I don't suppose you can fill us in on any of the others? Like, Phyllis Dennehy - she was in and out of Greta's house all the time, because of Humphrey."

Emer sipped her tea and ruminated.

"Phyllis – I've actually met her before. Before Humphrey, I mean. She's an odd fish. About three years ago, when I was still fairly unknown as a writer, before I won the Golden Knife Award, she was PA to Mark Kerno, the British writer. She was devoted to him, it was borderline creepy. But then, according to him, one day she just upped and left, barely gave notice. That's when she went to work with Humphrey in the USA. Mark said he couldn't understand it, how she would go from a best-selling, award winner like him to a has-been like Sterling – his words, not mine. I think it was partly the lure of the States, to be honest, and that she thought Sterling would be moving in Hollywood circles."

"Phyllis is Irish, isn't she?" Eve shook her head. "She doesn't seem very happy to be back here."

"Well…now, if you want the *inside,* inside scoop…" Emer lowered her voice and leaned forward. "I think our Phyllis left a bit of a mess behind her. Publishing is a small industry, ladies and in Ireland it's minuscule. Everyone knows everybody. But I feel a bit mean repeating this, because she was quite young at the time. So don't spread it around unnecessarily."

"We won't. But anything might be helpful," Eve pleaded.

"Okay. So, before she decided to become a personal assistant to various writers, she was an aspiring writer herself. And she had some initial success, modest stuff – like winning a local competition for short stories, or getting a story published here or there. She was working for – well, one of the big literary agents here in Dublin. It was more an internship, from what I gather…doing a bit of admin, making coffee, running errands. I assume she hoped it would give her a leg up towards being published herself. Then one of the mainstream publishers announced the *"National First Chapter"* competition – remember that?"

Eve did, vaguely.

And Dymphna broke her silence to say, "I remember it well. That must be almost ten years ago now. The winning first chapter would have their novel published."

"That's the one. Everyone who ever thought they had a book in them entered it. I did myself – didn't get past the first round! But Phyllis got through a few rounds to the semi finals. Sixteen "first chapters" were in the running, and the whole event was far more popular than expected. When they saw the level of interest the organizers decided to publish the entries, for the public to read, before choosing a winner."

Dymphna banged the table with one bony hand, rattling the china cups and causing the prim ladies at the next table to tut tut loudly. They tried to glare at their table, but one sharp look from Dymphna convinced them to return to their own gossip.

"*Now* I remember."

"Aha. Eve, ringing any bells for you?"

"No, I'm sorry. I recall the competition, but didn't pay a lot of attention at the time. What happened?"

"The chapters were published, and all hell broke loose. A young woman came forward asking why her chapter had the wrong name attached to it. It was accredited to P. L. Dennehy. Of course, it was really Phyllis. The story didn't take long to unravel. Phyllis had found a manuscript in the slush pile at the agent's office, it had been submitted ages before. She read it, realized its potential and reworked the first chapter."

"And submitted it under her own name?" Eve gasped. "But – that's insane, she couldn't have hoped to get away with it?"

"Ah. See, there was no talk of showing the public the chapters when she entered the competition. My friend – the one who told me all this – he thinks she fully intended to rewrite the novel enough so that she could claim any likenesses were coincidental. Ego, you know – her version would of course be so superior, et cetera." Emer took a bite of her bun and said somewhat indistinctly, "It's a bit like athletes taking performance enhancing drugs, isn't it? There's a chance of being caught and disgraced, but there's a chance you'll end up on the winner's podium…"

Eve could see her point. "Still, it was mad, so risky."

"The girl whose chapter it actually was, Elaine Merchant, she didn't win the competition but her work was taken up by an agent – oh! Actually, the agent was Damian Burke." Emer pursed her lips. "Now, that's interesting, don't you think? But then Ireland is so small, there's not that many options. It could be pure coincidence?"

Eve grinned. It was clear Emer had the instincts of a detective, probably a useful trait in any writer.

"You should try your hand at crime fiction," she remarked. "Yes, it's both interesting and possibly totally irrelevant. That's the problem, isn't it? How to tell the important bits from the red herrings in any investigation."

"So ye *are* investigating!" Emer said triumphantly. "I knew it. I did a bit of research this morning. Two murders in this area in the last twelve months – and both solved by the same two Gardaí? I said to myself, there's more here than meets the eye. And then when news broke of the murder, people started mentioning you lot. "

Dymphna leaned forward and frowned at the excited writer. "It's not a game, Emer."

"Oh, come on." Emer didn't seem a bit fazed, even by Dymphna's infamous beady eyed stare. "I'm as sensitive as the next person, but don't tell me you're digging into this case solely out of civic and moral duty. It's okay to want to help people, and get enjoyment from it at the same time. If you have a talent for singing, isn't it okay to enjoy singing – even at a funeral? Well then. You have a knack for finding things out – I'm the same myself. And I won't pretend I'm not interested or it's all some huge burden. I like snooping around, and I like helping people."

Eve braced herself for the hurricane of Dymphna's wrath, but the old woman just smiled.

"Very sensible approach. Okay then. We have been known to …help out our friends and neighbours. Discreetly."

"Hmm. I suppose that young detective – Ronan?- he's a neighbour isn't he? And a friend?"

"He is. As is his fiancée."

"And Greta Goode. I've listened to her podcast for yonks…I know she definitely has an interest in this sort of thing."

Eve decided to intervene before the morning had passed them by entirely. "Yes, yes. There's a whole group of us. You can help too. We generally congregate in my house on Bramble Lane. Kimberly Cottage – say, around 7 pm? Any special dietary requirements?"

Emer threw her head back and laughed. "Yes, please. I'd love to be involved. I eat anything, prefer coffee to tea and I'll bring anything I can dig up on the Literary Festival – organizers, attendees, and guest speakers. Fair enough?"

"Fair. But not a word, Emer, not to anyone. Ronan could get into a lot of trouble if his boss thinks he's involving himself in the case."

"I promise. Look, I know I like to joke around but I can be serious when needed. Damian Burke was a decent sort, I want to see his killer caught too."

Dymphna patted her on the shoulder. "Welcome aboard. Now, you just make sure you pull your weight."

"I will faithfully interrogate every single person who so much as handed out a programme at the Festival. Don't worry, if there's a shred of info to dig up on anyone, I'll find it."

Chapter 11

Claudia Warren had never fluttered her lashes at a man in her life. Even her courtship with her dear, departed husband had been full of passion but very little coquetry. Claudia was a woman who knew what she wanted, and took the straightest path to get it. Many years ago, she had informed the object of her heart's desire that she was interested in him, and his delighted response, whilst very flattering, had been accepted with a calm grace and unruffled demeanour. Until the day he died, he never had cause to regret his decision, nor doubt her devotion, but as a couple their love language had been cups of tea and volunteering to do the dishes.

However, sitting opposite Humphrey Sterling brought to mind several extremely romantic and heart-throbbing moments in her favourite Jerusalem Hill books. There was no denying that he was still a fine figure of a man, trim of figure and quite youthful looking, she reflected as she poured them both another cup of tea. While Eve and Dymphna held their conference with Emer, Claudia had chosen to concentrate on the man at the heart of the mystery. He had jumped at her invitation to "elevenses" in her house, smiling like a Cheshire cat as she pressed another of her very *special* recipe scones on him.

Her scones combined her award winning baking skills - three times the Irish Women's Brigade Home Baking gold medal winner for small baked goods, no less - with her other talent, that of a skilled potion maker. She had briefly considered offering him a glass of her famed cordial – Eve called it her "truth serum," – but thought even Humphrey might baulk at alcohol before midday. In fairness, she couldn't recall seeing the author with more than a glass of wine in hand but the image of a fast-living, hard drinking, man of the world was deeply ingrained in his fans. No, she would stick to tea and cake, she had decided, but put out a decanter of the good sherry as well, just in case he took a fit of wild writer-like creativity on himself and demanded hard liquor.

She need not have worried. Humphrey was quietly delighted with her spread of traditional buttermilk scones with butter, jam and cream. Her secret ingredients, the ones that loosened tongues and encouraged confidences, were undetectable.

"I love her dearly," he confided as he piled one half of a scone with strawberry jam, "but my niece eats like a rabbit. The fridge is full of lettuce and some class of rice made out of cauliflower! It's a crime to even call it "rice." Don't get me wrong, it's lovely staying with her, but I miss Greta's if I'm honest."

"Ach, that's her wedding diet. I've seen that girl put away an entire pepperoni pizza in one sitting. Wait until the honeymoon is over and you'll see – she'll be back to normal."

"Well, I hope I won't be imposing on her by then!" Humphrey looked rather alarmed. "Surely, the police will clear up what happened to poor Damian by then."

"It's only a few weeks, Humphrey. Murder investigations can take a long time. But they'll be finished with Greta's house soon I'm sure, and then ye can move back in…"

Humphrey paled.

"Of course. Although – I confess, I'm not sure I'd quite like to be – well, it would be very difficult to sit watching TV in the same room where he died… he *was* a very dear friend, you know."

"Of course. Of course. You and he had a bit of a row, didn't you? Always extra sad, when someone dies and you're not on the best of terms. My Aunty Philomena popped her clogs in the middle of a row with her sister Constance. Connie was distraught – said Philomena always had to have the last word."

"I – I didn't row with Damian," Humphrey protested weakly. "Not a row, per se."

"Did you not? Oh, I'm sorry. Greta said she thought she heard the pair of you having words."

"Oh. It was something and nothing. Business, you know – publishing is a difficult business. As you know, I've just written a new book and Damian was supposed to be touting it around publishers. He was a great agent in his day, no question about it, but in recent years – I feel that the industry has moved on, without him. He didn't seem to be able to get a meeting with the kind of publishing house I'm used to, let alone sell them the book. I told him, I'm not going with some rinky-dink, provincial little press – my books belong with the Big Five."

Claudia raised an eyebrow in query and Humphrey added, "The main publishing houses. We in the business call them "the big five." Anyway, I did get rather cross with poor Damian. In fact, I was about to – to sack him as my agent. There, I've said it. He was very angry, of course, and begged me not to give up on him…and I promised him a second chance. We parted on the best of terms, I assure you. He swore he would move heaven and earth to get "Devil's City" in front of the right people."

Claudia was prepared to swear Humphrey was telling half-truths, but she held her tongue.

"Ah, well, at least ye parted on a good note. That's the main thing."

"Yes, I would have hated it if the last thing I'd said to him was in anger. No, he was perfectly happy leaving the park, he reassured me that he would keep working on the book deal for at least another month." There was a ring of truth about that last bit, Claudia felt.

"That's nice," murmured Claudia. "More tea? Have another bit of jam on that scone."

"Thank you! Mm, heavenly, you're a dab hand with the auld baking, Claudia." His rich and cultured tones had slipped somewhat and the unmistakable cadence of Dublin city rang through. "Damian was a decent auld sod, I have to admit. The amount of second chances he gave me over the years, despite everything. I haven't been an easy client, I know that. I get very protective of my books, Claudia. I know exactly how I want them, and how my characters should be – hate when the publishers force an editor on you, chopping and changing and criticizing everything. Poor Damian, he was always in there smoothing things out and sticking up for me."

"A good friend."

"The best. The very best. If he had followed though on his threat and dropped me, it would have broken me heart. The fact he was prepared to give me one more go –" the author dabbed at his eyes with his napkin –"I'll always remember that."

He seemed oblivious to the fact that he had contradicted his earlier story, but Claudia pretended not to notice. Instead she changed tack, and distracted Humphrey with a question.

"Tell me, now. Is there much money in writing?"

"Not enough," Humphrey said fervently. "Oh, you get your advance all right and if the book sells well, you'll manage but it's not like it used to be. And it's harder to get a share of the market now. It's all serial killers and gore and dark thrillers – or them sci-fi fantasy romances, that's what young people want. I just like to write thrillers, good old fashioned ones, with a bit of glamour and lots of action."

"There's still a lot of us who want to read them. I like a good serial killer myself, from time to time, but I prefer books like yours."

"Ah, my loyal fans are the only reason I keep going. I would have broken my pen and given up years ago, if it wasn't for them. But it's hard to keep your head above water as a writer nowadays. I don't mind telling you – just between us, you understand – I need this book to be a success. Things are – tight. I owe a few people, not nice people. Back in New York. And London. And one or two here in Dublin, but that's only in the last few weeks so I'm not too worried about them…yet. I'm hoping if we sell this book, I'll be able to clear it all off."

"Oh!" Claudia didn't hide her dismay. "But- that's awful. You could be - you could be in danger, surely? If they're on the shady side of the law, I mean? And with your agent – well, you know – how will you sell the book?"

Humphrey's face clouded over. "I don't know. It'll take a while to find another agent for Ireland and the UK. My American agents aren't too pleased with me at the moment, so no joy there. I suppose I'll have to go for plan B. I really don't want to go for plan B."

Claudia eyed him a trifle anxiously. He had had quite a few of her special scones and while there was nothing in them that could be harmful physically, you could get quite a dose of magic from them. She was aware that she had a real talent for making potent "truth serum" and that Humphrey had probably had more than most people. On the other hand, she thought, he was an author and that meant he essentially lied for a living. It'd be grand. He'd have a nap and sleep it off.

"What's plan B?" she prodded gently.

"It's not nice. Not nice at all. I thought it'd be easy but that was before I actually met her. She's an awfully nice girl. But then again, he inherited everything and that wasn't fair, was it? They could have left a bit to me! Margaret won't mind, not really. Once she sees how badly I was treated, how unfair it is. Don't you think? She'll definitely want to make it right."

Claudia stared at the man.

"Plan B, then – it's to get money out of Margaret?"

"Just what I should have got from my parents. What her dad got instead. My share of it. That's all."

Claudia sat back and sighed. Ronan was going to explode when he heard this. The question now was, should they even tell him?

* * *

"Where to now?" Eve asked, once they had parted from their new friend.

"Coffee morning at St Augustine's." Dymphna responded. Eve's surprised look in response prompted her to explain,

"Emer is the perfect person to talk to the literary types, but we need the local take on things. Every auld biddy in the area will be there, gossiping."

Dymphna's prediction proved to be accurate. The coffee morning usually attracted less than a dozen dedicated mass-goers, mainly the elderly parishioners who liked the routine of near daily mass, or popped in to light candles and pray. Fr Aloysius made a point of attending, to listen to their problems or gush over pictures of grandchildren, but it rarely lasted more than forty minutes, and it never required more than one urn of hot water.

When Eve and Dymphna arrived it was already clear that this was not the usual coffee morning. At least thirty people were crowded into the room, and three red-faced, harassed parish volunteers were desperately wrestling cups back from the guests to wash and hand out to the next wave. There were scuffles over the custard creams and the shortage of chairs threatened to cause serious rifts in the community.

"Look at them," Dymphna hissed. "Most of them haven't seen the inside of this church since they were baptized."

"Eh, you're not exactly a regular attendee yourself," Eve pointed out.

"Sure that's different. We're here on official business, not like this shower. And I've no need to shuffle into Mass every week, I'll have you know. My conscience is in perfect order. Would you look at that? That's Olivia O'Mahony, the poor auld thing. She's half crippled with arthritis. Why is she standing while that big gallute of man sits?"

Elbows out, Dymphna made her way through the crowd, leaving a murmur of agonized yelps in her wake. She reached the aforementioned Olivia, a frail woman with a noticeable stoop who barely reached Eve's shoulder. Dymphna paused and glowered at two middle aged men seated at a rickety table beside them.

"Have you no seat, dear?" Dymphna's voice rang out across the crowd, despite the fact that she did not raise the volume. Somehow, the quietly spoken statement managed to ricochet around the room, and echo slightly. "Wouldn't you think any able bodied person would be ashamed to be sitting on their plump behinds while a woman of your age was left standing?"

Eve wondered if Dymphna realized that Olivia was at least ten years younger than her. Like her mother Niamh, along with Claudia and Greta, the woman seemed oblivious to her own age.

One of the men in question shifted slightly in his seat, trying to avoid eye contact with the stern woman staring down at him. He lifted his tea cup to his lips in a fair imitation of nonchalance, which was thoroughly spoiled when the handle came away in his hand and he was forced to leap to his feet to avoid a flood of hot liquid. He was not entirely successful, grabbing paper napkins to repair the damage as a dark tea stain spread around the crotch of his light coloured chinos.

As he stood, Dymphna's hand shot out, grabbed the back of his chair and pulled it from under him.

"Why thank you," she said sweetly, gesturing to the other woman to sit. "Appreciate it."

She turned to the other man and said pointedly, "I'm sure you'll want to follow suit?" He stood rather quickly and relinquished his seat, backing away with a murmured apology.

"Not at all," Dymphna said graciously as she took his place. A flurry of activity could be observed around the room as those seated hurriedly offered their seats to the regular, older congregation members.

"Thanks, Dymphna," Olivia said gratefully. "Do you know, I've been standing for twenty minutes? I was about to give up and go home. Normally I can sit on my rollator but I don't bring it to mass – it's a bit of a nuisance with the narrow benches. Honestly, I don't know half these people."

"Here for the gossip," Dymphna said. "Not like us. Although, because it happened in my friend Greta's house, I probably know better than most…" Olivia's eyes lit up and she lent in for a comfortable chat.

Eve left the two women to it, braving the knot of people around the tea station to secure three cups of hot but weak tea and a handful of cracked Digestives. By the time she found her way back to the table, there was a circle of eight senior citizens and Dymphna. She placed the tea on the table, Olivia exclaiming in delight.

"Aren't you a good, kind girl?" It was a while since anyone had called Eve a girl. "Dymphna, is she one of yours?"

"No, no. This is Niamh Caulton's girl. That's Niamh Boyd, that was. This one's the artist."

"Ooh!" The entire table favoured her with a long, appraising stare.

"She doesn't look like an artist," a short, stout man with a balding head said in a disappointed tone.

"Oh, she dressed respectable for today. You should see her normal outfit – overalls, covered in paint, hair standing on end, floaty scarves everywhere. Like something out of Montmartre."

This went down well, the idea of an artist looking like a nice, middle class, middle aged woman apparently being too much of a let down for the crowd.

"I'd say it's a fierce interesting life," one old biddy elbowed Eve in the ribs and winked. "Very…*free*."

Eve opened her mouth to protest but gave up when she saw the hopeful expressions on the faces of the elderly parishioners.

"Um, well, I've had my moments, I suppose," she managed weakly.

Heads nodded wisely.

"Artistic temperament," the short bald man said with relish. "Ya can't expect the rules to apply to them lot."

"Can't help themselves," agreed a tiny bird of a woman, who wore a miraculous medal pinned to her lapel and was never seen without her rosary beads. "Sure, it's how God made them. Great passions, am I right?"

Eve, who could count the number of dates she'd had on one hand and had been married for twenty-five years before her ex-husband found a younger companion, tried to assume the look of a woman who had "seen things," and "been places."

"Like the writers," Dymphna murmured. "Sure, aren't they all mad too?"

As if on cue, this innocuous remark opened the floodgates of local opinion. Bald man had been at every event during the festival and held the reputation of being a deep thinker and something of a literary connoisseur. He held forth for a solid five minutes on the state of the poets – the individuals themselves, not their work – and how in his day a poet looked like one, with a romantic air, long hair and maybe even a cravat. They certainly didn't wander around in torn band tee shirts and ripped jeans. He had been tempted to leave when he saw the lack of organization, at the Poetry in the Park event, but thank heavens for that young woman stepping in.

"Tall girl, with a clipboard?" Dymphna asked.

"The very one. Liam Quigley nearly boxed her ears for her, but she was right – the entire thing was a shambles. He didn't have the seats put out, and the writers were all milling around."

"She had to step in at the last event too," one of the women remarked. "He had a right go at her then."

"Officious little git."

"Ah now, he did a great job getting the festival off the ground. Sure, it was him got the funding. He annoyed them down at the council until they gave in and gave him a grant. And he had Brendan Kavanagh plagued."

"The Minister?" Eve was surprised. Minister Kavanagh was a big noise in politics, and not given to mixing much with the lowly voters. He held the Arts portfolio, but any attempt to get him interested in her community arts projects had been met with a polite but firm request to go through official channels.

"Yes! My eldest is friends with Kavanagh's young fella. They're in the Hurling together – the seniors at St Paul's. Didn't Quigley turn up at one of the matches, and seat himself beside the Kavanaghs? Bent the poor man's ear until he looked fit to strangle him."

"Did it work?"

"I dunno, but he got everything he needed for the Festival in double quick time," their informant gave a wry smile. "I bet Kavanagh helped him, just to get rid of the man. But whatever you think about him, or his methods, there would have been no Merrion Literary Festival without him."

"Maybe he didn't realize how much would be needed then on a day to day basis, and it just got away from him?" Eve sipped her tea innocently. Long association with the ladies had taught her the fastest way to get their generation to tell you something was never to ask a direct question. Instead, make a statement they would be sure to disagree with and wait for them to tell you how wrong you were.

It worked a charm.

"Oh, come off it. Isn't he on every committee in the area? He's organized enough lectures and those endless resident association meetings…he knows you need seats for people to sit on and a drop of tea afterwards."

"He was all over it the first few days! Oh, down the hall three hours in advance, throwing his weight around. He practically measured the gap between the chairs to make sure they were all the same distance from each other. No, he lost interest by the Poetry day, that's what it is."

Eve made a mental note of this. "I wonder what made him think of a literary festival?"

"Oh, I suppose seeing he's such good mates with that writer – Jerusalem Hill."

"Humphrey Sterling, Biddy. Jerusalem is his main character."

"Is it? Well, him. I bet he wanted to impress him, and maybe give him a platform to promote the new book."

"Oh. I didn't think they knew each other that well…"

"Ah, I'd say it's back in the days when they were both young. He called him by his real name once or twice – Pat, Paddy? Something like that. Heh, your man didn't like that, I can tell you. Said very snippily, 'Humphrey, if you please." Biddy shook her head. "Very snippy."

"Well, you shouldn't go around calling people by their old names if they want to change it. I was in school with a girl, Gobnait Murray. God help her, she got an awful slagging over her name. It was very old fashioned, even back then. Met her years later, she was introduced as Gabrielle. Nearly died when she saw me, but I just said, "Oh, I think we were in school together, Gabrielle?" and she was delighted. Poor woman, I'd change my name from Gobnait too! Why shouldn't Humphrey Sterling change his name? I bet he wouldn't be as famous if he was plain auld Paddy from Dublin."

The birdlike woman smiled at Eve and appealed to her, "Amn't I right, love? The young people now, they just let people be. Call yourself whatever makes you happy. It's the way forward."

"It is, you're right. But it's interesting all the same, that they know each other. Or course, Humphrey knew that poor man who was murdered too…"

"Ah." A few looks were exchanged around the table before the bald man addressed himself to Dymphna, as respectfully as possible. "We did hear – was it that Greta Goode's house?"

Everyone present was well aware that Dymphna and Greta were fast friends, and there was a general air of treading very carefully over wafer thin ice, as her name was mentioned.

"It was. Poor Greta found the body, terrible shock for her."

"And – I suppose, there's no truth in the rumours…it wasn't her did it?"

There was always one gobdaw who couldn't read the room, Eve thought.

The look Dymphna gave the poor man would have pierced concrete.

"None. And I am sure you will make sure to quash those lies whenever you hear them."

"Oh we will, we will," the entire group chorused hastily.

"We never believed them, you understand! But just thought you should know, like, what ignorant people might be saying. I expect someone broke in, then?"

Dymphna shook her head. "The Gardaí don't seem to know what happened. And no one has any idea why the man was there, at all. We can only assume he was looking for Humphrey, and ran into an intruder."

"Or was he perhaps attacked on the street outside, and went inside looking for help?" Biddy suggested. "I read a book once, and the heroine found a dead man in her hallway – stumbled in off the street, with a knife in his back!"

"That's…that's a theory, all right." Eve conceded diplomatically.

"I have a ring doorbell," a white haired lady, who looked about a hundred and two, suddenly spoke.

Everyone looked at her pityingly. "That's lovely dear," Biddy said, patting her hand.

"Don't be a twit, Biddy. I meant, lots of people do now. It's a brand of doorbell. They record when they sense motion, or sound. Mine records people passing by the garden gate. I wonder now, do any of Greta's neighbours have the same?"

Eve looked at her in awe. "That's a brilliant idea."

Of course, the Gardaí would probably already have asked but it wouldn't hurt to make sure. Ronan could chase that up.

"You can go nowhere these days without surveillance," the woman continued. "Of course, it used to be all neighbourhood watch and twitching curtains…doesn't Greta live on Merrion Avenue? Her neighbour is Marian Fitzpatrick – she's very old now, of course, the poor dear, and practically bed ridden but she likes to watch the comings and goings in the area. She started the first neighbourhood watch back in the eighties. I bet she would have seen something. You should start with her."

The group looked at Eve and Dymphna rather expectantly.

It was beginning to dawn on Eve that they had acquired something of a reputation in the area, as amateur detectives.

"That's very helpful, thanks." Dymphna stood and added, "If any of ye think of anything else -"

"We'll let you know!"

"Thanks. Come on, Eve, drink up. Can't be sitting around all day, gossiping!"

* * *

Niamh waited patiently in the little park behind Bramble Lane, admiring the flowerbeds and the beautifully maintained gravel paths. She spotted the green and grey uniforms of the local secondary school, as students spilled into the park for their lunch break. Only seniors were allowed to use the park during school hours, and it was a privilege enjoyed to the full during good weather. It wasn't long before she saw a tall girl, with long red hair and a lanky young man with a shock of dark curls. They were accompanied by a shorter, slim girl with a head of shining black hair that hung loose to her shoulders and several other teens, all at that awkward, in-between stage of growth. Not quite adults, but definitely not little kids any more.

She raised her hand and waved, and the red haired girl immediately responded, setting off across the grass to where Niamh sat. The group followed, laughing and waving.

"Howya, Mrs. Caulton!"

"Niamh, please. How's things? Good day in school?"

"Horrific." The redhead, Ashleigh, threw herself onto the bench beside Niamh and hugged her arm. "If I hear one more lecture about the exams, I'll scream."

"Sure, they're only fifth year exams. What are they plaguing you over them for?"

"See? I knew you'd understand. Now next year, that's the leaving cert. That's the big one. You'd swear we were doing it this year, the way they go on about it. Our English teacher actually shouted at us, I swear to god. *"Yiz'll all fail, FAIL..."* Mad woman."

The dark haired girl, Jenny Chan nodded. "We had the same in Geography. Miss Lowry said she couldn't sleep at night worrying about us, that we're the laziest bunch she ever had through the door."

Niamh chuckled. "Ah sure, they said the same back in my day. My class were told we were the worst in the history of the school. I went to an all girls, convent school and the nuns told us we were all going to hell because we said we wanted careers."

"I wouldn't mind," Jenny remarked, "But I got an A plus in geography at Christmas. It's not like any of us are failing."

"They're just trying to keep ye on your toes. Boyd, how are you finding it?"

The tallest of the boys, with the dark curls, grinned down at her. "Coming from the wilds of Illinois, you mean? I've caught up, thanks. Tom was a great help, he got me up to speed on European history over the Christmas."

"Good, good. I saw ye all helping out at the Literary Festival, too. Very community spirited of you."

A burst of laughter greeted this and Ashleigh smiled at Niamh. "We wondered when ye would get around to us. Oh, we know you're all investigating again. Don't even bother to deny it!"

Boyd sat the other side of Niamh. "If you guys hadn't helped me last Christmas, I'd be doing my studying in a cell. So whatever you need, I'm in."

"Well, right now I need to know if you saw or heard anything, no matter how small, that struck you as odd during the festival? We're trying to get a handle on who had dealings with this agent, Burke, the man who was killed. And Ashleigh, not a word of this at home."

"Cos my mam is dating Detective Cullen? Hah. Don't be daft, I wouldn't say a word. Although Cullen's no eejit, I'd say he's well aware of your antics. And Ronan…"

"Ronan has been told not to touch this with a barge pole," Niamh informed them. "So officially, even where Cullen is concerned, he's not involved at all. Understood?"

"Got it. Right, the Literary festival. I'll go first. Boyd suggested we volunteer, he said it would be a nice gesture and also, it would earn us Brownie points with Sister Marion - she's our civics teacher and she gives you a homework pass when she sees you helping out around the area. So, yeah, sounded like a good idea. Until we met Mr. Quigley, he's a right pain in the - well, he's pretty hard to deal with. Nothing we did was right."

Boyd chimed in. "He sure didn't want us around, from what I could see. He actually said if he could get anyone else, he would."

"But he couldn't, hah!" Ashleigh grinned. "None of the auld ones would volunteer, they all knew him too well. So, he had us running around everywhere, completely disorganized. I don't know why he even wanted to have a Literary festival, to be honest. He didn't seem to like writers very much, if you ask me."

"The way he treated them was unreal," Jennie interjected.

"That poor Helen one, the poet. He called her a simpering hen, I heard him. She was in tears. That's when that nice Mr. Burke stepped in - the poor man who died."

"Damian Burke?" Niamh tried not to sound too eager.

"Yeah. He was in the community hall, before the opening night. Quigley was up to high doh, he was like a headless chicken. Roaring at everyone, bullying them. That's when he took a pop off Helen. Burke took her aside, had a chat, and she cheered up. Then he went right up to Quigley and snapped at him, *"You're a jumped up little weasel, and if you spoke to me like that, I'd box your ears."*

"Oh, wow. And what did he say?"

"Nothing, just glowered at him. He's not so brave when someone stands up to him."

"Like that Dennehy one - she was brilliant. I enjoyed listening to her have a go at him, the last evening."

Niamh agreed. "She took no prisoners. I thought he'd have a heart attack."

"I thought he'd hit her," Boyd said grimly. "If he had -"

"You'd have had to stand in line. He'd have regretted it." Niamh looked smug. "He may well yet."

Ashleigh and Boyd shared a quick knowing look, having inside knowledge of just how the local busybody might find himself punished, but the rest of the teens were too interested in the gossip to read much into her statement.

"Anyway, after Dennehy took over at the poetry event, things ran much more smoothly."

"Until that journo started annoying her." Jennie contributed eagerly.

"Journo?"

"Face like a smacked bum, sleazy manners, creeps around the

place…"

"Ah. Journalist. You mean Aidan Lowe?"

"Yeah, him. He turned up *everywhere*. We were sure he was stalking her."

"Phyllis?"

"Yeah. He tried to get her alone, kept pestering her."

"Jennie's right," Boyd said. "I heard her tell him to get lost, at least twice. In the end, Charlie Goode and me went over and stood beside her until he got the message."

"And how did Phyllis react?"

"She was rattled," Ashleigh said firmly. "She didn't let on, but if you ask me she was scared of him."

"Scared?" Niamh was surprised. Lowe was horrible but she found it hard to imagine that woman really afraid of him. She hadn't even flinched when Quigley had been aggressive to her. Still, it was hard to say what might upset a person.

"Yeah, I'd say so. Oh! Lowe had a row with Mr. Burke too. I'd forgotten." Ashleigh frowned. "It wasn't at a festival event, that's why I didn't think of it. It was the Friday night, right here in the park. Let me think - they were standing over there, beside the wildflower section. Remember, it was drizzling out? I was in a hurry to get home and thought, what are they doing standing in the rain? Aidan Lowe had his back to me, so I only saw it was him when I was up close but I could hear him from the far side of the park!"

"Shouting?"

"Roaring. Red in the face. Burke was calm, he just stood there, like he was waiting for Lowe to stop shouting. He wasn't making much sense, though - Lowe, I mean - he was saying something like, "You can't tell me what to print." And he mentioned something about someone being like, a hack and fraud, and then I heard "If you try to stop me, you'll be sorry."

"Oh."

"Yeah. Now I think of it, that's a threat - isn't it?"

"Well, let's not read too much into it. People say things like that all the time, but don't mean anything by it."

"True. I tell my brother all the time that I'll strangle him," Jennie Chan agreed, "but I don't actually do it. I just hide his x-box controller."

"Exactly. Still, it's interesting. Thank you, my pets. I'll have to have a word with the bold Aidan, see what he has to say for himself."

"Let me know when," Boyd said firmly. "I'll go with you."

Niamh patted his arm. "Ah, thanks. But if anyone should be nervous, it's him."

* * *

"I suppose we should track down this Marion Fitzpatrick?" Eve asked. Dymphna nodded, but it was clear her attention had wandered again. Feeling a little worried for her friend - after all, she was over eighty, and they had had a busy morning - Eve slowed her pace. Immediately Dymphna spun to face her. "Come along, I can't abide dawdling."

"Dymphna, there's no mad rush. And you look - tired. Sorry, but it's true. I've noticed you seem a bit distracted and -"

Dymphna rolled her eyes. "I'm not doddery, for goodness sake. Nor am I tired. I was - and you might like to practice this some time, young woman - I was listening. With all my brain, not just the fraction of it most people employ."

"I was listening too!" Eve protested.

"No. You heard what was said, which I'll concede is more than many do. But listening - really taking things in, *isteach* - is a different kettle of fish altogether. I heard what was said, what was unsaid, and what they didn't know they were saying."

Dymphna set off again at her usual brisk pace, and Eve trotted beside her. Her curiosity was fully piqued now.

"How? I mean, how did you hear things unsaid?"

"It's in the music, in the sound. When a person is anxious, or scared - they can say very convincingly that they're not, but the timbre of their voice changes, the inflexion rises or lowers in pitch. If you have ears to hear, it's all there."

"Okay. So - what did you hear that I didn't?"

"Well, for a start - Emer. That young woman was determined to join our group from the moment she saw us. What we don't know is, why? Is she just a naturally nosey woman, a born detective, or - "

"Or does she want to be on the inside for a reason," Eve finished.

"Exactly. And while she was very open about her dealings with that Lowe person, the journalist, and the story about Phyllis rang true, there was a false note in there somewhere. Now it could be innocent, or it could be that she's hiding something. But I will be keeping my eye on her."

"Anything else?"

"Well, every member of the parish is convinced Humphrey is the murderer. You could tell that by how they avoided speaking about him. They were quick enough to bandy Greta's name about but not his. Of course, that's probably just bad-mindedness too. There's no soul more prepared to believe in the wickedness of their neighbours than a holy Joe."

Eve chuckled. "I did like that old woman, the one that looked like a wee bird."

"Laura McGillycuddy. She's ninety five if she's a day, and all her wits about her. Strong woman - married to a brute of a man for nearly twenty years. One day he got tired of tormenting her and raised a hand to the eldest girl instead. Laura bashed him over the head with a coal scuttle and threw him out. The Parish Priest at the time was a terror, turned up the next morning telling her to take back her husband or be read from the altar as a bad, unrepentant wife. She asked him what would be the penance for an unrepentant wife and he said, "Climb Croagh Patrick in Mayo, in your bare feet." Well, off she went, and up that mountain she went, and she came home with a letter from a priest in Westport to say she had done it. Her husband stayed gone and the priest never mentioned taking him back again."

Eve stared at Dymphna. "Wow."

"Yup. My generation, dear, we've seen it all. You can't shock us. Laura McGillycuddy would outwit the divil himself, even now. Ah - here we are." The old lady stopped outside the house opposite Greta's. "Let's hope Mrs. Fitzpatrick is at home."

They were in luck - not only was Greta's neighbour at home, she was only delighted to receive visitors. Her door was opened by a teenager, who ushered them in and called out cheerfully, "Granny, there's people here for you." As an aside, she whispered to Eve, "She doesn't get many visitors, she'll be made up!"

Marion turned out to be a plump, cheerful woman with shoulder length white hair and bright green eyes in a pale, lined face.

"Come in. It's Dymphna Moriarty, isn't it? Sure, I remember you knocking around with Greta Goode, back in the day.

Wasn't it you pair who set off the fire alarm in Sister Mary's class?"

"It was. She was a dreadful auld gasbag."

"Was this at school?" Eve smiled as she asked, imagining her friends as impish schoolgirls. Both women looked at her strangely.

"No, dear. This was when we were all young mothers together. We were all in our twenties. Sr. Mary ran the mother and baby classes in the community centre. Oh my goodness, she was irritating."

Dymphna looked smug. "If we hadn't set it off, we'd have missed the All Ireland Finals. I'd never have forgiven her. Dublin beat Kerry, it was mighty."

"Sr. Mary threatened us all with the parish priest if we didn't tell her who was responsible. She caused a stink for days about it - in the end, Greta's fella paid the young Kelly lad and his mates to say *they* did it."

"Heh! Her face when they confessed - she was raging. She was full sure it was me and Greta, the cheek of her."

"But - it was you and Greta…" Eve pointed out.

"But she didn't know that. Cheek of her, assuming. Anyway, sure it all worked out for the best. Young Sean Kelly was thrown off the altar boys roster, he was delighted with himself. Freed up his weekends nicely. Not to mention the two shillings he got from Donal Goode."

"Didn't he become a priest though, in the end?"

"No, no. That was his brother, Liam. Sean Goode has a chain of shops - retired last year and gave the whole lot to his daughter Katie."

Eve managed not to roll her eyes. The next ten minutes passed in an exhaustive exchange of news about people from the long distant past of the Merrion area. It was fascinating really, how even the housebound Marian knew what their old friends and neighbours were up to, and more, how their kids and grandkids were doing in life. This one had a degree, that one had had some troubles, your wan had had two kids and your man had two divorces - no mean feat even now in Ireland, where divorce still took an average of four to five years! "Speaking of divorces…" Marion turned to Eve and arched an eyebrow. "I hear you and that Peter one parted ways."

"A few years ago now, yes." Eve felt a familiar mixture of embarrassment and defiance answering. "It was for the best."

"Of course it was. You were always far too good for him. I told your mother, twenty-odd years ago, that man is jealous of Eve and her talent." The elderly lady pointed to the mantelpiece, grinning. "I'm a fan, you see."

Eve turned to look, and felt her cheeks grow red hot. There, hanging over the ornate, marble-clad, period fireplace, was one of her early works. A misty spring morning, by the canal, the outline of the city as it was then just visible but the focus centred on the nesting pair of swans that she had discovered one morning, among the reeds by the Portobello bridge.

"Oh."

"I was waiting for you to notice it," Marian chuckled. "I snapped that up at your first exhibition, and do you know when my daughter got it appraised for insurance, it had more than quadrupled in value?"

She mentioned a figure that made Eve blush even harder. It was a strange feeling, hearing her work rendered in euros and cents, but that was tempered by the genuine pride and affection in Marian's voice as she told her.

"My husband said I was daft - he had no eye for art, bless

him - but I loved that painting at first sight. When I die, it'll go to my daughter and then to Kylie-Anne - you met her, as you were coming in - but if you ever need it for an exhibition, just ask. We'll happily lend it."

Eve looked to Dymphna for help before she burst into tears. Dymphna looked wryly amused, but stepped into the breach.

"You're embarrassing the poor girl, Marian. You know artists and their temperaments. Here, what class of a name is Kylie-Anne?"

Marian sighed. "Don't. Her brother is Carlton. And her cousin, my Phelim's boy, is Keanu Leslie. I ask you, what's wrong with the good old Irish names? I mean, not even the ones like Fiachra or Domhnaill, but Sean, and -and Conor and so on."

"I agree. But you can't turn back time, I suppose. Young people now, they're obsessed with "unique" names." The acid tone in which Dymphna said "unique" made it clear what she thought of the current fad for unusual names. "They'll regret it though. My daughter's friend called her kid "Daisy-Moon" and when that kid hits an age to understand…"

"She'll change it to Mary." Marian laughed. "Ah, Dymphna, you're a tonic. I haven't enjoyed a chat as much in a long while. But truth be told, I'm tired. Not able for too much any more, sadly. So…what is it you need to ask me?"

Dymphna looked at her old friend. "I'll be back soon, Marian. I'm ashamed I haven't called more often and that's the truth. And it feels so rude to admit we came here for a purpose but there it is - we need to ask you something and there's no getting around it."

"Ask away. But I'll hold you to your promise, yes? You'll pop in again?"

"Regularly. Right so - yesterday evening there was an incident across the road -"

"Greta's house? The murder? Hah! I knew that was it. Well, didn't I have a fine specimen of a detective around here earlier, asking me what I saw? I told him, so I don't suppose there's any harm in repeating it to you…I saw a lot of comings and goings from that house yesterday…"

"And earlier? the last few days, to be precise?"

"Ah. Okay then, now that's something the detective didn't ask me. Right. Let me start at the beginning. I noticed Humphrey Sterling last week - Saturday, I think it was - he rocked up to Greta's with a small suitcase, a tall brunette with a sour face, and a bunch of flowers. Greta let him in, and then a load of people started arriving - Kylie-Anne said it was some class of a party, for the author. Part of the Merrion Literary Festival. Everyone left by eleven, except Humphrey so I assumed he was staying there. I saw the sour-puss leave with the last few guests - not that she wanted to, mind you. The writer was on the doorstep for ten minutes, ushering her out. I heard him tell her several times to stop worrying, everything was in hand, to go back to the Bed and Breakfast and get some sleep. She was very agitated."

That was the night Margaret Furey had discovered that Humphrey was in fact her long lost uncle, Paddy - Eve knew the sour-faced woman had to be Phyllis. Interesting that the news upset her…

"Over the next few days, there were lots of comings and goings. That poor man, the one who was killed, I recognized him on the news. He came on the Sunday, and again on the Monday. On Monday, he and Humphrey had words on the doorstep. Not very aggressive, nothing like a fight, but just -

words. The writer fella looked fierce upset. Tuesday was quiet enough but on Wednesday, I heard Greta asking Humphrey what his plans were - they were passing right by my window, you understand - and he said, "Flat out all day, dear lady," and something about the organizers needing to see him. I assume he meant the organizers of the Festival, I'm nearly sure he mentioned Quigley. "

That took them up to the Poetry in the Park even, Eve noted. They had to ask Greta what exactly Humphrey had told her about his movements on Wednesday.

"Let me see - the young woman, the sour one, she was back in and out all week. I had a doctor's appointment here on Thursday so I missed a bit of the action - but Thursday evening, I saw the poor man - Damian Burke - I saw him come back."

Eve perked up. This was new. According to Humphrey the last time he saw Damian was the Wednesday at the poetry reading.

"And he saw Humphrey?"
"Ah no, he saw the woman. I thought she had to be the secretary, or PA or whatever it's called nowadays?"

"Yes, his personal assistant." Dymphna replied. "Phyllis, she's called. So she met Damian Burke on the Thursday. How interesting."

Eve added another point to her mental notes. "Ask Cullen what Phyllis said about Thursday. And ask Humphrey if he knew Burke had called to see him." She only hoped she could remember all this - she could see why the Gardaí carried notebooks.

"And on Friday…?" Dymphna prompted.
"Ah. Well, I wish I could say I saw everything that happened but I wasn't feeling great and I nodded off a lot. Sorry. But for

what it's worth, here it is…" Marian rummaged in her pocket and produced a folded sheet of A4 triumphantly. "I wrote it all down you see, in case the Gardaí needed it. I was afraid I'd forget. Would it be any use to you?"

Eve held out her hand for the paper. "It would be brilliant, thanks. Marian, you're an absolute marvel."

* * *

A quick meeting of the sleuthing committee was called for. The plan was for everyone to congregate at six o'clock at Kimberly Cottage, Niamh texted.

"Don't be late, Eve, for goodness sake." her mother added.

Eve was conscious of the time pressure. She had a class at five, teaching art to her senior citizens in the community hall, and with Margaret always needing help to finalize wedding details, she wanted to bring everyone up to speed and have a few hours free to help the bride out afterwards. She popped into Wisteria Cottage on her way home, and told Margaret to expect her after eight o'clock. The bride-to-be was grateful, not least because entertaining her uncle Humphrey was proving to be more of a strain than anticipated.

"Claudia took him out this morning, which was lovely, but he came home and went straight to bed for a few hours. When he got up again, he was a bit odd - honestly, he's been following me around like a puppy, offering to help which is sweet -"

"But he'd help more by leaving you to it?" Eve smiled. "I understand. I'll be over later and we'll get it all under control. There isn't much left to do."

"I can't believe I'll be getting married in three days time."

Margaret beamed from ear to ear.

Humphrey chose this moment to wander into the hall. "Ah, Eve. How are you? How is poor Greta holding up?"

"She's doing okay, thanks. How are you?"

"In shock. Shock. Poor Damian, he was a good man." The famous author drooped rather theatrically. "I feel quite worn out. And it's such a worry - he was in the middle of very delicate negotiations…but never mind, that's hardly important at the moment. I shall just have to manage."

Eve tried not to be uncharitable but she couldn't shake the feeling that the writer was hamming it up. Margaret was instantly solicitous, patting her uncle's arm and murmuring sympathetically. Eve left them to it.

The art class proved to be a welcome distraction. Her students were all retired, full of life and willing to try anything. Eve's long cherished plan was to mount an exhibition for them and now, inspired by the Indie authors she had met, she was fired up with the idea of also producing a book of their paintings, a couple from each student from this class and from her teenagers. The two groups often had classes together and were firm friends, so the enthusiasm for a joint project was high. She hurried home in much better spirits, despite the fact that she was running slightly late.

Kimberly Cottage was already full of guests by the time she arrived. Niamh had let herself in, as usual, and made herself quite at home. Eve loved her mother dearly but she really was a typical Irish mammy - no boundaries when it came to her adult children. Or their stocks of fancy biscuits, she thought bitterly, eyeing the loaded plates being passed around. Everyone she expected to see was present and a few she hadn't expected. The quartet of Dymphna, Claudia, Niamh and Greta were centred at her small kitchen table, while Tom and Finn acted as waiters, wandering around with food and pots of tea. Ellen and the two teenagers from Holly Cottage, Boyd and Melly, were squeezed into a corner with Ashleigh, who was fast becoming Niamh's protege. She could do worse, Eve felt. The young girl had innate talent and better her mother taking her in hand than someone like Greta. Greta was marvelous, of course, and very skilled, but she had a worryingly flexible approach to many things including truthfulness and legalities. Niamh was straitlaced in comparison.

Also present was Ronan, looking rather bullish and his detective partner, Cullen - looking sheepish and distinctly uncomfortable. What on earth was he doing here? Surely the whole point was to investigate under the radar…She noted Emer O'Neill seated on a stool beside Ellen, looking delighted with herself. Eve caught her eye and the author grinned at her and gave a thumbs up. It seemed no introductions were necessary, the woman had slipped right in like she belonged there.

Her attention was claimed by Humphrey, who looked around him with undisguised interest. When he caught her eye, he also grinned and followed it up with a wink. He looked as if he was thoroughly enjoying himself. He really didn't allow anything to keep him down for long, Eve thought wryly.

"Eve!" Niamh called out to her. "Finally. We've been waiting ages for you."

"I had an art class to teach…anyway, ye seem to have made yourselves perfectly at home in my absence."
"Well, someone had to organize things. Really, Eve, when you invite people over, you can't expect them to sit hungry waiting for you!"

Eve would have pointed out that usually *she* had never actually invited them, they just turned up as usual and assumed Kimberly Cottage would act as the Headquarters for their little gang. She would have pointed it out, but didn't bother because she had tried many times before and Niamh simply didn't listen.

"Well, I'm here now." She sat on the arm of the sofa, accepted a cup of tea from Tom, and looked around the group. "Let's get started."

She could tell by their smug expressions that both Niamh and Claudia had something to share but there was one thing she needed to get out of the way first.

"Before we do anything else, we need to start writing down everything. Can someone take notes?"

Ellen stuck her hand up, only delighted to find a role. "I'll be the secretary!"

"Good woman. We need to sort out who spoke to Burke, and when, and where everyone was at time of the murder. Ellen, I'm relying on you - take it down, and then compile it all into a coherent timeline, okay?"

"Will do."

Eve was about to offer her neighbour paper and a pen, but Ellen whipped out her phone, opened an app and sat poised for action.

"Ready? I'll go first, if that's okay. Myself and Dymphna had a very productive morning, and I think with this -" she waved the neatly written report that Marian Fitzpatrick had supplied -"We can lay down a basic idea of what happened, at least around Greta's."

She felt rather than saw a look of discomfort on Humphrey's face. Looking at him rather sternly, she added, "If anyone remembers anything they forgot to tell us, now would be the time. It's vital to know who spoke to Burke, and what about."

The author shifted in his seat but remained silent. Perhaps he really didn't know that Burke had called to see him on Thursday but she could feel it in her bones, he was hiding something.

"Jump in at any time," she couldn't keep a touch of sarcasm from her voice. "Anyway, this is what we found out."

With a few interjections from Dymphna, she recounted their morning's activities and the various bits of information they had gleaned, up to visiting Marian. Niamh made her report, but Claudia just shook her head slightly when Eve turned to her. "Later," her expression said as clearly as if she had spoken. After a bit of chat, and contributions from all present except for the silent Cullen, Eve stood up again and began to summarize.

"It boils down to this - several points of interest came out of the morning. Emer there has given us details about Phyllis Dennehy and her attempt to steal another writer's story. Thanks, Emer. We also know that she had some kind of confrontation with Liam Quigley at the Poetry on Wednesday, and at the finale on Saturday, just before the murder. She doesn't seem to have had any row with Burke, but she did speak to him on Thursday - Humphrey, did you know that he called around?"

"No, absolutely not." Eve glanced at Dymphna who gave an almost imperceptible nod. It would seem he was being truthful.

"Okay, so she didn't pass on the message, for some reason. Detective Cullen - I know you can't comment but in case any of this is news to you - "

Cullen nodded. "I'm listening."

"Okay. Phyllis also has some problem with Aidan Lowe - from what Emer told us, that could be because he's a creep, or it could be something else. Considering that Lowe also rowed with Burke on Friday night, we need to pursue this."

It was a little embarrassing to be talking about pursuing leads with Cullen sitting right there. She cast an anxious look in his direction and hesitated.

Cullen heaved a sigh and stood up.

"I'm not here," he said by way of explanation. "I certainly am *not* helping my partner investigate a case that he's been expressly told to leave alone. I wouldn't risk my career and pension, and I absolutely would never listen to the rantings of a bunch of amateur sleuths. Is that clear? Grand so, carry on. And I'll take a copy of your notes when you have them ready, Ellen, thanks."

The large detective sat down heavily, winked at Ashleigh and added, "Not a word to your mother, mind."

Eve bit back a laugh.

"I'm glad you cleared that up, Detective Cullen, or we'd be in danger of thinking you were putting yourself out on a limb to help your partner there. I'm sure Ronan appreciates your …lack of involvement, as much as the rest of us. " Ronan gave his friend a pat on the arm, and nodded. "Okay. Following up on Lowe, that's a priority. Yes, Mam?"

"I'll take the wee *Sleeveen*," Niamh said. "Boyd here has already volunteered to come along."

"Grand so. Ashleigh, you and your friends have been a great help, and I want ye to keep asking around the volunteers. Concentrate on the last event, who arrived on time and where everyone was. Someone was missing, they had to be, unless Burke was killed by a random stranger who walked in off the street! We need to nail down the whereabouts of every player."

"So, Quigley, Lowe, Dennehy and …" Ashleigh stumbled to a halt, blushing. "And um, anyone else…" She cast a glance at Humphrey and Greta. "Not that anyone else is under suspicion. At all."

"Everyone," Eve said gently. "The clearer a picture we have of that evening, of the comings and goings, the better."

She turned to Greta. "You know what to dig into." She didn't want to specify in front of Humphrey, no need to let him know they were digging into old stories from his past. Still, it would be remiss to ignore the old rumours about a murdered publisher, now they had a dead agent on their hands. Greta nodded, and for once resisted the temptation to remark.

"Okay then, let's get to it."

She knew it would take everyone a while to stop chatting and say their goodbyes and she was conscious of the time. But she was anxious to know what Claudia had discovered that couldn't be said in front of the group. Hoping the Brigadier would hang back and spill the beans, she was dismayed when Niamh insisted on waiting for her. Claudia reluctantly allowed herself to be led away, giving Eve a tiny shrug of the shoulders and mouthing, "Call me later," and Eve had to be satisfied with that.

Chapter 12

Eve had hoped a few hours on wedding related activities would act as a welcome change from the serious business of investigating, but on arrival at Wisteria Cottage, she was greeted by a white-faced Margaret, who looked as if she had been crying. Or was about to very shortly.

"Eve." She waved her mobile phone in the air, pointing at the screen. "Read this!"

The terse strained voice worried Eve more than any display of hysterics. She took the phone and saw it displayed an email from Bountiful Bouquets, Dublin's famous wedding florists.

"Dear Ms. Furey,

It is with regret that we received your order of cancellation today. Please note that the deposit of €380 is non-refundable. I trust your new florists will be more to your satisfaction,

Kind regards,

Maura Flynn, Manager."

"What?" Eve exclaimed. "Margaret, did you cancel your flowers?"

"No! Of course not. I tried ringing but they're closed. I don't understand it at all."

"Okay, okay. Let's not panic. It clearly says, they received an order of cancellation. If you didn't cancel, then I bet they accidentally sent an email to you that was meant for someone else."

Margaret looked at her doubtfully. "Really?"

"If a bride had a similar name, and this was fired off in a rush - or a temper, judging from the tone of it - they probably hit the wrong email. Just ring them in the morning, and sort it out. Come on, no company would throw away a big order for a wedding. They'll be mortified that you got the email, and it'll all be fine."

"Oh my god. You're probably right. I mean, what else could it be?"

"Nothing. Nothing else that I can imagine."

Margaret whistled. "Whew. I was in a terrible panic. Like, there is no chance of getting another florist at this point."

"I know. But, pet, think about it. If you had no flowers, we'd pick you a bunch from the garden. You don't need flowers to get wed. You have a lovely hotel, one of the best in Dublin. You have a car, a church, a groom, a kick-ass dress…"

She was relieved to see Margaret smile. "Okay, I get the point. It's only flowers. And you're right. I didn't cancel, so it can't be meant for me."

"Good woman. Now, what's left to do?"

There really wasn't much, Eve was pleased to note. The worst task left was the dreaded order of service. Once the readings and songs were chosen, the couple were expected to print off and collate a sort of missalette, listing all of them and who was reading them. The Prayers of the Faithful, if it was a Catholic church wedding, were usually distributed among friends and family, and if there was any glimmer of musical talent among the guests, they would be pressed into singing a hymn or playing for the instrumental bits. Everyone had to be acknowledged and the missalette should be pleasingly presented, according the "Wedding Etiquette" website Margaret was following.

Thanks to modern technology the task was a lot easier than in Eve's day but true to age old tradition, the moment you tried to print it out, the printer would either stop working or print the pages out of order and upside down.

"My boy calls it a "CND,"" Eve said, as they struggled with the laser jet printer. "A "Critical Need Detector." It detects that your need to print is critical and it stops working just to mess with you."

It took over two hours to print a reasonable amount of legible pages and by then, they were too tired to attempt to collate them.

"That's a job for tomorrow," Margaret said. "I'll have it after school."

"I'll help, if I can. I'll let you know."

"How's it going? The investigating, I mean."

"It's…getting there. We're at the stage where we know a lot of different facts but seeing where they all come together, that's the hard bit."

"Keep at it. I would love to have it all settled before Saturday morning. No pressure."

"Hah! We'll do our best."

* * *

Greta was used to having to dig deep to get at obscure facts for her true crime podcast, but even for her, finding information on the mysterious death of a publisher in Humphrey's past was proving highly annoying. Just as she thought she had a solid lead, it would turn out to be the wrong place, the wrong person. She was sure she had the basics right - a newspaper article from the period stated clearly, Cornelius Watkins of Brighton House Publishers died in his house, in a mysterious fire that the Fire inspectors were sure was caused by the new microwave he had installed. It was the mid eighties and microwaves were in their infancy, but even so - it was highly unlikely that one would spontaneously combust. There were a few articles after that, but none yielded anything of real interest, and no further theories on the cause of the explosive fire.

She had tried to track down everyone mentioned in the reports - neighbours, investigators, friends - but either they were deceased, couldn't be found, or had nothing further to add. The last line of inquiry was colleagues of the poor man - but as Brighton House Publishers were long defunct, Greta didn't hold out much hope.

She hadn't become Ireland's most successful true crime podcaster by giving up easily. She opened her file marked "Sterling and Watkins," (it sounded like a firm of solicitors, she chuckled to herself) and revised the entire thing over the course of the afternoon.

The facts were simple enough. Humphrey had been on his last legs, financially, when he submitted a manuscript to Brighton House. As luck would have it, Watkins was assigned to his book, read it, and discarded it. Humphrey was not pleased, and was rather vocal about it, but as an insignificant, unpublished author that hardly troubled the agent.

Then Mr. Watkins met with his unfortunate end - an explosion ripped through the house and the subsequent fire gutted it. There was no reason to think Humphrey had anything to do with the crime, none at all - no one ever officially suggested it. Greta's initial interest in him had been, as she assured Eve, purely the hope of getting some insight or leads into her true crime story, from someone who had been acquainted with the victim. Then when murder struck here, with Humphrey at the heart of the mystery, she had suddenly wondered if after all there was some connection with the long distant demise of Mr. Watkins…

But sadly, she admitted, it looked increasingly unlikely. There wasn't a shred of evidence to connect Humphrey to the cold case.

And yet - she thought suddenly the extract he had read out from his new book, the change in style, the sense of menace and authenticity to the description of Jerusalem Hill creeping through a house in the dark…

"I wonder," Greta mused, staring into space. Her mind whirled, turning over various possibilities before finally set-tling on one. It was a mad idea but every instinct told her she was on to something. If only she could persuade Humphrey to tell her, but how to persuade him?

She remembered a bottle in the back of her kitchen press, a small green bottle that Claudia had made up for her. A little dash of her friend's special ingredient and Humphrey would be *singing like a canary*, as Jerusalem Hill would say. Feeling rather pleased with herself, Greta trotted off to the kitchen to whip up a batch of biscuits, Humphrey's favourite while he had been staying with her. She added a few drops of Claudia's special recipe then added a few more. And a few more to be on the safe side.

Sure, what harm could it do?

* * *

Eve fell asleep without much trouble, but spent the night dreaming, her head full of a strange mixture of wedding dresses, bouquets and murder weapons. She woke in a start, and her first thought was that she had completely forgotten to ring Claudia! It was only half past seven, and far too early to be ringing people, but she got up, washed and dressed anyway. She felt a strange sense of urgency, and hanging out with her mother and friends had made her more willing to listen to that instinct.

She had just made her coffee and wandered out into the April sunshine - a rare Spring day in Dublin, with bright blue sky and not a hint of rain - when her mobile rang.

"Claudia! I was just about to ring you."

"What part of ring me later did you not understand?" Claudia asked grouchily.

"I'm so sorry." Eve explained what had happened with Margaret the night before. "I'm sure it's all a mistake, but she was in bits. She's going to ring them first thing today and sort it out."

"Oh. That's awful. But it must be some error on their part, you're right. I hope. Anyway, I need to tell you what I found out yesterday and I couldn't say it in front of Ronan. And to be honest, I didn't want to tell anyone but you until we're sure what's the best way to go about this..."

"Claudia, you're worrying me. What?"

"I asked Humphrey his plans. He told me that either he sells this book, or he gets money from Margaret."

Eve was speechless for a moment. No point in asking if Claudia was sure - she knew her friend - but she found it hard to believe nonetheless.

"Money from Margaret? But - she's hardly rich, Claudia."

"Ah. She owns a nice property, we all know what our cottages are worth in this market. She has the inheritance from her grandparents, not to mention the life insurance from her poor parents, and she has a good, steady job. Teachers don't earn a lot but she has no rent, and she's thrifty. Humphrey feels that he should have inherited some money from his parents but they left it all to the son who stayed behind, and minded them. Legally, at the time, he might have had a case actually - I asked my Jennie - but he obviously can't do anything about it now."

"Except guilt his niece into giving it to him." Eve said flatly. Her blood boiled at the news. Poor Margaret, all she had wanted was some family and all her only family member wanted was her money.

"Ronan was right about him."

"Ah. Well, he certainly was right to be suspicious but I don't think it's as clear cut as all that. Humphrey is genuinely fond of Margaret, whatever his original intentions. He really hoped Burke would come through for him on the book."

"Do you think - is it possible that Burke turned him down and Humphrey lost his temper? I mean, if he is capable of trying to con his own niece out of money…"

"I don't know." Claudia sounded sad. "I still think there's good in the man, Eve. But we have to proceed with caution. And we have to work out how best to tell Ronan."
"Ronan will destroy him," Eve exclaimed. "We'll have another murder on our hands."

"Well, get your thinking cap on. Someone has to break the news and soon."

* * *

Greta noted that Humphrey was on his third biscuit, and he was loosening up nicely. Her podcast tactic was to ask leading questions and let her interview subjects waffle on, sifting the wheat from the chaff as she listened back. Humphrey needed very little prompting as long as the subject was himself. She nudged the conversation along here or there but within minutes had him on the subject of the early days in America. A rambling anecdote about agents and their philistine ways made it easy to insert a gentle questions about the late Mr. Watkins of Brighton House Publishing.

"Watkins? Oh." Humphrey put his finger to his lips and shook his head. "My lips are sealed, dear lady. Sealed. Poor man. He wasn't the worst - although he was pretty awful, if I'm honest. Publishers back then - they were more powerful than they are now. Now it's all business, bottom line, profit margins - not interested in literary quality, you see, just bestsellers. But back then, they were like petty kings. No self publishing, then. You were at the mercy of the agent, and then of the editor and in the end, the House always wins. The Publishing House, get it?" He snickered at his own joke, and then resumed, "I hated the way they made us crawl. Watkins could be very cruel, very. I submitted a great story to him, beautifully written. Heart and soul I put into that book. He dismissed it as "derivative.""

"How mean..."

"Yes. But I had the last laugh, eh? That story became Angel City, you know. I decided to rewrite it and make it more exciting, and Jerusalem Hill was born."

"How interesting." Greta noticed with some alarm that he had eaten at least half a dozen biscuits. She had been a little heavy handed with Claudia's special recipe…but sure, what harm? "But your new book…it's based on the events back then, isn't it?"

Humphrey stared at her. "My- my new book? Oh no, not at all, whatever gave you that idea?"

"The way you describe being in a house, in the dark, looking for something. You wanted your manuscript back, didn't you? If you were going to write it up in a different form, the last thing you needed was Watkins showing everyone how it stated."

"It wasn't that -" Humphrey blushed and continued. "I'm not admitting anything, mind. But it wasn't like that. Watkins wouldn't have done that - but the truth is, I was so broke I could only afford one copy of the manuscript. I typed it out, on a cheap electric typewriter but I hadn't the money to get it copied, and I was so sure Watkins would take it - my agent swore he would - I just handed it in as soon as possible. When he turned it down, I couldn't ask him to return it…"

"He would have made you a laughing stock?" Greta guessed.

"Yeah. Imagine everyone knowing I was so broke I needed the book back! No computers back then, no saving a book to the cloud. Just a typewriter and a ream of paper. People forget what it was like before computers."

"So you broke in that night, to look for it? What happened? Humphrey, what happened to Watkins?" Greta was aware of her heart thumping uncomfortably in her chest.

"Watkins? Oh, the poor man was as drunk as a skunk. He was snoring in an armchair when I went into the living room - I just backed out quietly and found his study. My book was in a pile on the floor, so I grabbed it and ran."

"Oh." Greta looked blank. "You just left?"

"Yes. The poor man, we were told afterwards he got up to make something to eat and used his microwave. Put it on for an hour instead of ten minutes - it was a dial timer, you understand, not like the modern ones. Blooming thing had a fault in the wiring, and an hour of cooking a bowl of sauce was the final straw - it exploded, set the house on fire. He was passed out, mercifully, so never knew what hit him."

Greta shook her head. "So it was just an accident?"

"Of course. What else? Anyway, when I went to write my new book I remembered that night and I wrote about it - always felt sorry I hadn't woken the poor fella, but of course, I never dreamed he'd end up setting the place on fire..."

Greta was conscious of a great relief, a lightening of her heart. "There was nothing you could have done, Humphrey. Here, leave those biscuits. Have a bun..."

"No thanks, I'm quite stuffed. And I must be getting back to Margaret's"

"Sure I'll see you home - we'll have a nice walk to Bramble Lane, shall we? I'd like to call in to see Margaret. and see how the wedding planning is going."

And tell the others that there was nothing to worry about after all - the old story was just that, a garbled old tale. Humphrey could remain their hero.

* * *

Niamh was touched to see Boyd Marrinan waiting for her at the end of Bramble Lane. He had insisted on accompanying her to interview Aidan Lowe, from the moment she had mentioned it. Ellen also insisted her son act as bodyguard and indeed, was only short of sending Finn too, but Niamh refused.

"Honestly, it'll be fine. Lowe is a bully and I'm the wrong woman for him to try it on with," Niamh had said. She had meant it but a little part of her was rather glad to have the tall, well built young man beside her. Having seen him wield a hurl on the pitch, she had no doubt he could handle the older man with ease - not that it would come to that. She suspected the sight of Boyd would keep the journalist in check.

It took a good half hour to track him down - she had expected to find him among the media pack haunting the area around Greta's house but he was nowhere to be seen. A friendly young woman from one of the local papers confided that she had seen him around the community centre.

"He's interviewing the poets and authors, from the festival - *"Death of an agent through a literary lens,"* is how he put it. Pretentious git. You'll probably find him there."

They retraced their steps back to the main road and headed for the Community Hall. The posters advertising the festival still hung from the railings, but a team of volunteers were hard at work removing them. Niamh greeted a few familiar faces as they entered. The hall's interior was still set out in rows of chairs and she spotted Liam Quigley on a stepladder, wrestling with the festival banner. Obviously tidying up after the event had been delayed by the tragedy.

Boyd hissed in her ear, "There he is!" Niamh looked around to see Aidan Lowe deep in conversation with a visibly uncomfortable Helen Dunphy. They were seated, the man leaning over her, his arm along the back of her chair. The young poet had the body language of a woman trying to avoid being stung by a scorpion, and she greeted the appearance of Niamh and Boyd with obvious relief.

"Mrs. Caulton!"

"Hello, Helen." Niamh had of course made fast friends with the younger woman, as she seemed to do with everyone who crossed her path. "Helping out with the clear up?"

"Yes - they couldn't get to it until today, so I thought I'd help. Actually, I'd better give Mr. Quigley a hand, he looks like he's about to fall off that ladder. Excuse me…"

Flashing a grin at Niamh, she sidestepped the journalist and made good her escape. Niamh met Lowe's eyes with a sharp glint in her own. She was somewhat mollified to see the man looked wretched, his skin pale and waxy and he winced as he shifted in his chair. His left arm was bandaged and his right thumb looked swollen and slightly green. She hid a smile as she sat down, taking care to keep a chair between them. Boyd remained standing, looking rather like a trainee bouncer in a nightclub, hands clasped in front of him and a stern expression.

"Mr. Lowe."

"Yes?" He looked at her with undisguised contempt. "Do I know you?"

"We met at Greta Goode's reception for Humphrey Sterling," Niamh said pleasantly. "The night Humphrey met his niece? Margaret is a close friend."

"Ah." If he recalled the elderly lady, he hid it well. Niamh wondered what he would say if he knew he owed his current discomfort to that interaction. Probably best if he didn't, with his nasty temperament, but she made a mental note to point out to Eve how right they had been to punish him. Eve was far too ready to disapprove of her mother and the other ladies. Wait til she has our experience of human nature, Niamh thought smugly.

"I was hoping to have a quick word with you, Mr. Lowe. You being the expert on all this literary stuff, obviously, you'd have a better idea than I would about these people. I mean, you hear a lot about writers, don't you? And I'm sure most of it is exaggerated, but then again…"

"What?" Lowe interjected. "What are you on about?"

Boyd shifted slightly at the man's tone, and the journalist glanced up at him. Whatever he saw in the teenager's expression, he continued in a far politer manner. "I mean, I'm not sure how I can help…?"

"Well, it's the question of people in your home, isn't it? Look at Greta. Took in that writer fella and a murder happened. She seems like a nice girl, but I don't know if I want to take the risk. I'm sure you can see that?"

"Take what risk?"

"The risk of having her in my home, of course. I mean, she's Humphrey's assistant and that's probably better than being a writer, but she says she's also a writer…"

"Are you talking about Phyllis?" Lowe sat forward eagerly.

"Why yes, didn't I say? Phyllis Dennehy. I don't mind helping out, obviously, but I just want to be sure before I offer to put her up. I don't know anything about the girl, do I?"

"I completely understand." His voice turned oily and ingratiating. "You are right to be wary - people are often not what they seem. And that young woman is a prime example of it!"

"Oh! Oh dear. I am sorry to hear it, I promised Greta I would…but you don't think it'd be a good idea? Oh dear."

"I wouldn't want to alarm you, and I never spread gossip, but I couldn't let a nice lady like yourself be taken in by a weapon like Phyllis. It would weigh on my conscience." He paused, obviously hoping to be pressed. Niamh obliged.

"You have to tell me, please."

"Well, she's not a trustworthy person at all. She was caught out years ago, lying and plagiarizing another writer's work to win a competition. Lost her job, and pretty much fled to London."

"How awful…but I suppose that was a long time ago? She's surely not the same person…"

"She's the same, if not worse." Lowe's malice was evident in every syllable. His eyes burned as he spoke. "Let me tell you, you'll be a fool if you trust her. She lies the way other people breath - constantly and without thinking. She spread her lies about me, at one point. Tried to get me fired, just because I took an interest in her. She gets obsessed - hah! you should hear how her last employer talks about her. He said she was practically a stalker. Couldn't get rid of her, she took over his whole life. Threw a tantrum if he made an appointment without her - even to see friends. He was relieved when she switched to Sterling, I can tell you."

"That's fierce alarming," Niamh agreed. "I think I would be better off not having her to stay, I really do. I'll make some excuse. Thank you, I'm most grateful."

Lowe preened himself. "You're welcome. It gives me no pleasure, you know, but I do think you need to be warned."

"Of course. Well, we should get a move on. I'm sure you're very busy. And of course, condolences on your loss."

Lowe blinked. "My loss?"

"Your friend. Damian Burke."

"I-I didn't really know him. Just in passing."

"Really? Oh, I'm sorry. I must have got it wrong. Just, people are saying the two of you knew each other well. In fact, if I'm honest, people are talking about the row you had with him…"

The effect on the journalist was electric. He sat bolt upright and looked even greener, a sheen of sweat breaking out on his upper lip.

"Row? I didn't - I never had any row with him."

"Did you not? Not in the park on Friday night? Isn't that strange - I heard you and he had a right barney."

Lowe stumbled over his words. "No, no. I mean, perhaps they saw us chatting. I mean, we were old mates…not close mates, I mean, but we used to have a laugh now and then. Probably someone misunderstood…"

"Probably. If you say so. Of course, it can get garbled in translation. I heard you were shouting at him, something about printing what you want…" She tipped her head to one side and smiled. Lowe stood up abruptly, standing over Niamh at first but quickly taking a step back as he realized just how tall and broad young Boyd Marrinan was up close.

"I can assure you, I had no row with anyone. Certainly not with Damian Burke."

"If I were you," Niamh said cheerfully, "I'd go and tell the Gardaí all about it. That Detective Cullen is very sympathetic. I'm sure if you explain it to him, he'd understand."

"There's no need for that! Honestly, this is ridiculous…I may have had a wee chat with the man but that's no one's business."

Niamh said nothing, just smiled calmly and waited.

"Look, I - I was talking to him about Humphrey. About him employing someone like Phyllis as his assistant, for one thing. About how his last book tanked. I just wanted to confirm the rumours I heard, about Burke finally giving up on the man. I outlined my story and asked him for a response…"

"And he told you to stuff it?"

"He was a self righteous little git. Just because he made a few appearances on the telly, thought it made him god almighty! He said if I printed anything about his professional relationship with Humphrey, he'd sue me."

"Ah."

"I am a serious journalist. No one tells me what to print. I told him that." He winced and stood up. "Now if you'll excuse me, I'm feeling quite unwell."

Niamh chuckled quietly as the man stomped off, his face like thunder.

"That explains his row with Burke, anyway. Now, while we're here, shall we have a chat with Liam Quigley?"

"Lead on," Boyd said.

* * *

Claudia and Eve decided to tackle Ronan together, in private and away from Margaret but the fates did not smile on them. Ronan wasn't at home in Copper Beech Cottage, although his car was parked in the driveway.

"He's probably at Wisteria." Claudia looked at her anxiously. "Should we go over?"

"I think so. Let's call in, and see if we can't get Ronan on his own."

They found the young Garda Detective in Wisteria Cottage, but any thought of breaking the news about Humphrey's plans had to be put aside. There was a complete air of chaos in the house, and the young couple were distracted, to put it mildly. Ronan had his phone clamped to his ear, and was deep in conversation, his tone exasperated. Margaret was slumped over her laptop, and looked as if she had been crying.

To their surprise, a third person was stalking up and down the living room, having an animated conversation over her mobile - Phyllis Dennehy.

"What on earth?"

"Oh, Eve!" Margaret leapt up and threw herself at Eve. Hugging her, she could feel the young woman's body heave in silent sobs. She pulled Eve into the kitchen. followed by Claudia, and shut the door.

"Eve, something awful has happened. Someone canceled my entire wedding. Everything. The flowers, the hotel, it's all gone. The only thing they didn't manage to get to was the honeymoon - the travel agency refused to cancel without speaking to me. The rest though - they all fell for it. They have emails from my account, as if I did it, but I didn't!" She ended on a wail, and Eve waited patiently while she let out the pent up emotions. "I didn't, Eve - but they say I sent emails and they're keeping our deposits..."

Claudia gasped. "Who would do such a thing?"

"I don't know. Ronan is trying to sort them out now, and Phyllis, she called in and when I told her she volunteered to help."

"That was kind of her," Eve said. "But I don't understand, how on earth could they have an email from your account?"

"Phyllis says it's probably not from me - it's a fake account that looks really similar. She says it's what hackers and scammers do. But, what would anyone gain from canceling my wedding? I don't understand."

Before Eve could reply, the front door banged and Humphrey's voice rang out. "Margaret, dear!"

"Uncle Paddy." Margaret opened the kitchen door and seeing both Humphrey and Greta, gestured to them. "Shut the door,

Greta, there's so much noise in the sitting room I can hardly think. You won't believe what's happened. Someone has canceled our wedding."

She launched into a more detailed explanation, Humphrey reacting with genuine outrage and sympathy. "But they can't just do that, surely? Once they see it was from a fake email…"

Margaret shrugged helplessly. "They keep saying they're within their rights…"

"Margaret!" Ronan called suddenly from the living room.

She ran in, but one look at his face dashed any hopes she had that he had sorted the mess.

"Oh Ronan!"

"I'm sorry love. They insist it was from your account, and that's it. Can I look at your laptop?"

Margaret flushed a dark red.

"I'm not - I didn't send those emails."

"Of course not. Don't be daft, Mags. You've been hacked or someone has had access to the computer, and I just want to see if I can see any trace of it."

His matter-of-fact reply did more than anything to calm his fiancée. She handed over the laptop and waited patiently for him to search her emails, all the while Phyllis continued to argue with someone called "Tonya" about the flowers. The others sat in somber silence, occasionally exchanging significant glances.

Ronan leaned back in defeat. "Well, they're not in your sent file, but that proves nothing. I asked the Hotel to send me on the email they received…hang on!" He stood up, took out his mobile again and punched the screen with his index figure. "Powers! He's the man for this. He's a whiz at technology, he's part of a special unit but we know each other from way back.

He'll help."

Margaret's eyes followed him as he walked out of the room, talking in a low urgent voice to the mysterious "Powers." He reappeared a few minutes later, picked up the laptop, and disappeared again into the kitchen.

"It sounds like this guy could help," Eve said encouragingly. "If we can find out who sent the emails, surely the vendors will have to honour their side of things! After all, they'll lose a lot of money if they don't."

Margaret and Humphrey sat close together, the author's arm wrapped protectively around his niece. Eve frowned. How could he be so duplicitous? Pretending to be upset for the young couple while planning to con Margaret out of her inheritance…she froze as a horrible thought occurred to her. What if Humphrey was behind the wedding chaos? If Margaret married Ronan, he had to know the chance of getting money out of her would be slim to nil. His new detective garda nephew would soon put paid to that. Maybe this was "plan b" in action…

"Humphrey!" It came out a lot sharper than she intended, but Eve ploughed on regardless. "I don't suppose you know anything about these emails?"

As luck would have it, she chose the very moment that Phyllis hung up on her call, and Ronan walked back into the room. Her voice rang out loud and clear, and she caught the look of astonishment on both Ronan and Margaret's faces.

"Me?" Humphrey stared at her. To her surprise he didn't seem at all put out by the question. Instead there was a kind of relaxed quality to his demeanour. Suspiciously relaxed.

"Oh no, I wouldn't do that."

"Right. I thought maybe you - maybe you had some

objections to the wedding." Eve cursed herself, this was coming out all wrong. She had meant to be subtle but had charged in like an elephant. She cast an imploring glance at Claudia but her friend just smiled.

"You're on your own," the smile said, and her raised eyebrow added, "And you'd better not screw it up."

"I am delighted about the wedding, although it was a bit inconvenient at first." Humphrey was still unnaturally calm. A suspicion began to whisper at the back of Eve's mind. He seemed…entranced. If she didn't know better, she would have sworn that Claudia had dosed him again. But she couldn't have, the man had been with Greta all morning. She shot a look at the incorrigible old woman, and was not one bit reassured by the innocent look she got in return.

"Humphrey, why did you want to reconnect with Margaret?"

"I needed money."

A gasp from Margaret smote Eve's heart. She wished she could pull back but it was time to get the truth out.

"And you thought she would give it to you?"

"I hoped so. After all, part of what she inherited should have been mine."

Margaret pulled away, staring at him in confusion. Phyllis made a sharp tutting noise, and seemed about to intervene, but a stern look from Ronan silenced her.

"Uncle Paddy?"

"Humphrey, please. Oh, I was very pleased to meet you again. I really was. And now that I know you, I can honestly say I love you. If I'd had a daughter of my own, I would have loved her to be like you. Getting to know you has been the joy of my life, Margaret. But it does seem to me that you benefited greatly from my parents' cutting me off. They couldn't accept that I wanted something different from life, instead of a boring old nine to five. No offense to your dad, but it wasn't for me. And for that, they left me out of their will. I should have had half that house, for a start. But I didn't and no point crying over spilt milk, eh? I wouldn't expect that much, no."

"But you expect her to give you something? How much, exactly?" The edge to Ronan's voice would have cut glass.

"Oh, ten, well really, twenty thousand would do it. All I need is enough to cover me until I get back on track. I'm absolutely sure this book will sell…" He beamed at the group, no trace of embarrassment. "I'm sure Margaret agrees, don't you?"

Everyone turned to stare at Margaret. She was completely still, her face shuttered. Eve could only guess at the thoughts going through her head. She braced herself for the outpouring of hurt and anger, ready to comfort her young friend.

"Uncle Pa-Humphrey," Margaret said quietly, "I do agree."

"You what?" Ronan spluttered.

"I agree. It was unfair. I've often thought so," she said stoutly. "And twenty thousand is very reasonable, it's only a small part of what you should have been given. Dad always said Granny and Granddad were wrong not to look after him in their wills."

"Margaret, did you hear the man?" Ronan asked. "He admits that he only looked you up in order to sponge off you."

"He didn't know me then," she said. "Now, it's different. Isn't it?"

"Of course. I'm terribly fond of you, even though it's only been a short while since we met." Humphrey nodded at Ronan. "There's nothing to be annoyed about."

"Hang on." Margaret leapt to her feet, and moved swiftly to the bureau that sat in the corner of her living room. She rummaged through it, and extracted a slim cheque book and a biro. "I'll do it now. Twenty thousand - and if you need more, we'll talk again. Ronan, you agree with me, don't you? Please?"

Eve watched Ronan's face change through a range of strong emotions, from exasperation to pride, to affection, to annoyance, and then as he looked at his future Uncle-in-law, grim determination.

"Whatever you think best is fine with me." He watched as Margaret scribbled a hasty cheque and handed it to Humphrey and added pointedly, "I'm sure Humphrey will be content with such a generous gift."

Humphrey stared at the piece of paper, with its bank logo and "twenty thousand euros" printed in Margaret' neat handwriting. He seemed a tad bewildered. Out of the fog, it was dawning on him that he had not only confessed his ulterior motive in being there but had achieved his goal. Thousands of euros, in his hand.

He lifted his eyes to Margaret's. "I - I can't thank you enough. This is the nicest thing anyone ever did for me."

Ronan snorted, then hastily covered it up at a glare from Margaret.

"It's fine, Uncle Humphrey. And I totally understand - you were in a very awkward position. But this is much better, sorting it out between us rather than having solicitors and courts involved. You could have challenged Granddad's will, and upset Dad but you didn't - I appreciate that."

Eve didn't need to use her second sight to know that Claudia and Niamh were glaring at Humphrey too. Only the man himself seemed unaware that he was the subject of their intense scrutiny.

"I didn't - Well, I had plenty of money at the time. I never begrudged your dad getting the bit our parents had to leave. I truly didn't."

"I understand."

"But now - I really couldn't see any other way. If this book didn't sell, I couldn't possibly pay off my debts." There was a note in Humphrey's voice that no one had heard before - humility.

"It's my pleasure." Margaret linked arms with her uncle and faced the room, her usually placid expression replaced by one of mulish determination. "We *all* understand, don't we?"

Claudia and Greta muttered something that could charitably be interpreted as "yes," while Eve tried to smile her agreement. Phyllis looked disinterested - Eve wondered what she really made of all this drama over her employer's inheritance - but murmured, "of course." Ronan looked like he might choke on the words but out came "Hmm," with a nod, and Margaret seemed happy enough with that.

"I feel - If you'll excuse me, I think I need to lie down," Humphrey was still clutching the cheque to his bosom. "I feel quite done in…"

Eve caught the guilty look on Greta's face and with a nod to Claudia, dragged her friend into the kitchen. Claudia followed, her face alight with curiosity.

"What the - Why on earth did he blurt all that out? I was full sure we'd have to beat the truth out of him!"

"I think Greta can answer that," Eve said.

"Me? Well, yes - I had some of Claudia's special recipe in my stores and I wanted to get at the truth of all this cold case stuff - it's all quite innocent, by the way, Humphrey didn't murder anyone in the USA. Or at least, not that poor publisher. But I admit, I may have been a tad heavy handed with the auld mixture…"

"Oh Greta!" Claudia exclaimed in dismay. "You never dosed him? Didn't I do the very same thing a few days ago? No wonder he blurted everything out."

"Oh. Well, I didn't know that. Why didn't you tell me? Anyway, it's grand. He got it all off his chest and now Margaret knows."

"She knows, but she just gave him a huge chunk of money!" Eve replied.

"It's her money," Greta pointed out. "If she prefers to keep her uncle happy and not fall out over it, that's her business."

Eve looked to Claudia for support but to her surprise, the other woman shrugged.

"Greta's right, dear. It's Margaret's choice and in many ways, it's a wise one. She has money, and no family. Now she has a little less money, but keeps her closest relative happy. There's nothing wrong with that."

"But - he deliberately targeted her," Eve pointed out, "and he meant all along to cheat her out of money..."

"That's not true. You heard the man. He loves her. He couldn't lie about anything right now, and he clearly said he cares about his niece. Possibly more than he even realizes. No, Margaret did well today. There's hope for the man yet."

Eve gave up. You just never knew with these auld biddies. At their age, they seemed to see life from a totally different perspective.

"Well, you'd better tell us about the cold case anyway. At least we can scratch that off the list. But it doesn't get us much further with the investigation, does it? And what about the wedding stuff? It's all still canceled."

"Fingers crossed this friend of Ronan's comes through," Greta said. "I think we need to regroup. You get home and put the kettle on. I'll get on to the others."

* * *

Dymphna decided that it was time to pull out the big guns. With the wedding only days away now, and the specter of Damian Burke's murder hanging over them all, special measures were needed. She thought about all the people wandering through the story - Helen Dunphy, Emer O'Neill, Phyllis Dennehy, Liam Quigley and of course, Humphrey. Of them all, one struck her as having the ability to truly hear - to listen to things and hear the false notes, the jarring chords. It was time for a chat with the young poet.

She found Helen by the simple and mundane expedient of checking social media. There, on the girl's Insta-photo page, was a picture of her in the Merrion Community Hall, beside a small pile of books. The caption read, "Sold more than I ever hoped! Clear up still underway at the Hall."

Dymphna strolled in, giving a nod of approval to the various volunteers still hard at work clearing the debris. She was only mildly surprised to see Niamh and Boyd in conversation with the loathsome Aidan Lowe; it was clear that they didn't need her to disturb them, so she wandered around until Helen appeared carrying a stack of books.

"Hello," Dymphna greeted her, "Last of the books? I hope I'm not too late to buy one?"

Helen turned pink. "Oh! Of course not. Only, I don't have a card reader today. So it'd have to be cash?"

"Cash is fine."

"Tell you what, let's call it five euro." Helen smiled at her, and the words "Poor Auld Dear," popped into Dymphna's head as clearly as if the woman had spoken them out loud. On the one hand, few people could get away with calling Dymphna Moriarty "auld" or "poor" and remain intact. On the other hand, it was nice to know that the young woman wouldn't take advantage of an Old Age Pensioner. Dymphna approved of people being kind to frail old women as long as they didn't make the mistake of thinking she fell into that category herself.

"That's very sweet, dear." She handed over the five euros and took a slim, glossy volume in return. Helen carefully deposited the stack of books on the edge of the stage and offered, "Would you like me to sign it?"

"Of course!" Dymphna waited while the poet signed the book, a neat signature with very little flourish. "How nice. I did enjoy your reading at the Festival. And your contribution to the questions and answers session."

"Ah, thanks. To be honest, I'm usually a big wimp when it comes to public speaking but I have to admit, this festival went better for me than I could have hoped. Oh! Doesn't that sound awful, considering what happened? I don't mean to sound callous."

"Not at all. When you reach my age, you learn to celebrate any good that comes your way. You can't let the bad over-shadow everything."

"I like that. I admit I have a tendency towards the gloomy. I'm trying to be more positive, though. And -" she cast a quick glance in the direction of Liam Quigley, now berating a volunteer for not being quick enough in moving his ladder - "And more assertive."

"Good for you. You'll meet people like him everywhere, you know. They can only treat you badly if you let them. Like most pompous asses, Quigley backs down if you roar at him."

Helen laughed. "I should take lessons from that Phyllis, the one who works for the thriller writer? My goodness, she gave Mr. Quigley back as good as she got!"

"She certainly did. He really took a dislike to her, didn't he?"

"She wouldn't let him talk to her boss, that's why. For the first couple of days, none of us could get any attention from him - he was obsessed with Sterling. He followed him around the place, until Phyllis told him to get lost. He couldn't stand her after that."

"Oh. I imagine she wasn't very tactful in doing it?"

"She went through him for a short-cut. But you can't blame her, it's her job to a degree. She's supposed to make sure people don't bother the great author." Helen's eyes twinkled, "Or at least, the wrong people. He likes adoring fans, I've noticed, but old friends like Quigley, not so much."

"That's not the first time I've heard them described as old friends," Dymphna remarked.

"Hmm. If you ask me, Humphrey didn't recognize him. Oh he made the right noises - "Lovely to see you again," and so on - but no. You could hear it, he didn't really."

"Do you think Quigley noticed?" Dymphna prodded

"Not at first, but he must have realized in the end. I heard them talking and Quigley kept bringing up "the class," and "their shared interests" but it was clear poor Mr. Sterling hadn't a clue what he was on about."

"How interesting. Sure, it's always a bit awkward meeting people from the past, isn't it? They remember such different things from you."

"Tell me about it!" Helen gave a heartfelt sigh. "I met up with friends from college recently, and they were on and on about someone in our English tutorial that they disliked. I always thought he was lovely, but to hear them tell it, he was as dull as a bucket of ditch water."

"I suspect Liam Quigley would fall into that category. Ditch water, I mean, not lovely."

"Yeah, I can't imagine him ever being young and full of life, can you? Although, according to him, only circumstance kept him from being the next big thing in writing. That's why he's so snippy with all of us, if you ask me. Hates that we're making a living doing what he couldn't." Helen looked aghast almost immediately. "Ah, ignore me, I'm being horrible!"

"No." Dymphna patted her hand and grinned. "You're being honest. You keep working on that, and you'll soon find it easier to stand up for yourself. Good girl."

She strolled away, her new purchase in hand. It was a fiver well spent, she thought, worth every cent.

* * *

Niamh and Boyd waited until Dymphna had left the hall before approaching the festival organizer. His mood had worsened as the clean up continued, and a lot of the volunteers had downed tools and left him to it. Only a handful of stalwarts remained, the ones who were the backbone of every committee and event. Even they looked mutinous and Niamh wondered how long it would be before Quigley alienated even them.

"Liam?" She greeted him with her friendliest smile, the full wattage of her charm on display. "I can't get over what an achievement it was, the Festival I mean. Everyone is talking about it. You must be so proud!"

His face was a battleground of warring emotions. The desire

to snap at this interruption looked momentarily as if it would win out, but his ego couldn't resist this level of flattery. He managed a brief and chilly smile, coupled with a gracious nod of the head in acknowledgment.

"It did go rather well, at least until the end." The sour note was evident in his voice. "I'm surprised anyone even remembers the Festival, they're all too busy gossiping about the…*incident*."

"Ah. Well, I suppose vulgar minds will focus on something like that. But those of us who appreciate a bit of culture, we're all so impressed!"

Quigley looked at her suspiciously. "You are?"
"Of course. What a triumph for the area, its own literary festival. You brought all these wonderful writers to our doorstep, so to speak. Obviously what happened afterwards to that poor man was dreadful…but it really had nothing to do with the Festival, did it? It's not your fault."
Boyd's lips twitched but he managed to turn his head before Quigley could notice. If Niamh was laying it on too thickly, the target of her flattery didn't seem to care.

"That's right, that's right!" he responded eagerly. "That's what these plebs can't seem to grasp. The festival itself, that was the important thing and it went perfectly well."

"It was superb."

"No one understands how much effort went into this. The emails, the lobbying for grants, the endless red tape - just so people around here could enjoy the cream of Irish writing." He looked around angrily. "And now it's all over, they can't even take down the bunting properly, without me standing over them."
"It must have been such a strain, so much pressure!" Niamh

sympathized. "Did you have to oversee everything yourself?"

"Naturally. Oh, there are some who thought they could just barrel their way in and take over - but I soon put them in their place."

"I can't tell you how much I admire what you achieved. And to see someone do all this, just for the love of literature - well, it's amazing."

"Yes! See, that's what they don't get. It wasn't for personal gain, it was for Literature." He emphasized *"literature,"* in the same way that wild eyed preachers emphasize the word "religion."

"Are you a writer yourself, Mr. Quigley?"

The man blinked rapidly. "I- I dabble. I did at one time cherish dreams - but I had a lot of responsibilities. I had to work for a living, not like some. Yes, once I did really think I might break into the world of literature. "

"What a pity, I'm sure your work is fascinating. But you obviously haven't lost your love of reading. Anyway, I'm so glad I got a chance to tell you how much some of us appreciate all you've done. I did try on the last night, but unfortunately I couldn't find you before it started."

"I was here," Quigley said sharply. "Herding authors on to the stage and people into their proper seats. Chaos, utter chaos. And people interfering, telling me I didn't know what I was doing!" He looked set to launch into a fresh litany of grievances, so Niamh cut him off with a hasty excuse about time and needing to be somewhere. She and Boyd made their escape, and once outside, her young champion whistled softly.

"Mrs. Caulton, I don't mind telling you - that dude is a few hamburgers short of a picnic. He's not a nice man."

"Lowe or Quigley?"

"Both. Where to next?"

Niamh glanced at her phone. "Eve's. Greta has called a meeting. Let's hope they've turned up something. Other than confirming that Lowe is a creep and Quigley is bad tempered, I not sure how much good we did here."

Chapter 13

The meeting, such as it was, consisted of the older ladies and Eve, with Ellen Marrinan. The latter had arrived clutching a neatly printed sheet, that she proudly gave to Eve.

"Your timeline, as requested. I've included everything that I could, but there's space there if you need to add anything in. I sent a copy to Detective Cullen too. Boyd, go home. You left a pile of crockery in your room, it's disgusting. Clear it all up and put it in the dishwasher."

The teenager left in high dudgeon at being excluded but Ellen was unmoved.

"He's a good kid," she informed them, "and I love him. But he's a divil for leaving every cup in the house, unwashed, in his room. And the pile of dirty clothes…"

"It's my fault," Niamh defended him. "I kept him out longer than I expected."

"Did you break into my house, make endless cups of coffee and leave them half drunk to fester in his room? No? Then it's no one's fault but his own."

Eve listened with half an ear as the ladies exchanged views on teenagers, their mess and ways to persuade them to clean up. She knew, knew at some basic level, the answer to the mystery was in front of them. The familiar prickling of excitement and frustration at not being able to see it yet was strong, but no matter how she wracked her brain, nothing was clicking into place.

Dymphna's lecture on listening, on taking in what was said, and truly hearing it, sprang to mind. Instead of leading the meeting, she leaned back and let the women recount their activities, to whom they had spoken and about what. She could see them in her mind's eye, Greta talking to Humphrey and her mother listening to Aidan Lowe. Dymphna told everything that Helen had said, and Claudia explained what had happened at Wisteria Cottage, the group gasping in horror at the disastrous cancellations of the venue, florists, and cake.

All these things, whirring around in her head. All that noise. But where were the false notes, and where were the true ones?

Without realizing she was doing it, she started to hum. The high notes, they rang true. They were the details they were sure of, knew for a fact, had evidence of. The middle notes were the noise, so much of it, so many people and so many stories. All the stories. Like the chatter in the room, rising and falling. She read the sheet again, and low notes crept in, and then one odd note, one note that didn't belong…

She glanced at the sheet Ellen had given her, read through the timeline one more time - and knew.

* * *

While the ladies convened in Kimberly Cottage, Ronan and Margaret had retreated to Copper Beech Cottage, giving Humphrey the run of Wisteria Cottage for the evening. They sat huddled together on the couch, both too wound up to do more than stare at the TV and try not to fret over their ruined wedding. Eventually Ronan's hand reached out for his fiancee's and he said quietly, "You know, it'll be okay. I promise. We'll sort it all out."

Margaret managed a smile. "I know, love. Maybe we'll just do the marriage ceremony and arrange a reception some other time. We'll have to let people know, though. I can send out emails…"

"Not yet." Ronan said firmly. "It might sound daft but - let's wait."

"But if we have nowhere to host the reception-"

"I know. I know. Look, I can't explain it but I've seen some stuff that beggars belief. If anyone can save the day, it's those old bats. Let's just keep our fingers crossed and see what Eve and the ladies come up with, okay? And maybe Powers will get back to me soon."

Margaret shrugged. "Okay. But I don't know that even the Ladies can fix this, Ronan."

"Trust me." He kissed her hair and hugged her close. "Let's just keep hoping for a while yet."

"And you understand why I gave Uncle the money?"

There was a short silence, before Ronan answered.

"It's your money, pet. I don't mind what you do with it. But if I'm honest, no. I don't really understand."

"I knew he was in trouble. I didn't tell you, because I didn't want you to think badly of him. I could tell you weren't mad about him, as it was."

"I admit, I've been - a little suspicious."

"I understand. I do. But I heard him on the phone one afternoon, and it was awful. He sounded scared, and he was pleading with them - a man his age shouldn't be worrying about how to pay his bills, Ronan. If he hadn't left, if he'd stayed home and lived in Ireland, we'd be minding him anyway. He would have had family to rely on. So - when he said he needed the money, I was relieved. I would have offered to help him if I thought he would accept it."

Ronan kissed her. "You're right, as ever. He's your uncle and it's only right that we help him. Hopefully now we can keep an eye on things, and make sure he doesn't get himself into another mess."

Margaret snuggled in and sighed. "I can't wait to marry you, Ronan Desmond, even if we have to have the reception in a field."

"It won't come to that." Despite his confidence, her future husband crossed his fingers.

* * *

In their own way, each of the ladies took time that evening to send some good wishes towards the young couple.

Claudia took a sensible and practical view of the situation, feeling that while receptions and fancy flowers were all very well, the really important thing was to actually get wed. She sat and watched her fire burn low, thinking about her own wedding - the pale yellow satin jacket and dress that she had bought for the occasion, the Vicar saying the vows in front of a tiny gathering of her parents, in-laws and a few good friends. Her Sam smiling at her in his navy suit, that he wore for funerals and weddings for a good ten years after. Their wedding breakfast in the Gresham Hotel, just twenty people sitting down to a meal. It was a poor show if judged by the standards of today, when couples spend tens of thousands and dance into the night, but she had loved every minute of it. She wished with all her heart that her young friends had that joy, not the trappings and glitter but the happiness that lasts.

Greta was furious for the young people, thinking of her own children's weddings, of the planning and effort that she had poured into them. These huge family gatherings were her expression of love, and pride. She was looking forward to her grandchildren settling down next. The mere thought of anyone interfering with their happiness made her blood boil. Ronan and Margaret were almost family to the old woman, and she was not about to let anyone harm them either. Her eyes narrowed and she plumped a cushion viciously. She wished a blight on the person tormenting the young couple.

Niamh sat on the side of her bed, and thought about her long dead love. There had never been anyone after him, not for her. Raising two children had filled her life, the daily struggle to put food on the table and keep a roof over their heads, but even if she had had time and leisure - no, there was no second love for her. She wasn't sure what she believed in exactly, but the one fixed star of her existence was the feeling that she would see him again, someday. And that was enough. Love was so important, she thought. Eve laughed at her fussing over Conor and Ray, but she just wanted them to be happy. Everyone deserved to be loved, and loved truly. She sent the warmth of her love towards Margaret and Ronan. They had already won, in her opinion, because wedding or no wedding, they were loved.

Dymphna too was pondering the mysteries of love. She had been frustrated that she wasn't present when Humphrey had confessed to wanting money, and it had taken some effort to persuade her that Margaret had been happy to give it to him.

She worried about the young woman, and about how Ronan would really feel. It bugged her all evening until she had to give in, and slipping out into the night, took to the skies. She found her way to Ronan's house, perching on the edge of the front window. She listened, and she watched, and before she made her way home, she blessed the pair with all her heart.

And as night fell over Bramble Lane, Margaret and Ronan held each other and comforted each other, and promised each other that no matter what, come Saturday morning they would be married.

* * *

Thursday morning dawned grey and rather drizzly but mild, in typical Irish Spring weather. Eve had passed a restless night. She was fairly sure that she had cracked the case, but the problem was proof - and that was thin on the ground. The first step was to talk to Ronan, and get his opinion. Could they persuade Cullen to move on this based on the admittedly slender argument that Eve had a strong hunch?

She planned to call into Copper Beech first thing but before she could, there was a knock on her front door. Ronan was on the doorstep, looking as if he had had as little sleep as Eve.

"Sorry, I know it's early."

"It's grand. Come in. Any word from your friend?"

"Powers? Not yet. I think we have to accept the hotel and florist are gone at least. I thought I'd ring around and see if I can find anything…"

"Good, good, but before that - I need to run an idea past you. A theory, really." Eve set out her thoughts as succinctly as she could, while Ronan listened. When she finished, he pursed his lips.

"I see. It's - interesting. It's plausible. What we lack is actual evidence…"

"I don't know. Cullen must have checked CCTV footage and ring doorbells and so on by now. Don't you think there must be footage somewhere, something that would back it up?"

"I'll ask. If you're right…well, I'll be glad. One less thing hanging over us."

"It'll be okay, Ronan. I promise you, we will sort this wedding out somehow. But let's get this out of the way first?"

"Agreed. Let me ring Cullen. "

While Ronan conducted an intense conversation over the phone with his partner, Eve continued to muse on everything. Her theory explained a lot, but there were still some loose ends. The wedding - the maliciousness at play there, the cruelty, it didn't fit. What was she missing?

"Eve!" Ronan broke her train of thought. "I'm going to meet Cullen, he has some footage that might help - he's not completely convinced but he's interested."

"Good. Keep in touch…"

It was frustrating, sitting around waiting to hear what the Gardaí had found out. It might be hours before Ronan got back in touch. Eve decided to do something productive with the time, and what better than to visit Margaret and start operation "Rescue the Wedding"? She grabbed her laptop and made her way down the crescent to Copper Beech Cottage - where she was greeted by a red-faced, wild eyed Margaret.

"Eve." Her friend gripped her arms so tightly Eve winced. "Ronan's friend rang. The tech genius. He tracked down the owner of the fake email, the one that canceled the wedding vendors."

"Oh my god! But - who? Who was it?"

"I'll kill her Eve. I'll pull every strand of hair off her head and -and I'll box her ears for her!"

Thoroughly alarmed now, Eve tried to calm her down. "Margaret, let go. I need the use of my arms, thanks very much. Now, take a breath and tell me - who was it?"

"It was her!" Margaret waved her hands, stumbling over the actual words. "Humphrey's PA. Phyllis!"

"What? No. Really? Ronan's friend is sure?"

"Positive. He couldn't get on to Ronan, he kept going straight to voicemail -"

"Ronan was on the phone to Cullen," Eve interjected.

"Ronan gave him both our numbers, so he rang me instead. He has absolute proof and - and it was her. Oh Eve, why? Why would she do this?"

"Because she's a dangerous, mean, rotten person," Eve said furiously. "But we'll get her. We'll get that snake."

She rang Ronan, thinking perhaps it would be better for him to concentrate on the home front right now rather than solving the murder but his excited response changed her mind.

"Never mind all that - I mean, tell Margaret I'm raging and we'll get that wagon - but Eve, I think we've cracked it. Cullen said once they knew what they were looking for, it sped everything up. You were right. Although, I admit I'm still not quite sure why…"

"You leave that to me," Eve said firmly. "I'm pretty sure I know why."

The trick would be getting them to admit it, she told herself.

"There's more. We know why Burke called to Greta's that night. He had great news for Humphrey - he sold the book.

And not just sold it - there was huge interest. Some Hollywood star mentioned Humphrey in an interview, said how he wanted to play an old style gumshoe like the great Jerusalem Hill. That was enough to tip the balance."

"So, Humphrey had no reason to kill his agent. In fact, Burke dying is the last thing he'd want."

"Yeah, it certainly looks that way. I think I've finally persuaded Cullen that he's not in the picture."

"I'm glad. I wonder where he stands now, with the book? If Burke secured the deal, it will probably go ahead, don't you think?"

"I have no idea. I hope so for his sake. The main thing is, if Humphrey had spoken to Burke even briefly, he would have known his friend had pulled it off."

"We'll just have to hope for the best. Time enough to sort it out after. For now - let's get some justice for that poor man."

Chapter 14

If Cullen thought it was an odd request, to gather the main players together in the community centre, he kept it to himself. He had followed Ronan to Bramble Lane, where he listened carefully to what Eve had to say. While he didn't say much, he treated her with respect, and gave her theory due consideration. She appreciated his faith in her, or possibly his faith in his partner. Ronan had lent his largely silent, but very visible support, as Eve pleaded her case, nodding in agreement whenever she looked at him. Finally he weighed in with one statement.

"Cullen, this is our chance to get this over and done before it ruins my wedding." Ronan knew his friend wouldn't be able to withstand this final argument. To Eve's relief, it worked and the Garda gave in with a heavy sigh.
"Fine then, I'll have them there. Is this going to be one of them denouement thingies, where the great investigator unmasks the villain and the bungling cops take the credit? Because if so, I'm fine with that. This is a headache of a case."

"I can't promise anything, but I'll do my best. Thanks, Cullen, we won't forget this. And if I'm right, it'll get the press and your Super off your back."

"Oh, I'm in. But you'd better be right. And as ever, I don't want to know how you found out whatever it is, unless you can provide a chain of evidence that will stand up in court."

Eve was glad he was taking this very sensible attitude to their help, because she deeply suspected that "Dymphna overheard it while flapping around last night," or "Greta saw it in a dream," really wouldn't pass muster. At least this time she could point to actual evidence and a proper theory.

True to his word, Cullen arrived at the hall promptly at two o'clock, and ushered in the people Eve had listed for him. Emer O'Neill was visibly excited, grinning at the ladies as she took a seat. Eve winked at her, but made a gesture to indicate she should remain quiet. Humphrey just looked weary as he filed in. Liam Quigley made no secret of his annoyance, tutting and fussing over the seating arrangements. Phyllis Dennehy was calm and collected as ever, a derisive smile on her lips as she noted Quigley's agitation. Aidan Lowe was truculent and made veiled threats about what he would publish. Eventually Cullen had to tell him to sit down, and be quiet. Finally Helen Dunphy took a seat, her expression nervous.

Before anyone could speak the hall doors opened again and Finn strolled in, accompanied by his son Boyd, and Sergeant Jo Maguire. It opened one final time, and Eve waited until the last person entered - her neighbour and friend Margaret. They exchanged a look, and to Cullen's visible surprise, Eve stepped back and allowed Margaret take centre stage. The young teacher reached into her bag and pulled out a wad of paper.

"These are the emails from my hotel and florist, and other vendors, claiming I canceled their service. I printed them off so you could see them. The ones that seem to be from me, canceling, are highlighted. As you can see the email address is very similar to mine but not identical. Someone created an account to contact these vendors." She stood in front of her uncle's personal assistant and paused.

"Phyllis," Margaret's voice was surprisingly calm but the hand holding the sheaf of canceled invoices shook slightly. "How could you?"

Phyllis raised an eyebrow.

"I beg your pardon?"

"How could you do this to me? To Ronan? and why?"

"I have no idea what you're talking about."

"Oh yes, you do. Don't bother denying it. Ronan sent the emails to a Garda tech unit and they traced them directly to you. There's no point in lying now."

Phyllis shrugged. Her expression remained as cool and detached as ever, but she admitted, in a nonchalant way, "All right then. Well done, you caught me. I canceled your precious wedding."

The group gasped, all eyes on the two women. Humphrey drooped and laid his head into his hands.
"Why?"

The other woman looked at her defiantly.

"Why shouldn't I? Why should you get everything you want and I get nothing! For years I've slaved for your uncle. I did everything for him. *Everything.* He treated me like a dogsbody, but I was loyal to him. He promised me he'd take care of me. And then he finds some long-lost niece and suddenly I'm nothing? Nothing?"

The calm facade cracked and her voice rose hysterically. Cullen took a step forward, but she laughed.

"I'm not going to hurt your precious Margaret. Calm yourself."

Humphrey finally looked up, lifting his head out of his hands.

"Phyllis. I told you, I told you over and over – of course I would have looked after you. I paid you a good wage. I would still have employed you - Margaret getting married had nothing to do with you. You just didn't need to do this, any of this."

"Oh, pooh!" Phyllis sounded like a bold child. Gone was the cool, efficient assistant, and in her place was a petulant, angry brat. "I couldn't trust anything you said, not after we came here. First it was, *"We'll just look her up, I might not even say anything to her..."* next thing he was announcing it in the press. Then it was *"Oh we'll just stay for the wedding"* and then..."

"Then he announced he was moving here for good," Eve filled in the blanks as Phyllis trailed off, overcome by her rage and emotion.

Cullen shook his head.

"What I don't understand is – why kill poor Damian Burke? I mean, he was coming to tell Humphrey that the book was snapped up, that there was already talk of a film – everything that would have tempted him away from Dublin and back to his life in America."

Phyllis stared at the older detective. "What are you talking about? Burke had dropped Humphrey, fired him as a client."

Eve shook her head. "No, Phyllis. He intended to, but out of friendship and for old times sake, he decided to give it one more try. He sent the new manuscript out, pushed to get it actually read. A stroke of luck meant that Humphrey was back in the public eye, which made the manuscript more interesting. Once they read it, they loved it. It was a triumph, for both Damian Burke and Humphrey. And that is what the poor man rushed over to tell his old friend. He was back, on top and in demand."

"And Phyllis here killed him, not realizing she was murdering the one person who might change Humphrey's mind about staying here!" Cullen exclaimed.

"Ah. No. See, there's just one problem with all this." Eve said. She caught Finn's eye and nodded slightly. Immediately both he and Boyd moved to stand in front of the exit to the hall. The moment they moved, the action was mirrored behind her by Ronan and Jo Maguire, cutting off any way out through the stage area.

"Phyllis didn't murder Damian Burke." Eve announced. "She was in this very hall, organizing chairs and handing out programmes, we all saw her. Yes, she could have just about managed to stab him, and leg it through the park, across the playing fields and in through the back entrance here – but not in time to set up the event. We all remember it don't we? Mr. Quigley here, he was so angry with her for taking over."

"She's right!" Niamh interjected. "Liam here was spitting nails over it, weren't you? Called her an interfering, officious wagon if I recall correctly."

"That's right, Mam. And we all remember what Phyllis said in reply – "You can't complain about me taking over, when you weren't here to do it yourself…""

All eyes turned to Liam Quigley, who regarded them all with a defiant stare.

"Well, what of it? She was officious and interfering. I was perfectly capable of setting up, but I just had to get the authors settled first –"

"No." Helen said. "No, all the guest speakers were milling around backstage, not knowing what to do. Remember, we all complained about it – about the lack of communication and the chaos."

"Of course you did," Eve agreed, "because there was no one backstage organizing you. And he wasn't out here setting up the hall, Phyllis had to do that. Which begs the question, Mr. Quigley….Liam…where were you, exactly?"

Quigley's face turned puce red. "I don't appreciate your insinuation. How dare you."

Cullen took one step forward. "Answer the question. Where were you?"

"I was here."

"No, you weren't." Eve stood her ground. "You were not here."

"I'm telling you. I was – I was busy. There is a lot to do for an event like that, I was all over the place. People must have seen me…"

"No. No one can remember seeing you between the doors opening and your very public row with Phyllis. You came out of the crowd, shouting about how you only stepped backstage for a moment and she took over. But it's not true. When I stopped to think about it, that was just redirection. We all thought we knew where you were that night, because you told us. In fact, you had just arrived, red from running – and possibly from the shock of what you'd done."

"I thought he was having a heart attack, from rage," Tom remarked.

"We all did. It wasn't emotion though, it was exertion." She stared Quigley down, her sheer force of will keeping him rooted in his seat. "You killed Damian Burke."

The man in front of her shrank into himself, but he wasn't done yet.

"That's preposterous! Ridiculous. What motive could I

possibly have to kill him? I barely knew him!"

Cullen caught Eve's eye and frowned. She knew he was backing her, but she had to prove her case. Ronan shifted slightly behind her, a reassuringly solid presence.

"You didn't know Damian well, that's true. But you knew Humphrey well. That writing class you took together – to him it was just a small stepping stone, he hardly remembers it. It was insignificant – he was already destined for bigger and better things. Humphrey, what did you think when you heard from your old classmate after all this time?"

"Eh – Not a lot, if I'm honest. Um, truth be told I hardly remembered him. I thought it was nice he invited me here, and it meant I could visit Margaret without having to shell out for air fare and hotels." Humphrey sounded bewildered. "I took it all at face value, I suppose."

"Exactly." She looked at Quigley with something like pity. "He never gave a second thought to the whole experience. He took a class. He wrote a story. He submitted it and got praised by an agent. Later on, that agent took him on - several years later. But you, you have obsessed about it ever since. Why?"

Her tone was gentle, coaxing. Something had changed in the atmosphere. Coming from somewhere, there was a low hum, a soothing undertone. The four older ladies sat stock still, each with their hands on their knees, feet firmly rooted on the floor, eyes fixed on Quigley. Eventually, with something like relief, the man broke.

"He didn't just "*find an agent!*" Tell them, Paddy! Tell them how you met Damian Burke."

The author winced at the sound of his old name, as if hearing it from his old acquaintance brought back an unhappier time.

"He came to the class – he was a friend of the teacher, I

think. It was so long ago – he was invited to speak to us about publishing and how to find an agent. Then he asked for someone to read their short story…I volunteered."

"Short Story!" Quigley shouted. "It was supposed to be a short story but instead you read the first chapter of your bloody novel."

"But – I asked. The teacher said to go ahead…" Humphrey looked around at the rest of the group. "I don't understand. I really don't. Damian praised me for trying, but said it was immature. It was all tell and not show, it had too many adverbs, the dialogue was unnatural – the only really positive thing he said was that if I wrote something better, I should feel free to submit it to him."

"Liar!" Quigley reached into his pocket, ignoring the sudden movement of Cullen to restrain him. He pulled out a wallet before the detective could stop him and with one quivering hand retrieved a faded newspaper article, folded and browned with age. "Look! Two years later, here it is in black and white. You'd changed your name, but I recognized you immediately. "Irish born writer signs with top UK agent.""

"Liam. At that point, I had been in the United States over a year. I had an American agent. They set me up with Burke. He didn't even remember me, that's the God honest truth. Oh, he pretended when I reminded him, but I knew I was just one out of the hundreds – thousands – of hopefuls he met along the way. We became friends after he signed me and he only signed me because Leeman Goode – my American reps – asked him to. And they dropped me a few years back. Only poor Damian put up with me…" the writer's voice broke on a sob and he buried his face in his hands. "You murdered my only real friend, out of jealousy over something that simply never happened."

There was a silence that seemed to last for ever. Eve's heart broke for the poor man, vain and shallow and duplicitous though he was. Humphrey had his faults, but he had a heart too. To her surprise the first person to move to comfort him was Ronan.

"It'll be okay, Paddy, It'll be okay."

In the history of condolences, it wasn't the most eloquent attempt but it was rewarded by a look of pure gratitude from the older man.

Quigley however, was unmoved.

"Liar," he repeated. "I don't believe you. You stole the limelight that night, you cheated!" His voice rose to a near scream. "Burke too – he deserved to die!"

"Tell us how it happened, there's a good man," Claudia said quietly. "You went to Greta's to confront Humphrey?"

"Paddy!" Quigley spat. "Calling himself Humphrey Sterling – a ridiculous name. Yes, I'd had enough. I was going to give him one last chance to admit his guilt and if he didn't, I planned on telling everyone that night. In front of his precious niece and the press and the other authors. Hah! But I was too late, there was no one there. He left the door unlocked, typical selfish careless behaviour…I tried the door, just in case. It opened. It was - I only went in to make sure he wasn't just avoiding me, and then Damian Burke arrived. He was so full of himself, bursting with the news. Oh, he was so easy – I just flattered him, fawned over "my dear friend, Humphrey,"and pretended to be worried about him - that fool just blurted it all out. What great news he had, how this book was a return to form, better than anything he'd done in years, film rights – film rights- I nearly puked. He wouldn't shut up. They stole my career from me, between them. It should have been me." He was wild eyed by now. "He wouldn't shut up so I – I made him."

Before anyone could react to this terrible admission, the man sprang from his seat and made a dash past Ronan, still comforting Humphrey, and straight for Sergeant Jo. All four Senior ladies jumped to their feet and the air crackled with the combined energy of their wrath. Eve was just about to grab Tom and duck when – Jo calmly floored him with a punch straight to the jaw and Quigley dropped like a stone.

She gave a brisk nod at the ladies, and remarked, "It's fine, I can manage the likes of him no problem."

Chapter 15

The dust had settled to some degree, with Quigley firmly in custody and shadow of suspicion lifted from Humphrey – and Greta – but the problem of the canceled wedding still remained. Cullen had pulled Phyllis in for questioning, on general principles, but whether the woman could be charged with any crime was a moot point.

"It's more than likely a civil matter," Cullen whispered to Eve as they took their leave, "but we'll make a report, and she'll be stuck in processing for a long time. Least we can do."

Phyllis had retreated into icy indifference. Her only comment as she was led away was "Hope what's left of your big day goes well!" Her words dripped with malice and sarcasm, and Eve felt a shiver down her spine.

Ronan had insisted on accompanying Cullen and Sergeant Jo Maguire to the station - as much to prove a point to his superintendent as anything, in Eve's opinion. Tom and Humphrey had withdrawn to let the women comfort the bride-to-be, and to steady their nerves after all the excitement with a drop of good brandy. Now the shock of Quigley's arrest had word off, the reality of Phyllis' spiteful acts was settling in. Looking through the emails and invoices, Niamh gasped. The efficient personal assistant had been thorough in her destruction of the wedding plans.

"Twenty-four hours," Margaret wailed. "I mean – I know in the scheme of things, it's only a wedding…"

"Only a wedding?" Dymphna rolled her eyes. "My dear child. You're allowed be upset, for goodness sake. That bitter weapon canceled your flowers, your reception…"

"Dymphna, you're not really helping." Eve could see Margaret fighting back tears.

"Sorry, but I could spit, I'm so mad. I'll destroy that selfish little…"

"Dymphna! Not now."

But later, Eve thought privately, later on I'll help her hex Phyllis Dennehy until she *glows*.

"Right now, we need solutions. She didn't manage to cancel the church or Fr. Aloysius, so there's that. Margaret, you have your dress and veil, Ronan has his suit. The bridesmaid's dress and Cullen's suit are fine. That leaves – let me see…reception, flowers, transport and catering and the cake…"

Margaret shrugged. "I rang the hotel, and begged them. It's no use, they have given the date away and just said it's my fault for canceling. I explained til I was blue in the face that I didn't, that it was Phyllis, but it didn't matter. Same with the flowers and the caterer. We've lost our deposits, because of the short notice too. The woman I hired didn't even make the cake, she got the email before she started baking. It's all – spoiled. It's horrible to think someone hates me so much, they would try to ruin my wedding day. I feel like, even if by some miracle we got our vendors back and our hotel, it'd all be tainted."

Claudia gave the bride to be a bracing smack on the back. Ignoring the resultant yelp of pain, she squared her shoulders and announced, "Right. You've had a setback, Margaret, but the question now is – what are you going to do about it? Are you going to let this little madame ruin things for you? Call off the wedding? Disappoint Ronan, and the rest of us?"

Margaret looked a little taken aback by this sudden change of pace.

"Um, no?" she ventured.

"Good girl, that's the spirit. Now, I take your point about it feeling tainted - it's never nice to be ill-wished. But you leave that to us, we'll lift any bad luck for you. You trust us, don't you?"

Margaret nodded earnestly.

"Niamh, this is your area of expertise. What should we do?"

"Arrah, ladies. There's no end of good luck we can bring to a wedding, that's no problem. And maybe it's just as well the old vendors aren't available. Everything fresh and new, that's the ticket."

"Except there's no way we'd get a hotel with twenty four hours notice," Margaret plunged back into gloom. "I appreciate your efforts, I do, but –"

"Hush," Claudia said, "I'm ringing Jennie." Her daughter was a solicitor, a fact for which many present had on occasion been thankful. "Let's see if we can't get your money back, first off."

She wandered off, talking urgently into her mobile phone as she filled her daughter in on events. Niamh had drifted off into a reverie, which Eve knew from experience meant the wheels were turning in her mother's fertile brain. Best to leave her to it.

"Okay, Greta, it's you and me now. Any ideas?"

"Let me think. Well, my Una is dating a nice young man from the Vintners Association. He may have some contacts in local hotels. Flowers -ah here, don't we have Tom and his army of fanatical gardeners? You get him on that immediately, tell him we need as many as we can in – Margaret, what are the wedding colours again? Lavender, Lilac, Light pink…throw in some creams too for contrast. Doesn't matter what as long as it'll look nice in a bouquet or on a table. Claudia's Brigade ladies can do the arranging. Food – if we can get a decent hotel, they'll sort that for us. The cake - surely between us we can make a decent cake? And transport – my grandson Lorcan is a mechanic. He must know someone with a nice car."

Greta's fingers were blurs as she sent text messages flying, even as she spoke. "I'll put out a call on the Goode Hunters forum too – someone might be able to help us out."

"Good idea." Greta's fans were legion, spread across a wide demographic and fanatically devoted to their leader. "That leaves music?"

"I'll ask Teresa O'Brien, from the music shop in town. If anyone can help, she can."

Tom took to his task of sourcing flowers with enthusiasm. Every garden for miles around would be donating a few blooms, by the sound of it, although Eve worried whether there would be anywhere to actually put them. The Irish Women's Brigade were on standby for the following morning, to create masterpieces including the bouquets and buttonholes. A car to transport the couple from the church to a reception proved easy to arrange. Lorcan came through in spectacular fashion, promising a vintage Rolls Royce, fully restored, from the 1920s, belonging to a customer who willingly lent it for the day in return for a free service. Mrs. O'Brien of the famous O'Brien's Music Shop assured them there would be music in the church, if she had to wield a fiddle and play herself. Everything now hinged on Una Goode's young man, and his contacts in the hospitality sector.

Time ticked by, and Eve tried not to panic. Margaret had cheered up at each piece of good news, and was inclined to be hopeful. Eve didn't want to dampen her spirits, but it was beginning to look as if they might be pressing the community centre hall into service, and eating the wedding dinner off trestle tables and paper plates.

"Come on," She stood up and stretched. "We need to take a break. Margaret, you're as white as a sheet. Let's get some food and -"

Before she could finish, Greta let out a shriek, her mobile phone held aloft triumphantly.

"If Una doesn't marry that young fella, I'll disown her. Margaret, you're not going to believe this – sod Belleview Hotel and its snippy manager and its cancellation policy! Young Kojo – Una's boyfriend – he just texted me. He called into a hotel where he has friends working, talked to the events team and told them what happened to you. They have a wedding in the main ballroom tomorrow but they have another function room, waiting to be refurbished, and they'll let us use it."

"Oh, thank God." Margaret managed to cry and laugh at the same time. "That's brilliant."

"He says it's a bit shabby but it's still very nice, and we can decorate it any way we like, seeing as it's not used at the moment –plus they'll cater and they'll even do a special rate to help out. "

"Tell Kojo, when Ronan hears this he'll never have to pay a parking ticket in this city again." Margaret said fervently. "But where is it?"

Eve was expecting to hear one of the mid sized hotels on

the south side of Dublin, any one of which would have been perfectly acceptable. But Greta's grin almost split her face in two as she named possibly the poshest, prettiest and definitely the most expensive venue in South County Dublin.

"Finnslake Castle Estate."

The smile froze on Margaret's face.

"Greta, there's no way we can afford that. Holy gods, we couldn't afford to stand the guests a round at the bar there, let alone an entire wedding…"

Greta waved an airy hand. Eve deeply suspected the old lady was enjoying her role as Fairy Godmother immensely.

"Don't worry your head about it. I told Kojo your budget, and the clever boy made sure the hotel agreed to do it for the right price. In fact, because the room is strictly speaking, "not ready for use," they aren't charging for venue hire, only for the food and there's more."

"More?" Margaret and Eve chorused. The young bride looked as if she might faint.

"They're throwing in a suite for you and Ronan. Unfortunately, the other wedding has booked most of the rooms up, so we'll have to accommodate anyone who was expecting to stay overnight – but sure, I can take a few, so can Claudia and between everyone I'm sure we'll manage. But you'll have a fourposter with views of the rose garden…" Anything else Greta might have said was smothered by Margaret's fierce hug.

"I have no idea how you do it, any of you, but you're the best. I used to think I was alone, no family, no one to care about me. Now I have Ronan, I have ye – I have Uncle Pa- I mean, Uncle Humphrey." She squeezed Greta until the older woman protested. "Thank you."

"Get off." Greta tried and failed to hide her emotions under a gruff front. "I'm too old to be bear hugged, ya maggot. Right, we need to get to the hotel and start organizing this shindig. Ring Ronan and tell him to meet us there – all very well for him to swan off to the station with his mates, but it's time he pulled his weight."

Eve was moved to protest on Ronan's behalf.

"He's a Detective Garda, Greta and it was a murder investigation. He's not off having a beer with the lads."

"Want to bet?" Greta shook her head. "If you let them out of your sight, they'll leave everything to the women. No. He and that best man of his need to get their heads in wedding mode."

Margaret winked at Eve. "She's right, Eve. Don't be arguing with her. Now, let's go get me a wedding venue!"

* * *

The hotel proved to be beyond the loftiest dreams of the bridal couple, and so grateful were they to have a place to hold the reception at all, they were prepared to ignore the fact that the smaller function room was indeed a little shabby, and neglected. The manager, an efficient but kindly woman in her mid fifties, looked around it apologetically.

"I'm sorry it's not in better shape. The refurbishments have been planned for months now, but they won't actually start til the end of the Summer. But you're welcome to do anything you like to make it work for the day."

"It's fine!" Ronan assured her, but Eve shook her head.

"It will be fine, when we're finished with it." She said firmly. The artist in her was already hard at work, looking critically at the space. "We'll have flowers, and balloons – and would you mind if we hang fairy lights from the ceiling to the floor, behind the main table?"

"Anything you like," the manager repeated, "short of knocking a hole in the wall! I'll get the lads to look in the store room, I'm nearly sure we have some LED display lights that would look lovely."

Promising to return in the morning with reinforcements, they took their leave. There was still a lot to arrange, at very short notice, but Eve finally felt confident that they could pull it off. After all, one advantage of starting from a point of utter disaster was that anything at all was an improvement.

"You have someone to marry you, a place to celebrate it and nice clothes to wear on the day. That's all our parents had or expected, and their parents had even less," she told the couple as they arrived home to Bramble Lane. "Now, go take an hour to yourselves, finish off anything you need to get done and then get an early night. In your own houses, mind. It's bad luck to see each other before you meet at the altar."

"And mind you look straight ahead, until Humphrey taps you on the shoulder." Greta poked Ronan with one bony finger. "Hear me? No looking over your shoulder at the bride as she comes up the aisle. Don't turn your head an inch until she's at the altar."

Ronan opened his mouth, but Margaret got in first.

"He won't, I promise. Ronan, we need all the good luck we can get. It – it is going to be all right, isn't it?" She looked anxiously at Eve.

"We are going to load you with so much good luck, Phyllis Dennehy will choke on it," Eve said, and meant it.

Naturally, when she let herself and Tom into the house

she found that everyone – from the local teens, led by Boyd and Ashleigh, to her mother and neighbours – had crowded into Kimberly Cottage. Is there no other place to meet? She grumbled to herself. Not for the first time she wondered if she could change the locks and not give Niamh a key but the wrath of the Irish Mammy was not to be trifled with. There wouldn't be a decent biscuit left in the house, judging by the plates of goodies in front of the old women. Claudia had the grace to look slightly shamefaced as she stuffed a chocolate Mikado into her gob, but Dymphna just grinned like a bold child and made sure Eve could see her lovely haul of decadent snacks.

"Mam, I swear to God you're going to the supermarket this weekend and replacing all this." Eve said sternly. Her mother eyed her scornfully.

"Whisht. Didn't you bankrupt me as a teenager, you and your brother, eating me out of house and home? I no sooner unpacked a week's shopping but you had it ate. Don't you begrudge your neighbours and friends a measly biscuit. Anyway, everyone will be heading off soon. Oh, and I've done what I can about "you know what." " Her mother gave the most indiscreet wink-wink, elbow to the ribs. "We'll tackle the rest once we've cleared this place."

It took a good half hour to get the neighbourhood to go to their own homes, and Eve wanted nothing more than to curl up on the sofa for half an hour before bed. But Niamh produced an A4 sized sheet, filled with her scrawling handwriting and despite herself, Eve was curious.

"Right. I've placed wards around both their houses, and hexes – if Phyllis wants to send bad energy their way, she'll get it back and then some. It's a bit like bolting the stable door after the horse, though. She's already done a lot of damage."

"She has poor Margaret spooked." Greta remarked.

"We need to change the energy, ladies. That's something we can do right now. We need to make sure we generate all the good luck we can for tomorrow. Now, here's a list of things we need to do –" She passed it around for everyone to have a read. Eve recognized some of the piseógs – the little charms and superstitions – but some were new to her. And some struck her as eminently impractical. When she ventured to point this out, the older women looked at her pityingly.

"Where there's a will, there's a way. Don't be so defeatist. Right, item number one…that's your job, Eve. Assuming it's not too impractical for you, heh heh."

* * *

Eve rang the doorbell of Holly Cottage, praying that Finn or Ellen were home. To her relief, Finn opened the door within seconds, and greeted her with a smile.

"Hey, Eve. Good to see you. What's up?"

His rich American accent had already picked up some slight twinges of Irish, but he still looked every inch the tall, broad shouldered yank that had arrived into their lives barely six months before. It was hard to imagine Bramble Lane now without the Marrinans. After a rocky start, all the family had embraced life in Ireland with gusto. Recent events had proven they could be relied upon to help whenever possible.

"Finn, I need your help. We need the Child of Prague. We need one immediately, and we need it headless."

When he didn't respond, she repeated for emphasis, "A headless Child of Prague, we need you to get one. I'd do it, but

I've a load of other things to do. It's for the wedding."

Finn looked aghast.

"A *what?*"

Eve giggled at his expression. "A headless Child of Prague. Have you never heard of it? It's a statue, a little wee thing, of the Child of Prague. It's an old tradition."

Finn stared at her then shook his head. "No. Sorry. I'm just not following. Is this some mad Irish thing?"

"Yes. Look, you know the Child of Prague? No? It's a statue of Jesus as a little child that was supposed to be owned by St Teresa of Avila, then it made its way to Prague. So eventually they made replicas of it, little statues about the size of my hand. People here believe they bring good luck for a wedding."

Finn nodded. "Okay. But where does the headless bit come in?"

"Ah. See, it depends what part of the country you ask. But in Dublin, it should be a headless one. The heads used to fall off very easily, probably because people could only afford very cheap ones. So it was considered lucky and normal to have a headless Child of Prague. And the night before a wedding, you put him out under a bush …or just in the back garden, or in the tenements, they'd put him on a windowsill or in the yard. And he'll bring good weather and good luck to the nuptials."

Finn took a moment to digest all this.

"And you think it works, right?"

Eve shrugged. "Mam did it the night before I married Peter, and it rained on the day."

"So, it doesn't work,"

"I didn't say that. Sure, if she hadn't put him out, who knows how bad it might have been? Could have been a complete washout. The wedding day and the marriage, ha ha. We managed two decades together, so..."

Her neighbour tilted his head and looked at her for a long moment.

"Okay. I think I get it. So – where will I find a headless statue of Prague?"

"Headless Child of Prague. Your best bet is to go round the auld biddies of the area. Maybe up at the church, too, if there's anyone still around there at this hour. Dymphna had one but she lent it to her daughter in law for some family wedding. Mam has one, but can't find it and Claudia is a Protestant, so no joy there. And Greta doesn't like religious statues at all, so never had one. But I bet half the houses around here either have one or can get their hands on one. We need it this evening, so get to it."

One of Finn's best qualities was his ability to swing into action without arguing.

"I'll start up at St Augustine's and work my way around. Hey, if I see one with a head...well, I guess how it loses the head isn't so important?"

Eve paused. "Strictly speaking it should be by natural means."

Finn nodded. "Well, if a statue hits something hard, it's sure natural for its head to fly off."

Eve shrugged. "Do what you have to, Just get us that statue. We need all the luck we can get, this wedding has had enough hitches!"

She left him to it, there were still quite a few things to tick off the list and time was running out. Niamh's list had been extensive, and there was only one evening left to get it all done.

Phyllis could ill-wish all she wanted, Eve swore, but this wedding would be lucky and happy. And bad sess to anyone who thought otherwise.

* * *

Everyone was hard at work, working their way through the various tasks Niamh had outlined. Humphrey looked at the list and pointed to the only item left uncrossed.

"What's this?"

"Ah. Ignore that." Dymphna took the list from him and began to fold it up. "Years ago, before women had the right to work and when a single woman was seen as something of a burden to her people, they paid a dowry on the morning of the wedding."

"Her "fortune,"" Claudia said. "It's an old custom, and in some ways it gave a woman a bit of equality in a marriage. But awful hard on those whose families couldn't or wouldn't gift it."

"Awful for women to have to rely on it," Eve said flatly. "Thank heavens those days are gone."

"But it was considered very lucky," Dymphna said rather wistfully. "It would have completed the set, so to speak."

"How much – how much was considered a good fortune?" Humphrey asked.

"Oh, it varied. I mean, back then five pounds was a fortune. But five euro now would look a bit insulting."

"A good enough amount to show the bride was well thought of," Claudia said. "I remember my mother telling me about one of the local girls in her area, a child from the orphanage. Had a terrible time of it in that place, and was only able to leave because some farmer more or less bought her as a maid. All her wages were paid to the Nuns, she wasn't allowed anything for herself. So, of course, no man would marry her. Then the farmer died and his wife inherited and the first thing she did was fix a sum on the girl as a dowry. All the men wanted her then, and she said no to them all. If they didn't want her when she had nothing, she didn't want them now."

"Aw. What happened to her?" Eve asked.

"Sure, didn't the farmer's son offer for her. He was fond of her, and he had always been kind to her, so she accepted him. My mother always said, the widow was a clever woman. If the maid had married the son without a dowry, she would have been labeled a gold digger. If she had her pick of men but still chose the son – it was true love."

Even Humphrey looked moved by the story.

"Well then. It's not just a mercenary thing, is it?" he said quietly.

"No. In its own way, it could be a good thing." Claudia gave him a hard look. "Of course, Margaret has her own money. She's well set."

Humphrey looked at his feet, then without another word, left the room.

* * *

Chapter 16

The morning of the wedding dawned bright and clear, without even the threat of rain. For April in Ireland, this was a minor miracle.

Finn had come through for them, arriving on her doorstep at almost ten o'clock the previous evening, proudly carrying a perfect Child of Prague statue complete with a head separated from its body.

"Don't ask," he responded to her inquiring look, "It's headless, and it's in time."

"Fair enough," Eve took the statue gratefully. "Now to put it under a bush in the garden and pray."

The bright, clear blue sky was their reward.

The bride was in her boudoir, enduring the well-meaning ministrations of Niamh and Dymphna. Much to her frustration, the two older ladies had removed her full length mirror and replaced it with a small, oval one.

"Niamh," Margaret complained, "I literally cannot see myself in this yoke. It's ridiculous. I can see my top half, or if I stand on something I can see my bottom half, but I can't see the whole of me. Will you please get the full length mirror from my bedroom and -"

"No!" All the women chorused together, cutting the bride

off mid-request.

"Sorry," Eve said. "But, no."

"It's fierce bad luck," Niamh explained. "You shouldn't look at yourself full length in a mirror in your wedding dress. Just wait. You look amazing, and you know it. Ronan will be blown away. You can look after the ceremony, once you hold off looking til you're safely wed."

Eve and the ladies had gathered at Wisteria to escort the bride to the church, and they made a handsome group. Claudia had opted for a pale lavender outfit, with a matching fascinator, while Dymphna had chosen a smart navy and cream suit, as big a deviation from her customary black as she would allow herself. Niamh was elegant in a floral dress and mint green bolero, her hair held back by a velvet hairband. They all agreed that Eve was stunning in her bridesmaid dress, but Greta stole the show in a bright, cerise pink pant suit with a huge, wide-brimmed hat in a mix of bright green and pink. It should have looked ridiculous but instead, by some miracle of glamour and self confidence, she looked amazing.

Then Margaret stepped down into the hall and everyone gasped. Light streamed from the landing window at the top of the stairs, creating a halo of golden light around the bride. Her veil twinkled, all the tiny diamante pieces catching the sun, and her hair gleamed in ringlets around her face. The dress itself was deceptively simple, ivory satin in an a-line skirt with a boat-neck bodice, overlaid in lace with more tiny stones.

"You look like – like Maureen O'Hara if she was a brunette," Greta said.

"Pure glamour." Dymphna agreed. "I don't know that I've ever seen a more beautiful bride, honestly. And that includes my daughters, who were pretty gorgeous themselves."

Margaret blushed. "Ah, give over."

Eve glanced at her watch. "Okay, I hate to break this up but – time's moving without us."

Niamh glanced at her daughter, her face anxious. She pointed at the front door.

"It should be the back door, really," she hissed. "It's good luck for a bride to leave by the back door."

"Mam, we've gone over this already. Margaret is not climbing over a blooming wall to get out of her own house."

"No need," Dymphna said smugly. "Greta and I have solved the problem."

The old woman opened the front door with a flourish. "Ta -da!"

Eve stared and stared, her brain unable to quite accept what it was seeing.

"Dymphna. Greta. Did you – did you swap Margaret's front door for her back door?"

"We did."

"Well, in fairness Dymphna, we got young Boyd and his pals to do it. But yes, Eve, we had the doors swapped."

Margaret broke the stunned silence with a gurgle of laughter.

"Ye mad old bats!" She laughed. "I can't believe you did that!"

"Sure, why not? This way you go out the back door, without having to get over the back wall."

"See? Genius."

Even Niamh and Claudia looked a little taken aback at their friends' solution to the problem.

"And it fit?" Niamh asked. "I mean, you didn't…damage the doors, doing that?"

"These houses were built by sensible people, Niamh Caulton. Have you never noticed the symmetry? The front and back doors are the exact same width and height, and the originals looked the same. It's only in recent years that people put in fancy front doors. So I knew they would fit."

Margaret clapped her hands. "This is the best thing ever. I love it. I'll be telling my grand kids about this."

"Not if we don't get a move on!" Eve shrieked, looking in horror at her watch. "Or you'll be telling them how you stood Granddad up at the altar! Here, ladies, take the bouquet and Margaret's overnight bag. Someone take her flat shoes for later – out! Out, out!"

St Augustine's was only a few minutes away, and Margaret had chosen to save money on a fancy car picking her up. Niamh had seized on yet another way to avoid bad luck, this time an old belief from County Kerry - taking the long way around the church. So the entourage made their way across the new Marrinan Park, in the bright morning sunshine, following the path to the main road where St Augustine's imposing stone structure dominated the view. To their surprise, they did not make the walk unaccompanied. As they entered the park, Boyd and his friends, dressed in the distinctive green and gold of the Merrion Hurling GAA team colours, stepped forward and lined both sides of the path.

"Hurls up!" one of the teenagers roared, and each player raised their wooden hurleys, creating an arch for the group to walk under. Margaret grinned ear to ear, and practically danced under the canopy of curved ash.

Eve saw Boyd drop his hurl once they were past and take off at a run towards the main road, to take his place in the church with the family.

Once they had passed under the archway of crossed hurls, they were stopped by a large party of small children, shepherded by smiling parents. Each of the thirty kids held some kind of tribute – cards with glitter and hearts, paper flowers, and baskets filled with rose petals.

"Happy Wedding Day, Ms. Furey!" they chorused, then broke into excited chatter.

"Miss you look like a princess!"

"Ooh Miss, can I touch your flowers?"

"Miss, Miss! I made you a card, look! This is you and that's the garda you're marrying and that's the church…"

Eve was conscious of the time slipping past, but hadn't the heart to hurry her friend past the school children. These were the kids Margaret poured heart and soul into, day in and day out. Parents lined up to wish her well, and neighbours too – everyone seemed to bask in the reflected glow of the bride's happiness and beauty.

"Well, we wanted her to have good luck," Dymphna whispered. "I don't think you can get any more lucky than this."

Eve felt a prickling at the back of her eyes. "We're all lucky, Dymphna. Lucky to be here, lucky to be part of it."

Eventually Margaret tore herself away, a little tousled but looking all the more radiant for it.

"I can't believe they all came out to see me!" She slipped her arm through Eve's and squeezed. "Did you organize that?"

"No! That was all them. You're a very popular lady, Margaret Furey, and don't you forget it."

At last they were at the entrance of the church, and Eve stepped back. Humphrey Sterling stepped forward, emerging from the gloom of the little foyer, his face serious but peaceful.

"My dear! You look like a dream." He kissed her on either cheek and looked into her face, "Your father and mother would be so proud of you. I'm so proud of you. Thank you for letting me be part of your life."

Margaret hugged him. "Thank you for being here. I can't believe I get to walk down the aisle with my uncle, after all these years. Come on, let's do this!"

The strains of the Bridal March filled the church, the organist giving it a rather funkier rhythm than was usual. Niamh muttered, "We had to get a friend of Jennie Warren's in the end. He's a jazz musician, apparently. But he used to play organ for the Cathedral. He's very good if a bit…unorthodox."

Margaret and Humphrey didn't seem to notice, so Eve ushered the ladies into the church, hissing at them to sit down quickly. Ronan was waiting at the head of the aisle with his best man. Cullen was dapper in his suit, proud as punch to stand beside the younger garda.

She turned to the bride and raised an eyebrow.

"Ready when you are," Margaret beamed.

Eve turned and started to walk down the aisle, her bouquet clutched in front of her. She was conscious of some admiring glances as she went and Tom gave her a discreet thumbs up as she reached the top of the church, but without a doubt all eyes were firmly on the young woman in white behind her. A murmur of appreciation rippled through the church, and a smattering of applause. Eve could see Ronan's shoulders twitch but he was under strict instructions not to turn his head until Margaret and her uncle reached the altar. When they did, and Humphrey laid a hand gently on his shoulder, the young Detective Garda turned and his face lit up.

"Oh my God!" He couldn't stop smiling. "Howya, beautiful."

"Hi, Handsome." Margaret replied. Ronan was indeed handsome, in his light grey morning suit and ivory shirt. Lilac and blue accents in his waistcoat complemented the flowers in her bouquet and he looked a far cry from the harassed, weary cop they were used to seeing.

Eve and Humphrey took their seats, leaving the young couple alone, with the officiant, to say their vows and complete the wedding ritual. From the look on their faces, they only saw each other. Eve could almost fancy they stood in a bubble of glowing golden light, protected and safe together while the goodwill and love of their friends and family surrounded and supported them.

She dabbed a tear from the corner of her eye. Nothing could spoil this moment, not the ill wishes of a bitter woman nor the mundane, everyday irritations of life. She smiled and settled in to enjoy the event, as the words of the wedding ceremony rang out across the congregation…

"Do you, Ronan Turlough Desmond take this woman, Margaret Celine Furey, to have and to hold…"

* * *

Getting the beautiful hotel at the last moment had been nothing short of a miracle, Eve reminded herself, and the staff had pulled out every stop to make the event special. Staff had stayed after their shift ended to act as waiters and the manager herself was manning the bar, with the help of a young trainee. While the main ballroom was no doubt filled with glamourous socialites and high profile guests, Eve was willing to bet no one was having a better time than the people crowded into the old function room.

It was traditional for the guests to be greeted at the hotel reception area with a choice of champagne or tea and coffee, which was mainly a chance for the happy couple to take a few moments to regroup after the photographs and before the dinner. Eve was therefore mildly surprised to receive a text from Ronan just as she entered the foyer of Finnslake Castle.

"Can you meet us in the rose garden?" it read. "We are in the gazebo."

The white Victorian summer house was a local landmark, a favourite backdrop for wedding photographs. It was easily visible from the terrace of the hotel, and Eve paused only to let Tom know where she was going.

"I only hope nothing else has gone wrong," She whispered anxiously.

Tom grinned. "Arrah, sure, aren't they married now? That's all that matters. We can cope with anything else."

As she made her way through the pinks, cream and reds of the rose garden, she was relieved to see the couple smiling and waving. Ronan waited until she was within a few feet of them before producing a slim rectangle of paper, folded in half, from his breast pocket. She eyed it curiously.

"That looks like a cheque?"

"It is indeed a cheque," Ronan looked at Margaret, who nodded.

"It's a present from Humphrey to us. He – you know, I don't believe I'm saying this, but he very solemnly handed me over a cheque for twenty thousand euro, as a dowry for Margaret."

Eve couldn't believe the evidence of her own eyes and ears. "He did what?"

"I swear, it was like something from an old movie. He shook my hand, said he trusted me to value and honour his niece and presented me with the cheque. Mind you, it's the money we gave him in the first place – no, I'm not being snide, love, honestly. In a way it makes it even sweeter."

"It's his way of saying he loves us more than money," Margaret said proudly. "We'll give it back to him, obviously, but we wanted you to know. He really isn't as shallow as people think."

"He's…unique," Eve replied. "A complicated man, as Dymphna says. But he loves you, and he wants to do right by you. I wouldn't rush to give it back, though – you might hurt his feelings and besides, with all the buzz about his new book, he probably won't need it."

"Fingers crossed," Ronan said with feeling. "Maybe I'll get a rich uncle instead of a vagrant, unemployed writer."

"Ronan," Margaret tried to sound serious but it was clear she couldn't stop smiling. "You've married the niece of a famous writer, and don't you forget it."

"I'll leave you to it," Eve said, "Enjoy the moment's peace before the reception. Oh, just to warn you, Greta is talking about having a sing-song later and she's been practicing Dicey Riley all day."

On that somewhat alarming note, she left the pair to their bubble of happiness and returned to the hotel. The guests were now filing into the function room for dinner, consulting the famous seating plan pinned to a large board as they went. Eve was to sit at the high table, as matron of honour and bridesmaid, but she sat beside Tom for a quick chat before the newlyweds made their grand entrance.

"How are you, love?" Tom took her hand in his and beamed down at her. "Everything all right with them?"

"Absolutely perfect. They just had a nice surprise – and Humphrey seems to have redeemed himself in Ronan's opinion, which bodes well."

She looked around the table, where the bride's uncle was

happily holding court between Greta and Dymphna on one side and Claudia and Niamh on the other.

"I hear he's thinking of moving into Wisteria Cottage when Margaret and Ronan move into Copper Beech."

"That's good news! I could do with another man on Bramble Lane. I wonder if he's interested in gardening at all? I'll sound him out after…do him good to get out in the fresh air a bit more. Speaking of moving in together, what about us?"

Taken off guard, Eve stumbled over a reply. "I – I don't know, Tom. I mean, I'd love to – you know that – but it's just…"

"It's just that Kimberly Cottage is your home, and you can't bear to leave it? Of course not. You had a long hard road to finding peace and security, love. I wouldn't expect you to give that up. No, no. I was thinking I'd move in with you. Rent out my place to some nice young couple, or maybe a few young people sharing. You know how hard it is for people to find affordable houses around here – it'd be nice to be able to do that. I'd have to keep my vegetables, though, but I'm sure they wouldn't mind."

"If you're willing to rent it out at a decent price, I'd say people would offer to dig and plant it for you!" Eve exclaimed. "Are you sure, Tom?"

"Positive. I'm not much of a homemaker, Eve. I was happy wherever Fiona wanted to live, she made that house a home and after she died, I'd no heart to stay there. I downsized to Bramble Lane, thinking I'd live out my days alone. Now I've found you – sure, where you are is home now. If you'll have me, I'd be happy in Kimberly."

Eve was conscious that this was a moment, one of those rare shining gems that are scattered through life – precious chances for joy, love, and friendship that we regret if we fail to see their beauty or squander the opportunity. When she had arrived in Bramble Lane, it was as a proudly single woman, independent and ready to forge a new life. Now, that new life opened up in front of her, wider and richer and more exciting than she had dreamed possible. Unlike her ex-husband, Tom wouldn't dim her light, or drain her energy. Instead, she would be twice as independent and strong, because he was at her side.

"Tom MacDonagh, will you do me the honour of shacking up with me?"

"I thought you'd never ask!"

As they sealed the deal with a kiss, their friends gave a round of applause – having shamelessly eavesdropped, obviously. You didn't get to be Wise Women without a talent for sniffing out news. Any further discussion was postponed however, as the manager of the hotel clapped her hands and called for silence.

"*A Chairde*! Please be upstanding, charge your glasses and give a warm welcome to the happy couple, Ronan and Margaret!"

As one, the assembled guests sprang to their feet, raised their glasses in a toast to the newlyweds.

"Slainte!"

And as Ronan and Margaret entered to applause and cheers, the last word came from the famous author himself,.

"To my family!" he said proudly. "and to coming home."

Irish Folk Magic and Wedding Traditions

Irish weddings are full of traditions, some so familiar we barely even question them and others rooted in local customs. Even in this modern era, there are things that make a traditional Irish wedding - noticeably, a large family oriented gathering complete with distant cousins and kids, and elderly relatives. When Margaret and Eve wrestle with the dreaded seating plan, it's no laughing matter. Where people sit, and with whom, is a subject for intense and military style planning.

Another aspect of the average Irish wedding is that we tend to have smaller wedding parties than in some countries. It's the norm to have one or two bridesmaids, and a matching number of groomsmen. The couple usually pays for the bridesmaid and groomsmen outfits, including hair and makeup, and usually give each a little keepsake of the day. Bridal showers, like baby showers, are not the norm here, but couples will usually have a hen's night and stag's night.

The reception will go on into the wee hours, often with a sing-song or music session. It's an opportunity for everyone to show off their party piece and woe betide the person who "steals" another's favourite song! Family feuds have started over less.

The couple often stays around for the next day, having a

small gathering with close friends and family, and then go on honeymoon.

Many of the customs stem from a time when a wedding was held in the morning, with a "breakfast" afterwards. While in some areas, weddings were always big parties, in many and for many working people they were small affairs. My parents were married on New Year's Eve in the nineteen sixties, and they had a wedding breakfast in a hotel in Dublin, attended by immediate family and a handful of friends. Their honeymoon was a few days in Cork, a very normal type of honeymoon for the day. By the time their children were getting married, foreign holidays and large evening receptions had become the norm.

Also mentioned, although not a wedding tradition, is the climbing of Croagh Patrick. This is a famous mountain in Co Mayo, associated first with indigenous Irish traditions and then with St Patrick. Every August, pilgrims flock there to climb it, and it is a popular site all year round too. When I was a child it was common practice for penitents to climb it in bare feet, and it is a rocky, hard climb. However, managing this feat could wipe out any number of transgressions, and was considered to be a badge of honour. I've climbed it twice, but not in bare feet - I've never felt I've done anything bad enough to warrant that!

While mostly known now for its Christian associations there is a fascinating photo in the café in the car park, illustrating the famous "roll" of the sun along the mountain's peak at certain times of the year. As a historic site, it is of huge importance.

Folk Magic Traditions

There are dozens of traditions aimed at bringing luck to a wedding, or also, avoiding ill-luck. Duchas.ie is a fantastic website that contains stories collected in the 1930s from all around Ireland. These are the echoes of older traditions, and beliefs, and provide a glimpse into the rich culture of Ireland.

Among the most important wedding traditions are what day you choose, what month, who makes your wedding clothes. Not only should the groom not see you on your wedding day, but you should not look at yourself in a full length mirror. Good weather on the day (or at least until the marriage ceremony is over) is greatly prized, and the tradition of the Headless Child of Prague is very strong to this day! A family member or friend will put out the statue, overnight, to help ensure it.

All the precautions taken by Eve and her friends to save Margaret's wedding are real traditions from different parts of Ireland. Taking the long way to the church comes from Co Kerry, while leaving through the back door is found in Wicklow and the midlands.

In solving the crime, Eve and her friends talk about listening, about hearing the "notes" in what is being said, and about the way some notes ring true. There are several references to music and sound through this book. This is part of the Irish folk magic tradition of **Draíocht Ceoil,** (The Magic of Music/Sound) which is an intrinsic part of Irish Folk Magic. The practice includes the ability to tune into the "song" of a place, or situation, the ability to hear the unsaid, along with the use of sound to create magical energy, and the power of words - obviously important to the poets and writers of the Merrion Literary Festival!

The use of Draíocht Ceoil is an important part of the role of a **Bean Feasa.**

Bean Feasa means "Wise Woman," and they were found in

every community, rural and urban. In an era where the Irish population were denied access to legal or medical redress, they turned to their own practitioners for help. A Bean Feasa operated as a herbalist, an advisor in mundane matters, and a mediator between the average person and the supernatural. Our ancestors believed wholeheartedly in the existence of the Sí (commonly called fairies) and other magical entities. Even now, you will find roads diverted around Fairy Trees, and a fascination with the old stories and traditions still survives.

When dealing with a loathsome person, the Old Bats "hex" him. In modern times, people have come to see hexing as uniformly bad but that is not part of the Irish traditions. A Bean Feasa had a duty to protect and avenge her community. For much of the last 900 years of Irish history, the majority of the population were denied access to legal redress, medical aid, land ownership and education. This reached its height with the Penal Laws, which sought to outlaw every aspect of Irish culture. Thrown back on their own, ancient resources, the people relied on the Bean Feasa for protection and justice. Hexing is the modern form of an ancient poetic tradition of Satire, where the Irish poet (File) was able to challenge even the chieftain and bring him to justice. When we talk about a hex in Irish traditions, we are referring to justice. This is different from Ill-wishing, which is what Phyllis does to Margaret.

I hope you enjoy the authentic Irish magic and traditions in the Old Bat Chronicles, and if you are interested in further study you can check out resources like Duchas.ie (The National Folklore Collection) IrishFolklore.ie (Michael Fortune) Eddie Lenihan (Ireland's greatest living seanchaí or storyteller) and the Irish Pagan School which has a huge amount of free and paid content on Irish magical and spiritual traditions.

There will also be a book on Draíocht Ceoil soon, by Geraldine Moorkens Byrne.

About the Author

Nina Hayes lives in Dublin, Ireland. She is a teacher and writer as well as mother to two lovely boys and wife to a very understanding, long-suffering husband. Her teaching work is centered on Irish folklore, myth and folk magic. All of the magical or folk elements incorporated into her work are based on indigenous Irish traditions and beliefs.

Nina writes from her home in Dublin but loves to travel, around Ireland as well as abroad. She has several hobbies including knitting and paper crafts, gardening and music. She believes in writing books that feature strong female characters of all ages.

If you enjoyed this book, the author is happy to receive feedback from readers at author@ninahayesauthor.com or using the links below.You can also sign up for her newsletter, for special offers, free short stories and more.

You can connect with me on:

- http://www.ninahayesauthor.com
- http://www.twitter.com/ninahayesauthor
- http://www.facebook.com/NinaHayesAuthor
- http://www.instagram.com/NinaHayesAuthor

Subscribe to my newsletter:

- https://mailchi.mp/c5d9815e1c52/newsletter-signup

Also by Nina Hayes

The Kimberly Killing

First in the Old Bat Chronicles.

Eve Caulton is looking forward to a new life in Kimberly Cottage - until a body turns up in her own living room.

Lucky for her, her mother Niamh, and the feisty senior ladies of Bramble Lane are on hand to offer help. And their unique skills - a magical, fun Irish cozy mystery filled with authentic Irish folk traditions.

https://mybook.to/UN5elH

The Holly Homicide

Second in the Old Bat Chronicles.

When new neighbours move into Holly Cottage, everyone on Bramble Lane is excited. But they bring with them problems and upheavals that threaten the close knit community.

With the holidays fast approaching, a terrible crime seems set to ruin everything. But with the help of Dymphna Moriarty and the Old Bats themselves, can Eve save an innocent boy and restore the Christmas magic?

https://mybook.to/iBjTY

On the Fiddle!

First in the Music Shop Mysteries
    Writing as Geraldine Moorkens Byrne

Mrs O'Brien runs Ireland's oldest music shop and presides over her beloved West Stephen Street.   When new landlords threaten her neighbours, she is prepared for the fight and when the hated estate agent is found murdered, she has to solve the mystery. Aided by her colleague, Michael and mad cap teen Mai, she recruits the Super Ukers Ukulele group and sets out to save the street!

https://mybook.to/BkRg

www.ingramcontent.com/pod-product-compliance
Lightning Source LLC
Chambersburg PA
CBHW030818210726
48290CB00002B/652